The Fatherhood Mandate

The Unborn Child Protection Act

M.E. Wright

Merrywidow Publishing LLC

ISBN 979-8-9883566-1-5 (ebook)

ISBN 979-8-9883566-0-8 (paperback)

ISBN 979-8-9883566-3-9 (hardcover)

To Ruth Bader Ginsburg

You taught us that real change,
something that will endure,
happens one step at a time.

Contents

1. Chapter One   1

2. Chapter Two   5

3. Chapter Three   13

4. Chapter Four   27

5. Chapter Five   43

6. Chapter Six   59

7. Chapter Seven   75

8. Chapter Eight   95

9. Chapter Nine   109

10. Chapter Ten   129

11. Chapter Eleven   141

12. Chapter Twelve   163

13. Chapter Thirteen   175

14. Chapter Fourteen   187

15. Chapter Fifteen   197

16. Chapter Sixteen   211

17.	Chapter Seventeen	219
18.	Chapter Eighteen	239
19.	Chapter Nineteen	249
20.	Chapter Twenty	269
21.	Epilogue	287
	Author's Notes	301
	Acknowledgments	309
	About Author	311

Chapter One

Sam stood on the rocky beach, watching the small waves lap against the monochrome shoreline. It was late August, but the wind coming off Lake Michigan was a bit chilly. *Probably should have brought a jacket*, he thought as he shoved his hands deep into his front pockets.

He kicked at the pebbles that littered the beach, then pulled his phone out of his back pocket to check the time. 8:10 am. It was too early for this shit.

Sam shaded his eyes as the sun momentarily poked through the somber clouds, then slid the phone back into his pocket and glared at the horizon. Of course, Rylee was late. She was always late.

He sighed. Rylee was the kind of girl that you could love one minute and hate the next. Bright blue eyes that just drew you in. Long black hair and a saucy smile. Curves in all the right places. She knew what to say, when to say it, and what it took to get her way.

And that was the problem. Rylee always got her way.

Not this time, Sam thought as he kicked at the sandy pebbles at his feet. No more meaningless late-night texts. No more screaming fights over some imagined insult. No more scheduling and rescheduling his life around her ever-changing wants and needs. It was over. Done.

He heard her cuss as she stumbled across the damp rocks and pieces of driftwood that littered the beach, her complaints almost lost in the mindless hiss of the surf as she slowly made her way across the deserted beach. He ignored her.

"Sam, I'm cold," Rylee said when she finally reached him. That telltale whine warned him she was already in a mood. "Can't we go someplace else?"

Sam felt her tentatively reach for him. He pulled away and shoved his hands into his front pockets again. "Just tell me what you want, Rylee," he said, eyeing the darkening clouds that threatened rain out over the lake. "We broke up. It's over. There's nothing more to say."

"It's really chilly out here," she whimpered. "I can't talk when I'm freezing to death!"

She sniffed as if she was holding back tears. He turned and one look was enough. Melodramatic expression. Bloodshot eyes. Blotchy skin from crying.

That was the last thing he needed that morning. "Let's go," he muttered. He grabbed her arm and forced her to walk toward the trail that threaded its way through the woods surrounding the beach behind them.

Sam felt her stumble over a small piece of driftwood and glanced down. Soft leather flats peeked out beneath a long dress that were more at home on a riverboat cruise than on sandy terrain. No matter how many times they'd been to Tietjen Beach, she just couldn't take the hint and wear sensible clothes.

He released her arm as they slowly made their way through the overgrown trail to the stairs. Wild grapevines, goldenrod, and assorted weeds crowded the entrance to the limestone steps and made it almost impossible to reach the rough, wooden handrails as they climbed.

They approached the top of the bluff. Sam headed for one of the benches that used to overlook the beach below. Now, trees and small brush huddled against the hill, creating an almost impenetrable view.

He sat down. "Tell me what's going on," he asked as gently as he could. Sometimes it was easier to just go with it.

Rylee slumped onto a nearby bench. Almost on cue, tears started rolling down her cheeks. "We can't break up, Sam," she whispered. She brushed her long, black hair away from her face. "I need you."

Sam turned away, staring at the clouds that randomly filtered through the foliage around him. It was definitely going to rain. He could smell it in the air.

"Rylee, it's over." Sam ducked his head, staring at the sandy ground. "You broke up with *me*. We're done."

"No!" Rylee stood, fists clenched, as she screamed at him. "You don't understand. We made a mistake!"

Sam leaned back and wearily looked up at her. "How many times do we need to break up before you finally accept that it's over, Rylee?" he asked, lightly mocking her. "Two more times? Five?" He searched her face for any bit of understanding. "Breaking up was your idea." He paused for emphasis. "Both times!"

Rylee screwed her eyes shut and turned her face to the sky. "I was wrong," she whispered. She opened her eyes and wiped her face with both hands. "Things have changed, Sam."

"What things?" Sam demanded. "I'm really tired of this, Rylee! Tell me what's going on!"

She sat down and slumped against the bench, covering her eyes with one hand. "It doesn't matter, Sam," she told him. "I'm probably worried about nothing."

Sam sighed as he stood up. "Fine," he growled. And, with that, he walked away, trying to ignore the quiet sobs behind him. He had better things to do than to deal with the drama queen.

Chapter Two

T he next day, Sam was back in the zone. One last afternoon with his crew and then it was time to start packing up for his move back to campus.

"She did *what*?" Lucas snickered as he unwrapped his burger to set it on his tray. "After all the hell she put you through, she wants you back now?"

Sam clasped his hand against his chest, fingers spread as he looked at Lucas. "We made a mistake," he whined in a mocking imitation of Rylee. "I *need* you!"

Mason laughed. "Yeah, she needs you to stroke her ego!"

"That's crazy, bro!" Colby said with a snort.

"Nah," Lucas drawled. "That's Rylee!"

Everyone cracked up, even Sam. He took a bite of his burger, savoring the flavor and the company. For a moment, he sat back and listened to the easy banter. He had to admit that yesterday morning had been kinda crazy, even for Rylee.

They'd broken up twice already. Once because the college tennis season started up in January and he couldn't come home to visit on demand. The next time it was because he hadn't made a bigger deal about Rylee getting accepted into Wellesley College. Yeah, they'd done away with the whole 'automatic legacy admittance' policy, but her parents had made sure that her entire high school experience had been tailored specifically for Wellesley. Of course, she'd been accepted. It didn't seem like a big deal—until it was.

A woman in the booth across from them shot Sam a dirty look as she unwrapped a burger for her toddler. He nodded. The restaurant was almost completely empty, and they were probably making too much noise. Time to rein it in.

"So, Lucas," Sam cut in, "you're going to mentor the Mega Hawks this build season?" Robotics was always a safe topic. They'd spent all four years working in the Weston Prep School's robotics lab for high school students. He'd known Lucas the longest. They'd met in kindergarten and had each other's back ever since. Ryan, Colby, and Mason came later, after he'd joined the team.

Lucas nodded. "Yeah," he drawled, grabbing a few fries. "Looks good on the resume and, if the design team is able to work its magic, we might be able to get to the global championship this season."

Ryan elbowed him. "So, getting back-to-back Autonomous Awards while we were on the team isn't good enough for you?" he joked. "Or do you just miss the twelve-hour days during build season?" Build season kicked off every January. It was six grueling weeks of designing, programming, and building a robot for competition.

"Nah," Lucas responded, a goofy grin on his face. "Just trying to avoid going home on the weekends."

Mason laughed. "Dude. We go to the Milwaukee School of Engineering. It's only twenty minutes home, door-to-door!"

Lucas picked up his soda. "And?" he asked, an innocent grin on his face. He shook the cup and slurped the last of it.

Mason shook his head, laughing.

Lucas turned to Sam. "When are you headed back to campus?" he asked.

"Next weekend," Sam told him. Unlike the others, he attended an out-of-state college. "I am so ready. We scored a sweet condo just a few miles from campus." Four bedrooms. Right on the campus shuttle route. He couldn't wait to get the keys and settle in.

Sam's phone buzzed. He dug it out of his back pocket to check the caller ID. Not Rylee.

"Wendy," he mouthed to the group before he answered. "Hey, Mom—"

"Don't you 'hey, Mom' me, young man!" she snarled.

That didn't sound good. "What's wrong?" Sam asked, taken aback.

"I can't even—" his mom stuttered, her rage reducing her to a few simple sentences. "You get home right now!"

"Okay . . . "

"That effing whore!" The line went dead.

Sam looked down at his phone, confused. *What the hell?* he thought. *Effing whore?*

Lucas smirked, swirling a handful of fries around the splatter of ketchup on his wrapper. "Rylee?" he asked, then crammed them into his mouth.

Sam sighed. "Yeah," he said. "I'd better get going." He started to clean up the remnants of his lunch. The longer it took for him to get home, the worse it would be.

"I hope Rylee didn't throw a temper-tantrum at church," Colby said with a grin. "Before you know it, the ladies' Bible study group will have you back together again *and* planning your wedding!"

Sam snorted. "Not likely," he told the group. "Wendy can't stand Rylee. The last thing she'd want is for us to get married." He clutched at his fake pearls, then stood up. "I mean, what would the congregation say?!"

He grabbed his tray to dump it out before heading for the door, ignoring the laughter behind him. He could only imagine what Rylee had done to get his mom all riled up.

Sam told himself that it couldn't be that bad as he pulled up to the house. No sign of Rylee. Dad wasn't home. Just some strange car parked on the street in front of their house.

His mom appeared in the front window and beckoned to him. She looked pissed. He hurried across the driveway and let himself in. A nondescript blond stood in the vestibule, wearing a dark blue windbreaker with white 'Process Now' lettering near the shoulder. His mother glared at him, her hazel eyes almost bulging with outrage.

Sam looked from one to the other in rapid succession, frantically trying to figure out just how badly he'd screwed up. What did this Process Now person have to do with Rylee pissing off his mom? "What's going on?" he asked.

The woman eyed him. "Samuel Maxwell?" she said, the grave tone making it less of a question and more of a statement.

"Yeah, that's me," Sam said, hesitantly. Just the sound of her voice made his stomach churn.

The woman handed him a large manila envelope. "You've been summoned to Milwaukee County Children's Court to discuss financial support for your embryo. The initial court date has been assigned for next Monday."

"Wh-what?" he stammered, the envelope almost falling out of his hands. He heard the words, but they didn't make any sense. "Court date? Embryo?" *What the absolute hell?*

She held out a stylus and tablet. "It's all in the documents. Sign here, please."

In a daze, Sam juggled the oversized envelope and the tablet while he tried to scrawl something semi-recognizable with the stylus. Then, the process server pushed the tablet at his mom. "As the defendant is under the age of twenty-one, I'll need you to sign as well."

Wendy pursed her lips and looked like she was going to refuse, then shook her head and signed.

"Thank you," the process server said with a tight smile. "Have a good weekend." And then she let herself out, striding across the lawn to her car.

"I can't believe you got that whore pregnant," Mom snarled, the flush on her face almost matching her dark, copper hair. "How many times did we tell you to use protection!"

Sam turned to his mom. "I don't understand, Mom," he said. "She broke up with me. It's over. Rylee can't be pregnant." He stopped and thought back to yesterday morning. Rylee had insisted that she needed him. That things had changed.

Almost in a fog, he slowly walked into the living room and sat down, the envelope forgotten for the moment. Why hadn't she told him that she was pregnant? And why sue him for financial support? Her family lived in River Hills. They had money!

He looked up. "Okay," he said, giving his head a quick shake. "Let's just say Rylee *is* pregnant. Not a big deal, right? I mean, yeah, if it's mine, at some point I'll have to pay child support. But I'm still in college and don't have a job, so there's not a lot she can do to me. It's not like she needs the money!"

Wendy ripped the court documents out of Sam's hands. "Idiot child!" she hissed. "That new law was just upheld by the Supreme Court. If that baby is yours, your life is over. Don't you understand that?"

"How? And what does the Supreme Court have to do with it?" he demanded.

Wendy looked at him for a long moment and then turned away in disgust. "Just wait until your father gets home. At least *he* listens to me!"

A few hours later, Sam studied his dad's face as he methodically went through the documents. Andrew Maxwell was an intellectual property attorney, but had always prided himself on being a fast learner.

"Well," Dad said in that slow, melodic tone he used when he was trying to keep the peace. "The documentation seems to be rather straightforward. From what I can tell, Rylee went to the Faith and Prayers pregnancy crisis center to confirm an at-home pregnancy test. Once she'd tested positive, the center was required by law to notify Child Protective Services and she was taken into custody."

"Wh-what?" Sam leaned forward, digging his fists into the couch cushions on either side of him. "Why? Why would they do that?"

His dad shuffled through the papers on the coffee table until he found what he was looking for. "Well, Rylee is not legally married," he told Sam. "This new law requires pregnant women that are either unmarried, or in the process of getting a divorce, to be held in a medical detention center until their court date to prevent them from harming themselves or their embryo." He held up a hand to stop Sam from interrupting. "There's a psych evaluation, I believe, and the hearing is required to be held within three business days of detention.”

He placed the document back on the coffee table in front of him and looked up at Sam's mother. “I'm not sure what to say, Wendy,” he admitted.

Both men watched as she paced the living room as if she was a caged animal, arms crossed like it was the only thing keeping her from throwing something. “This should *not* be happening,” she snarled. “The Governor and I talked about this law during his election campaign. He repeatedly assured me that holding fathers equally responsible for their unborn child's welfare would have minimal impact on our community!”

Sam stared at his mom. *Equally responsible? What did that even mean*, he wondered.

“I know, Wendy,” his dad told her. “But this is what you voted for, unintended consequences and all.” He cleared his throat and looked down at the pile of papers on the coffee table. “I'm fairly confident that we'll know more when we get to court,” he said, his voice soft.

“Dad, I don't understand,” Sam said as he leaned forward to peer at the paperwork. “I know it's bad, but I don't get why this is bad . . . bad.”

Wendy stopped and planted herself in front of them. Her dark auburn hair seemed to reflect the rage in her hazel eyes. “Abortion is illegal in the state of Wisconsin,” she told him. “You know that, right?” She waited for him to nod. “Well, it's also illegal for that whore to travel to another state to get an abortion.”

Sam pursed his lips, trying to ignore the name-calling. “Why is it anyone's business if she gets an abortion?” He thought about it. The last time they'd had sex was mid-July, so Rylee couldn't be more than a few weeks pregnant, right? Which meant that taking a trip down to Illinois to get her flushed out shouldn't be a big deal.

Wendy started to answer, but his dad interjected. "Son, according to this, the clinic detected a heartbeat." He shrugged. "Well, not really a heartbeat. Right now, it's just a cluster of cells that have started to emit an electrical signal that was detected by ultrasound. But the law says it's a heartbeat and, as such, the embryo just became a ward of the state."

"A ward of the state? I don't understand, Dad!" Sam exclaimed, raking his fingers through his hair in exasperation. So what if the ultrasound detected something that looked like a heartbeat? That didn't mean anything!

His dad sighed. He put an arm around Sam and pulled him close so that their shoulders touched. "It means that both you and Rylee are responsible for making sure that those cells become a baby and that baby is your responsibility until he or she legally becomes an adult. The State of Wisconsin is going to monitor both of you every step of the way."

"I don't understand!" Sam scrubbed at his face, a feeling of raw panic making him sweat.

"I guess we'll find out on Monday," his dad said as he released him. "We should probably retain an attorney. Let me make some calls."

Chapter Three

Sam trailed after his parents as they slowly walked down the hallway to the courtroom. His mom had insisted that he wear his good suit, the one that they made him buy for special events, like the occasional formal dinners or funerals. He only had time for a light breakfast, just toast with some sort of nut butter, before they hopped into the car. Dad had said that they were lucky to be at the top of the docket. But that meant that they had to check in before 8 am.

As he stood behind his parents while they talked to the attorney, Sam looked around. The hallway was nearly empty. *Children's Court should start later in the day*, he groused.

The last three days had been sheer hell.

Wendy had been in high rage and spent the entire weekend in fall cleaning mode. That meant going beyond the usual dusting/vacuuming/floor scrubbing and into full-blown carpet cleaning/window washing/household sanitizing frenzy. Her outrage was palatable. She was a godly woman, she told him repeatedly. This was not supposed to happen to families like hers.

Sam had tried to stay out of her way, almost barricading himself in his bedroom. He vaguely remembered that the state's constitution had been amended a few years ago to include that life began at conception. But arresting Rylee just because she was pregnant sounded illegal. He needed to know more.

He had started with Reddit. Seemed like a logical choice. A quick search of 'forced pregnancy' brought up hundreds of individual posts, each of them overflowing with articles, opinions, and video clips. It was just too much.

Social media was a bust. Twitter was a nightmare of competing squabbles that seemed to flail around the ecosystem in a frantic quest for dominance. TikTok felt like a tsunami of short clips that seemed to alternate between an obsession with portraying pregnant women almost as if they were complete innocents in urgent need of protection and equating laws forcing women to carry unwanted pregnancies as fascism. Even YouTube let him down.

So many conspiracy theories. It was information overload. Sam had spent two days slogging through it on and off, but couldn't seem to make much headway, so he gave up.

After church on Sunday, he had tried again. An online article led him to Discord. He found a server called Bodily Autonomy, which led him to Prolife. From there, he found Forced Fatherhood.

Finally. The server included a number of channels, and he spent the afternoon delving into the dark side of things.

Apparently, according to Wisconsin's state constitution, not only did life begin at conception, but actual citizenship, with all the rights and responsibilities, was conferred with the embryo's first recorded heartbeat. And, just like Dad had said, unmarried women, or those who were getting a divorce, were automatically taken into custody to review their risk of hurting themselves or their embryo.

Assuming that Rylee was pregnant, and it was his, Sam still had no idea why he had to appear in court this early in her pregnancy. The channel talked about the need to establish paternity and some obligatory parenting program with mandatory mentorship meetings, but little else.

He took a deep breath, trying to ignore the acid eating into his stomach. *This was just a small delay*, he told himself. After this was done, he could start packing up his car for the move into that sweet new condo right off of campus. Yup, just a few more hours and things would get back to normal. Absolutely.

"Sam?" his dad said, his voice slightly raised so that it echoed in the marbled hallway.

"Yeah, Dad," Sam answered. "Sorry, just a lot going on." He walked around the bench his parents were sitting on so that he could join the conversation.

His dad sighed. "I know, son. But we need you to think. What day did you and Rylee break up? It's important."

Sam looked down and tried to focus. "Which time?"

Their attorney, an older woman with a perpetual frown carved into her face, leaned forward. "Explain," she said.

"Explain what?" Sam asked. "We broke up a couple of times, but somehow things just didn't end."

The woman nodded. "Think carefully about this next question. Were you exclusive? Or did Rylee have other men in her life that she might have been sleeping with in the last few months?"

"What?" Sam exclaimed. "Why does that matter?"

"Because if Rylee had sexual relations with anyone else, then we will be able to contest Rylee naming you as the alleged father," the attorney drawled, a wicked smile twisting that frown. "You may not actually be the biological father."

"We didn't talk about our relationship, but Rylee didn't sleep around," he responded. "At least, I don't think so." He thought about what he'd heard about Rylee and Kathryn and mentally shrugged. So what if she messed around with another girl. It wasn't as if they could get married or anything. It had been a few years, but hadn't the state passed some law that restricted marriage to just one man and one woman?

"What if he doesn't really know, Olivia?" his mom asked, her voice dripping with fake concern. "Rylee *does* have a reputation at church. Could that be a way to get him out of this until they're able to do a DNA test?"

Olivia shook her head. "The way that the law is written, at this stage we would need third-party testimony or the actual biological father to come forward to claim paternity," she told them.Third-party testimony can be very messy and expensive to litigate. The court will not accept social media statements or even photographs or videos of the alleged relationship because deepfake technology is so good. So, unless the biological father steps forward *and* Rylee agrees, Sam is on the hook until a DNA test absolves him."

His mom moaned and threw her head back to glare at the ceiling. "So, no matter what, he will still have to go through the motions and pay *that whore* money until we can get a DNA test done."

"Mom!" Sam gasped. His mom never really liked Rylee, but this was getting really old.

The attorney ignored him. "Unfortunately, yes."

Sam winced and looked over at his dad, hoping he would step in. Rylee might not be perfect, but the name calling was really beginning to get to him. *So much for being a godly woman*, he thought.

"Enough, Wendy," Dad said, impatiently tapping his fingers against the side of his leg. "Based on what I read, Sam will have to pay half of the expenses related to Rylee's pregnancy until a DNA test confirms paternity. Is that right?"

The attorney nodded. "Yes, but that's only part of it." She sighed, glancing up at Sam. "As unmarried parents, you will be enrolled in the Wisconsin Individual Family Education program. It includes classes like childbirth preparation, parenting, and even a finance class. If you are confirmed to be the biological father, you will also have to attend child developmental training on an annual basis until the child is three years-old."

Sam found himself sitting on the bench next to his dad. It was too much. He had a full plate this year.

Olivia held up one finger to get everyone's attention. "One more thing. Sam and Rylee are required to live together in a residence that is separate from either family beginning in Rylee's third trimester." She paused. "That way, you're close by when she goes into labor."

What the hell?

"What if I don't want to live with her?" Sam demanded. "It's too late for me to find another apartment near campus for just the two of us!"

"Cohabitation until the baby is a few months old is not optional unless there is documented proof of domestic abuse or a pending rape trial," she told him. "Be grateful that the girl hasn't claimed either of these or you'd be on the hook for 100% of prenatal expenses until it was sorted out at trial."

She glanced at Andrew, then made significant eye contact with Wendy. "Last thing to consider: grandparents are allowed brief visits only. No babysitting until cleared by the guardian ad litem because the legislation isn't clear on where the line is between the occasional sleepover and taking over parental care."

"So, if this *is* my grandchild, I'm not allowed to have a sleep-over or take them to church?" his mom snarled.

The attorney smiled, no doubt hearing the irony in his mom's indignation. "That depends on what the guardian ad litem allows. And that depends on you. So, be nice, Wendy!"

The bailiff opened the courtroom doors. "The judge will see you now," he said.

As they walked in, Sam noticed that the room was much smaller than he'd imagined. Gone was the elevated judge's bench, a jury box, and tables for the prosecution and defense like he'd seen on TV. Instead, the room had four narrow tables with a small desk for the stenographer tucked in the far corner. One desk, that he assumed was for the judge, faced the room, with two smaller tables directly in front of it. Another desk was off to the side, with a number of files neatly stacked on the far-right corner. Enormous monitors hung on the side walls.

Rylee's parents were already seated at the small table on the right, along with their attorneys. Sam's dad herded them into the room and, with a quick nod to Rylee's dad, gestured for them to have a seat at the other table. Almost as if they had come to an agreement earlier, Sam's mom wedged herself between the attorney and Sam's dad. Sam took the seat on the far side, nervously brushing his hand against his tie as he sat.

He looked over to try to get some idea as to how angry Rylee's parents were. Rylee's mom looked like she was on the verge of passing out as she leaned her head against her husband's shoulder, her bleached hair trailing off to one side. His black suit seemed to leach the color from her face, making her makeup a vivid and almost comical color against her ashen skin. Rylee's dad didn't look too well, either. He was on the River Hill's Board of Trustees. This probably didn't look too good for him.

A door at the other side of the room opened, and Rylee was escorted to her parents by a police officer. She was wearing an orange jumpsuit and her long, black hair was carefully braided down her back. No jewelry, and her ever-present iPhone was missing. She looked as lost as Sam felt.

Her mom sprang up and smothered her with hugs, alternatively smearing tears into her makeup and patting Rylee's back as if she was a toddler. Her dad eventually got up and briefly joined the family hug before urging them to sit. At no point did anyone in the family even look in his direction.

An older man stood in the doorway, watching Rylee's family for a moment before making his way to the side desk. He sat, sorted through the files, and pulled one of them out. The others were returned to the side.

"All rise," the bailiff said. "The Honorable Judge Christina Olson presiding."

Sam followed his dad's lead as the judge walked into the room, absently smoothing his tie as he stood. She was a tall woman. Her ebony skin and closely cropped hair made her expression seem much sterner than he had expected. Her white lace collar was stark against her black robe.

The judge sat down, cracked her gavel, and got down to business.

"Rylee Williams and Samuel Maxwell, you have been brought before this court because your unborn biological child has been declared a ward of the state. Under State of Wisconsin statutes, we are here to determine the facts leading up to Ms. Williams viable pregnancy, enroll you in the Wisconsin Individual Family Education program, and to ensure that you finalize post-delivery financial and placement arrangements for your biological child, which is expected to be born"—she paused and looked down at the file on her desk—"in approximately thirty-three weeks."

Thirty-three weeks? Sam screwed his eyes shut. That took him past the entire NCAA tennis season and into the National Playoffs!

He opened his eyes, leaning forward to try and catch a glimpse of Rylee. She was hunched over; her face buried in her hands as she rocked back and forth, silently crying. Her mom reached out to hold her, but Rylee shrugged her off.

Sam pursed his lips in sympathy. Rylee either needed to be completely smothered in hugs to be comforted or left alone. You never knew what she needed until you were in that moment.

The judge ignored the scene. "Attorney James Mueller has been appointed as your biological child's guardian ad litem," she said as she waved a hand to introduce the man sitting at the side desk. "He is responsible for representing the best interests of your child. This includes a financial resource assessment and participating in child placement negotiations or adoption, if you both agree to it."

Sam's mom had enough. "Investigate the facts?" she exclaimed, her face crimson with rage as she glared at Sam, then the judge. "We don't even know if this . . . this . . . this . . . girl is pregnant and, even if she is, that it's my son's!"

The judge banged on her gavel. "Order in the court," she said, sounding just a bit annoyed. "Mrs. Maxwell, I will have you removed if we have any more outbursts."

Dad put his hand on his mom's arm. "Stop," he murmured. "You're not helping."

"But Your Honor—"

Sam's attorney stood.

"Yes, Counselor?"

"Olivia Davis, Your Honor," the attorney said. She looked down at Sam's mom. "My client's mother is distraught, and with good reason. May we ask the Court to validate how we know that there is a viable pregnancy? Sometimes tests can be deceiving."

The judge took a deep breath. "I'll allow it, Counselor." The attorney sat down and the judge turned to the guardian ad litem. "Mr. Mueller, was there more than one ultrasound to confirm the embryo's placement and fetal heartbeat?"

Mueller looked surprised. "Of course, Your Honor. It's a standard procedure to repeat both the pregnancy test and ultrasound as a part of the intake process. Ms. Williams would not have been detained if we had not been able to validate that this was a viable pregnancy."

Judge Olson dipped her head slightly to acknowledge the information. "Thank you, Mr. Mueller. No issues found?"

He smiled. "Your Honor, my client is approximately seven weeks old and appears to be healthy."

"That's good news!" the judge responded with a slight smile, then turned back to Sam's attorney. "And, in answer to your next, obvious question, this court will rely on Ms. Williams' sworn testimony to determine the child's biological father." She gave Rylee a sardonic look. "I don't believe that I need to remind anyone about the penalty for perjury, do I?"

Rylee turned away and buried her face in her mother's shoulder.

Wendy began to sputter. The judge raised her hand to still her simmering outrage. "Unless you have pertinent third-party testimony or another man who is claiming to be the child's actual biological father, final determination will be made after the child is born with a court-mandated DNA test."

"Your Honor, will the Court allow us to request amniocentesis to test for birth defects and to determine if my client is the biological father?" Davis asked.

Judge Olson looked at the guardian ad litem. "Counselor, I know that there is a small risk of miscarriage, but will allow it if you agree."

Mueller looked down for a moment. "I will only agree to amniocentesis if Ms. Williams' physician finds just cause. There is no reason to put my client at risk if we don't need to."

"So ordered," the judge responded.

"I don't understand," Sam whispered to his dad. "They can do a test to verify paternity while she's still pregnant?"

Dad nodded. "Usually, people wait until after the baby is born to run the DNA test."

The judge cleared her throat, not so subtly bringing their attention back to the bench. "Ms. Williams, I need you to confirm your date of birth for the Court," she said. "According to your driver's license, you turned eighteen on December 22nd of last year. Is that correct?"

Rylee bit her lip. "Yes, Your Honor."

"Thank you for confirming that, Ms. Williams," the judge replied. "I'm glad we don't have to make a referral to criminal court for statutory rape charges." She paused and looked down at the papers on her desk. "I also see no report of rape or domestic abuse. Can you confirm this for the Court?"

Rylee stared at her hands. "Yes, Your Honor," she whispered.

The judge leaned forward. "Can you repeat that a bit louder for the Court?"

"Yes, Your Honor," Rylee said, lifting her chin.

"I need you to be very clear with me on this," Judge Olson told her, her dark eyes narrow with suspicion. "Did Sam Maxwell do anything physically or verbally that might cause someone to reasonably fear physical or sexual assault?"

Sam held his breath, looking from Rylee to the judge and back as he tried to swallow his outrage. What the *absolute* fuck?! Of course, he hadn't hurt Rylee. She always said 'yes' when he wanted to have sex. Isn't that what consent was all about?

After a long moment, Rylee slowly shook her head. "Of course not, Your Honor," she said. "I'm not afraid of Sam." He relaxed against his chair, struggling to keep his relief under control.

The judge nodded. "Thank you. Now, there are a few other items to discuss. You are an unmarried couple and, as such, your child's physical and developmental safety is at risk. Until this child is born, neither of you will be allowed to travel more than 50 miles from this courthouse."

"Objection, Your Honor!" Davis sputtered. "My client is not pregnant and does not pose a risk to Ms. Williams' pregnancy."

"Denied," Judge Olson snapped. "The statute is very clear. Your client will fully participate in his biological child's pre- and postnatal development. And he can only do that if he is local."

"Wait," Sam muttered, leaning forward to try to get his attorney's attention. "What?"

"She can't do this," Wendy growled at the attorney. "Sam is leaving for Northwestern in a few days!"

Sam's attorney leaned forward. "Objection, Your Honor. Undue burden."

"On what grounds?"

"My client is enrolled at Northwestern University in Illinois," Davis told her. "He will be forced to withdraw for a full year if he is unable to travel."

The judge stared down at Sam, making him squirm in his seat as he tried to maintain eye contact. "Counselor, I understand that this will have an impact on his life, much the same as it will for Ms. Williams. However, it is this Court's opinion that your client will be better served if he focused on preparing for the birth of his child. He always has the option of taking online courses or transferring to a local college. Request to travel outside of the state is denied."

Before Wendy could even open her mouth to object, the judge banged her gavel. "Bailiff, remove Mrs. Maxwell from the courtroom. I've had enough maternal outrage for one day."

The bailiff came to stand near their table and gestured with one hand. For a moment, it looked like Sam's mom would refuse to go, but the attorney whispered something urgent, and Wendy picked up her purse and marched out of the room.

"Next item," the judge continued, "I will need both Ms. Williams and Mr. Maxwell to surrender their driver's licenses and passports." She ignored the quiet murmur from Rylee's parents. "You will each be given a provisional driver's license so that you can travel to work, school, medical appointments, and your parents' homes until you have rented a place to live. In addition, you will each be fitted with a GPS ankle bracelet to track your location."

Sam stared at the judge in a confused rage. When did getting a girl pregnant become a crime? "What the hell?" he muttered beneath his breath. "They call this due process?"

Judge Olson looked at Sam, matching his rage with a determined glare. "As a matter of fact, it is, and we do, Mr. Maxwell," she told him. "This Court must always act in the best interest of the child, regardless of their birth status. As an unmarried father, you are also a flight risk, as this Court has learned the hard way."

Sam gulped and looked down for a moment. "Yes, Your Honor."

She pulled a document from the file and glanced over it. "Mr. Maxwell, I see that you have a birthday coming up. The provisional license includes a prohibition on the purchase or consumption of alcohol and CBD edibles," she told him. "Although you will soon be of legal drinking age, please be aware that you will be arrested and referred to criminal court if you so much as step one foot into a bar, dispensary, or liquor store until your privileges are reinstated after the baby's birth."

She paused, leaning forward to get his attention. "If warranted, you may be required to submit to regular drug testing to validate your compliance. Is that clear?"

Sam nodded. That didn't seem right, though. He wasn't sure what to believe anymore.

"I will also be issuing a court order to have all mail and packages for both households to be diverted to a special unit of the Children's Court before delivery to ensure that abortifacients are not sent to your homes," she continued. "As you know, abortifacients are illegal in this state. Please note that we are aware that this does not preclude individuals from personally delivering them to the defendants, but the Court will grant a standard request from the guardian ad litem for immediate criminal investigation if Ms. Williams miscarries. This includes an emergency access request for all electronics, including household security systems."

He could almost feel the glare.

"Next, you will be enrolled in a program designed to facilitate your transition to parenthood. These classes, including pre-natal, childbirth, and postpartum recovery, as well as essential parenting skills, will be taken jointly and at your own personal expense, unless your income falls below a certain threshold," the judge said. "The good news is that there are several low-cost programs that meet statutory requirements, and some online courses are included. These courses, along with weekly par-ticipation in motherhood and fatherhood support groups, are mandatory. Failure to complete these requirements within the timetable provided will result in mandatory jail time.

"Last item before you are fitted for your ankle bracelets and released into your parents' custody," the judge said, glancing at her watch. "Ms. Williams, you are required to provide this Court with the names of all medical providers within the next three weeks. I will be issuing a court order so that your physi-cian can legally provide copies of your medical visits and test results to the Court." She paused. "This is a standard waiver of pregnancy-related HIPPA that allows the state to monitor your pregnancy. You do have the legal right to appeal this request."

Sam sat back to look at Rylee. She'd dried her tears and looked like she was doing better.

"Any questions?" the judge asked. "If not, we're adjourned." Sam had never wanted to hear that gavel bang so bad in his life.

Chapter Four

It took hours for Wendy to calm down. She wandered around the house, crying on the phone to whatever sympathetic friend or relative she'd been able to hunt down. And just when Sam thought the worst of it was over, she would ramp it up all over again.

Typical Wendy tantrum, Sam thought as he retreated outside. He felt downright nauseous every single time she picked up that phone. It seemed like everything in their world had to revolve around her.

It had turned out to be another blisteringly hot day, baking the garden beds that hugged the deck. The closed window curtains provided him with some semblance of privacy, knowing that Wendy could come looking for him at any moment. For now, he was safe. He sat down on a couch in the shade and tried to think.

It didn't make sense that Rylee was pregnant. She'd complained about some kind of medical condition that had allowed her doctor to get her approved for birth control pills. Yeah, there was always a tiny chance of pregnancy, but Rylee had been so certain that she couldn't get pregnant. He'd believed her.

Rylee wasn't his first, but she was definitely the most opinionated. More than once she'd told him that she hated how condoms felt and he didn't question it. Why would he? When this was over, he swore to himself that he'd always glove up!

Sam laid his head back against the warm cushion and stared at the thin clouds in the distance. His attorney was already working on an appeal for the travel ban. She'd told him that this would probably take weeks and there was no guarantee that he would be allowed to travel out of state. If he couldn't travel for tennis matches, he'd lose his place on the team, and his scholarship, for sure.

He took a deep breath. It was a small scholarship. Just enough to pay for his meal plan and books. Okay. Time to focus.

He still had his academic scholarship. It covered about half of his tuition and had to be protected. Step one was to reach out to his adviser. Maybe Professor Carr could give him some guidance on how to adjust his course load. He sat up and pulled out his phone. Then, he took a deep breath and made the call.

"You've reached the office of David Carr—"

Sam closed his eyes and sagged against the couch cushion. He was still trying to figure out exactly what to say when he heard the beep. "Hey, Professor Carr," he said, hesitantly. "It's Sam Maxwell. I really need to talk to you about something that's come up and I really need your help sorting it out. It's urgent. Thanks."

He ended the call with a sigh. That didn't sound pathetic at all, right? Dammit, he didn't even leave his number! Sam thought about it for a minute. If he didn't get a call back from Mr. Carr, he'd call again tomorrow.

Next up, Coach Swan. Workouts started in a few weeks. He found the number and forced himself to make the call.

"Swan."

"Um, hey, Coach," Sam mumbled. "It's Sam Maxwell."

"Hey, Sam!" As always, the coach was brusque and all business. "Looking forward to getting some serious time back on the court?"

Sam leaned forward and covered his eyes with one hand. "Yeah, Coach," he said. "That's what I need to talk to you about."

"Sure. What's up?"

"I don't really know how to explain this, Coach," Sam said. He blew out his breath and straightened up from his slouch. "I'm not allowed to leave Wisconsin for a while."

There was a long pause. Finally, Coach asked the most important question, "For how long?" he asked, his deep voice raspy with disappointment.

Acid poured into Sam's stomach as if he'd just swallowed a Carolina Reaper whole. "I don't know, Coach," he whispered. "Might be a few weeks. Could be more than a few months. I really don't have an answer for you."

"What's going on?" Coach asked, and that was all it took for Sam to let loose. About Rylee's pregnancy. About not being able to leave the state due to that new Wisconsin state law. About how he was afraid of losing his place on the team and his scholarships. Maybe even forced to drop out of school all together. All of it because of Rylee.

Coach Swan let him ramble until he finally ran out of words, occasionally interjecting with a grunt of acknowledgment. After a long pause, he said the words that Sam knew were coming, but didn't want to hear. "If you can't leave the state, you won't be able to play in competition. And if you're not able to play in competition, we'll have to drop you from the team, and the school will pull back your scholarship. I'm sorry, Sam. There's nothing I can do."

Sam stood up and walked across the deck to the railing. "My attorney has filed an appeal. How long do I have before they take away my spot on the team, Coach?" he asked.

"A few weeks, maybe," Coach Swan warned, his voice as gentle as Sam had ever heard it. "I can't guarantee anything, Sam."

Sam closed his eyes. "I know."

"My next step is to let the athletic director know that you may not be able to return this fall," he told him. "I can hold your place on the team until after the quarter starts. As for your scholarship, you'll need to reach out to the financial aid department. It might not be too late for them to award your scholarship to the next person on the list."

"Oh, okay," Sam breathed.

"Thanks for letting me know," Coach said. "Hopefully, you'll get this sorted out and be back on campus in short order. Keep me in the loop."

"Will do, Coach," Sam replied. He could almost see the angry frown. Sam might not be his top athlete, but his forehand slice always gave him the edge.

"Don't take too long," Coach reminded him. "Workouts start in two weeks."

Sam nodded as he hung up. That scholarship—and his place on the team—were already gone, he was sure of it.

He walked back to the couch and slumped down, staring at the wilting flowers that crowded the garden bed. Tennis had given him the edge for getting into Northwestern. He loved his team. He loved the game. He put everything he had into every single match, and now every single thing that he had been working for was slowly being taken away from him.

Dammit, Rylee. Why the hell did you have to get pregnant?

The next round of painful conversations started early the following morning. Sam fumbled for his phone, barely awake. "Hello?" he mumbled, scrubbing at his cheek.

"Good morning, Sam. This is Professor Carr, returning your call from yesterday." The professor sounded way too cheerful.

Sam pushed the covers to one side so he could sit up. "Ah, good morning, professor," he said, trying to suppress a yawn. "Thanks for calling me back."

"So, what can I help you with, Sam?"

"It's kinda hard to explain, sir," Sam said, blinking his eyes in a vain attempt to wake up. "I may not be able to come back to campus this quarter and I'm not quite sure what to do."

There was a pause. "Are you dropping for the fall quarter?" Sam could hear the concern in his adviser's voice.

"I was hoping that I could move to remote learning, sir," Sam slowly replied. "Right now, I can't leave the state. And I'm not sure how long it will take to sort things out."

"You're a junior, right?"

"I am."

"Hang on," Carr said. "Let me pull up your curriculum path." There was a bit of typing in the background. "Okay, so, you've got Environmental Microbiology and Uncertainty Analysis this quarter and two electives?"

"Um, I think so," Sam said, thinking fast. "I know I'm taking Introduction to German Literature for my minor, and I think I have a leadership course as well."

"Looks like we might be able to move you to remote learning for Uncertainty Analysis," Carr told him. "I don't know about your other courses. You can look online or contact the Registrar's office for more information."

"I can do that." Sam scrubbed at the top of his head with his free hand, frustrated. Financial aid department. Registrar's office. Was there anybody at that school that he didn't have to tell that he was stuck at home because of Rylee?

"Since you might not be able to move all of your current courses to remote learning this quarter, we'll need to move some things around and get your study plan updated," Carr told him. "You only have a few days left to make the changes."

"I understand, sir." A thought occurred to him. "What if I can't make this work remotely? Can I drop down to part time for a quarter?"

"You could," Carr said, slowly. "But that might make it more difficult for you down the road. You'll either need to add additional classes in subsequent quarters or you'll have to delay graduation."

Delay graduation? Like hell! he thought.

"Thanks, Professor," Sam said, trying to sound calmer than he felt. "I'll email you when I get the information from the Registrar's office."

"Sounds good, Sam."

Sam sank back against his pillow, covering his eyes with his forearm, the phone forgotten as it dropped to the floor. It felt like he had lost his top seed ranking due to an unforced error. Rylee was just that one shot that landed out of bounds and cost him the match. What the hell was he going to do now?

Josh, he thought. Maybe talking to his brother would help. He really missed the days of being able to just walk down the hall, plop himself on the floor of Josh's room, and being able to just vent about life. If only Josh was still stateside.

He rolled over, scooped his phone up from the floor, then settled back against his pillow. 9:35 am. Sam screwed his eyes shut and tried to figure out the time difference. Berlin was seven hours ahead. That made it just after 7:30 pm there, right?

Praying that he'd gotten the time difference correct, Sam pulled up Josh's number and sent a quick text. *Gotta minute?*

Their family plan included calls to Europe, so he wasn't so much worried about the cost. The problem was that Josh was an architect. Even though Germany was pretty firm on the whole 'work-life balance thing,' Josh sometimes worked strange hours because his company's headquarters were in Seattle.

He stared at the phone and hoped that Josh hadn't left his phone in his work bag. Once, Josh had gone an entire weekend without calling home and Wendy had flipped out. She'd even tracked down one of Josh's ex-girlfriends, stateside, to raise the alarm only to find out that Josh had forgotten to charge his phone.

Almost immediately, his phone rang. "Hey, Josh!" Sam said, relieved.

"Hey, bro," Josh replied. "So, is it true?"

"Yeah," Sam breathed. Of course, Josh knew. Wendy and her big mouth! He closed his eyes and covered them with one hand. "I don't know what happened. She was on the Pill."

Josh laughed. "And you didn't wear a condom, huh? Dumbass."

"She hates condoms, Josh!" Sam shot back. "She doesn't like how they feel."

"Oh, man," Josh breathed. "She's got you wrapped around her little finger, dumbass!"

"What does that mean?"

"It means that she got you to not do the *one thing* that would stop her from getting pregnant!" Josh told him. If Sam didn't know any better, it almost sounded like his older brother was gloating.

"No way," Sam snapped. "She's always talking about how Wellesley is her future and how she can't wait to move to the East Coast and stuff. There's no way she wanted to get pregnant. Not now."

Josh snorted. "Then why did she go to a pregnancy crisis center instead of heading to Illinois to get it taken care of?"

Sam stared at the ceiling for a moment. "I don't know," he finally said. "I tried talking to her before things went south, but she was having her usual meltdown. I didn't want to deal with her crap anymore and left it at that. None of this makes any sense."

"Well, she's only what, seven weeks along? There's still time," Josh told him. "Hang on a second, lemme do a quick search." He paused, then said, "Looks like there's a Sanctuary Family Planning clinic in Waukegan. Maybe you could just give them a call to see if they can give you the pills to take care of it."

"Didn't Wendy tell you?" Sam asked. "They put a GPS tracker on us. We're not allowed to leave the state."

Josh grunted. "What about having one of Rylee's friends pick it up?" he offered. "I'm sure someone is going down there, if only to pick up some edibles."

Sam blinked. "Do you think that they can just give it to someone without seeing Rylee?"

"Maybe," Josh told him. "There's only one way to find out. Have someone other than you or Rylee give them a call. That way, they can't directly trace it to you."

"That might work," Sam said, turning the idea over in his head. Could it really be this easy?

"Don't take too long, though," his brother told him. "According to what I'm seeing online, the pill only works early on. The cool thing is that it doesn't show up in any blood work they do. That makes it untraceable."

"Lemme talk it over with Rylee," Sam replied. "I'm sure she wants out of this as much as I do!"

"Sounds like a plan," Josh said. "Now, can you try to stay out of trouble until I move back home, dumbass?"

Sam snorted. "Whatever, dude. I gotta go."

"Hang in there, Sam," Josh told him. "I know that Wendy will do everything she can to make you as miserable as possible. But things will sort themselves out. They always do."

They said their goodbyes, and that left Sam with a burning question: could it be this easy?

The rest of the day went by in a blur. The student portal didn't help, and it took multiple calls to the Registrar's office to get a live person. They were overrun with last-minute requests that could have been handled online, or so he was continually reminded.

Unfortunately, there were very few courses available for remote learning and none of them would apply to his major. However, he was able to confirm that his German Literature and Uncertainty Analysis classes were available for him to take via remote learning this quarter. His choice was to either drop down to part-time status or take a few filler courses that didn't count toward his degree.

He thought about it for a moment, grabbing a chewable antacid from his desk drawer. Did he really want to risk his GPA on some random online classes that didn't really count toward his major? Nope. Part-time it was.

He sent Professor Carr an email to advise him about the reduction in his course load and to request that his study plan be updated for departmental approval. Then, he left a message for Coach Swan. Obviously, his tennis scholarship was toast. But, if this didn't last more than a few months, maybe there was a way to regain his spot on the team.

Maybe.

That left one last call to make. Sam sat down at his desk, staring out the window as he waited for the antacid to kick in. Probably better to just get it over with.

AJ picked up on the first ring. "Hey, man!"

"Hey, AJ," Sam said. He could hear the uncertainty in his own voice. "You gotta minute?"

"Sure, man," AJ said. "What's up?"

Sam paused for a moment and considered his words very carefully. "Something's come up and I have to switch to remote learning for a while," Sam told him, trying hard to sound like it was no big deal.

AJ wasn't having it. "Dude! What the hell?" he snarled.

"I know," Sam said as calmly as he could. He couldn't afford to lose friends over this. "I've got a situation right now and I probably won't be able to leave the state for a while."

"So, what about rent?" AJ demanded. "This isn't going to work without you!"

"I know," Sam thought fast. "I can list it as a sublet, maybe?"

"This close to the start of the quarter?" AJ was pissed, no doubt about it. "You signed a lease with us, remember?"

"If I could get out of this, I would!" Sam told him, pressing one hand against his forehead. "There's this stupid court order that keeps me from leaving the state. I'm appealing, but I'm pretty sure they're not going to let me go."

AJ snorted. "What'd you do, murder someone?"

"Nah, man," Sam said with a sigh. "I hooked up with Rylee again, and . . . she's pregnant."

"Rylee, huh?" AJ said with a bitter laugh. "So, what if she's pregnant? Can't leave the state because it's a shotgun wedding? Her daddy all pissed at you?"

"No." Sam felt his gut clench as more acid flooded his stomach, overriding the pill he'd just taken. "Apparently, a new law went into effect. We had to appear before a judge, and I'm not allowed to leave the state until after the kid is born."

"That's insane," AJ retorted. "Do you even want to have a kid?"

"No!"

"So, what's the problem?" AJ demanded.

"I can't leave the state. The judge told me that I'm a flight risk," Sam told him. "I really don't understand what she means by that. I mean, Northwestern is just two hours south of here!"

"All because some bitch got pregnant," AJ said. He sounded resigned.

"Yup," Sam confirmed.

"What the hell, man!" Sam could hear the outrage in AJ's voice.

"I know! I don't even want to be a dad or be with Rylee anymore." Sam slouched down in his chair. "I have no idea what I'm going to do."

"I don't know what to tell you, Sam," AJ admitted. "I take it that abortion is out? She doesn't want one?"

"That's the thing. Abortion is illegal in Wisconsin," Sam reminded him.

"So, have her do a quick televisit and pick up some pills down here! Abortion is still legal in Illinois," AJ told him. "Hell, they even have that medical spa right over the border for women who are at high risk and might need an abortion if the baby dies before they're born. Problem solved."

"It's not that simple," Sam confessed. "She's not allowed to leave the state, either." He didn't want to go into too many details. Just the idea that Rylee's embryo was a ward of the state gave him the willies.

It was AJ's turn to pause. "Huh," he finally said. "I'm glad that I live in Illinois."

"Yeah . . . " Sam breathed. "Lucky you!" He paused for a moment and sighed. "Look, I'll reach out to the landlord and find out if they'll accept something from the Court that lets me out of the lease. If not, I'll find some way to get you the money until we find someone to move in."

"Maybe we should wait a few weeks," AJ suggested. "I mean, what if you win your appeal? You've already paid the rent for September."

Sam snorted. "I had to downgrade to part-time this quarter," he told him. "If I'm able to return to campus next quarter, I'm pretty sure that I can grab some on-campus housing."

"Okay," AJ groused. "Just lemme know."

"Will do." Sam hung up the phone and grabbed a sticky note off his desk. He scrawled a reminder and stuck it to the board on his wall. Just another thing to keep track of!

Dinner that night had been a disaster. Wendy had spent the entire time ripping the governor apart for lying about how the new law actually worked and yelling at Sam for having gotten her into such a horrible situation.

He fled the table as soon as he could. He wandered around the house for a while, then settled down in the game room. He snagged his XR goggles from the entertainment center and sat down on the couch. It was early enough that a few of his friends should be online. Maybe a game of Intergalactic Rogue would help settle his stomach.

What if Mom's right? Sam thought as he waited for the system to log him in. *What if it was someone else's embryo and, therefore, someone else's problem?*

No one was online. Sam briefly considered flipping to solo mode, but the game was so much better when you played in a group. He shut his goggles down, put them back on the charger, and grabbed his shoes. Maybe a good run was what he needed. Anything to get out of the house for a while.

As he ducked out the back door, he could hear his mom on the phone with yet another relative, fake crying about how her life was ruined. That she was too young to be a grandmother. That, somehow, Rylee had trapped poor Sam in an awful relationship and there was no way to get him out thanks to the Governor! First, the legislature let that ridiculous law from when Wisconsin first became a state stand as is. Then, they put laws in place, forcing boys like Sam to choose between fatherhood and his future! How dare they ruin *her* life! What will her prayer group say when this gets out?

It was just too much. *Not everything revolves around you, Wendy*, Sam bitterly thought as he popped his ear buds in. He paused long enough to pull up a random playlist before sliding his cell phone into his arm sleeve. Finally. Time to pound pavement.

He tried to settle into his pace, but he couldn't seem to focus. Obviously, people were making too big a deal about all of this. Sure, they'd had sex. And, okay, some of it had been wild, but so what? Why was he stuck raising some kid with her?

Sam increased his speed, heels slamming into the road. He was so screwed. Even if his attorney won the appeal and Sam could eventually return to campus, this quarter was a wash. Sure, if he was able to continue paying rent, he might still be able to move into the condo eventually, but then what? Take an extra class for a few quarters or try to squeeze something into the summer instead of his internship? Delay graduation?

His phone buzzed against his right bicep. "Rylee," his earbuds announced. Of course, it was. He slowed to a walk. For a split second, he considered pushing it to voicemail, but it was probably better to just get this over with. He touched his right earbud to answer the call. "Yeah?"

She sniffed. "Is now a good time?" she asked.

Sam gave his head a small shake as he bent over, sucking in air. Interesting. The Rylee he knew lived by one simple rule: never ask for permission.

"Sure," he panted. "What's up?"

"I've been going through the program information online and there's a lot of things that will need to be scheduled," she told him. She sounded like she was about to burst into tears again. "I created a calendar to help us keep track of this. I can share it with you, if you'd like," she told him.

"What's on the list?" he asked, staring at the pavement as he worked to catch his breath.

"We need to meet with a program social worker," she told him. "And sign up for the parenting classes. I mean, most of them are online and only take a few hours, but it looks like the in-person classes can be combined in a single day for each trimester or broken up into four-hour classes. We need to get these locked in so that we can plan other things around them."

"Like my regular classes?" he asked sarcastically.

"That, and medical appointments," she responded, completely skipping over how important his classes were. But, before he could call her on it, she added, "I made my first appointment with the doctor."

"Oh." He backed up until he found the curb and sat down. "When is it?" he asked, curious.

"September 12th," she said. Sam bit back a curse. Just a week before classes started. "It's the earliest I could get in. The nurse said there's a lot of paperwork that we'll have to complete online before we go. Because of the courts, you know."

Sam sighed. He looked down the street. "What kind of paperwork?"

"I don't know. She was kinda vague on the phone. Probably medical information from both of us. I know that I'll need to have blood work done and probably another ultrasound."

"Geez," Sam said. "How much do they need to do to make sure you're really pregnant?"

Rylee burst into tears. "I don't know, Sam!" she sobbed. "I'm just not ready for this!"

"Calm down," he told her, irritated. *Neither am I.* "Look, I've been thinking. Maybe we can have someone pop over the border and pick up some of those pills that the judge was talking about?"

There was a long pause. "I don't know, Sam," Rylee finally replied, sniffling. She sounded scared. "My lawyer told me that if I have a miscarriage that we could face premeditated murder charges."

Premeditated murder? "But it's just a cluster of cells that can't even look human at this point. How could they charge us with murder?" Sam fumed. Why was Rylee making a big deal about this?

"You heard the judge," she wailed. The sound almost overloaded his earbuds. He partially pulled them out to try to minimize the noise. "She said that if I miscarry, there would be a criminal investigation. I even have a list of stuff I'm not allowed to take without supervision. Like herbs that I've never even heard of and even stuff like acetaminophen!"

"That's insane!" Sam exclaimed. "What if you have a headache?"

"I know!" Rylee whimpered. "I can't believe this is really happening!" She started hyperventilating through her tears.

Sam dug his fingers into his forehead. She was overreacting, just like the time when the drive team lost contact with Invictus in the semi-finals for robotics. "Rylee, it's going to be okay," he finally told her. "See if you can get a friend of yours to call one of those clinics just over the border. Maybe all they need is for someone to drop off something from the doctor, confirming that you're pregnant."

"That won't work, Sam," she whimpered. "They're watching our every move. Maybe even listening to our phone calls."

"The pills won't show up in your bloodwork, so there's no way that they can charge us with something if we're careful," he told her, trying hard to sound reassuring.

Rylee sniffed, then pulled the phone away to blow her nose. "I'm not taking any more pills, Sam," she said. "I gotta go. My mom's calling me."

"Okay," Sam said. *Dammit.* He rubbed a fist against his forehead. "Talk to you later."

"Bye."

Chapter Five

"And there's the baby," the technician said, moving the wand along Rylee's stomach. Sam leaned forward, looking at the screen intently. "That's the gestational sac and if you look closely, there's where the baby is! Nine weeks strong." She sounded so cheerful. It was depressing.

Rylee took a deep breath. "It's so tiny," she whispered, looking a bit awestruck.

Tiny? Sam thought. It looked like a smear on the screen. Definitely not a baby.

The image moved on the screen and the smear enlarged to look like a tongue sticking out at them. Figures.

"If you look over here, you can see the heartbeat," the tech said. Sam could barely see something that looked like two tiny threads rapidly flickering on and off, like the filaments of an old-fashioned light bulb. "Your baby is 22 millimeters now."

Sam pulled out his phone and converted millimeters into inches. Almost 7/8 of an inch. That blob had ruined his life.

The technician pulled the wand away and handed Rylee a wet cloth to clean her belly. Then, she cleaned up the wand and put it next to the monitor. "Be right back," she said.

Rylee sat up and pulled the sheet higher on her lap. She looked at Sam, then placed a protective hand on her belly. "It just doesn't seem real," she said.

Before Sam could reply, there was a knock on the door, followed by the doctor and technician entering the room.

"I'm Dr. Zastrow," the man said, moving to sit at the desk. The technician closed the door behind her but stood next to it, almost as if she was blocking their exit. "I understand that you were referred to us by Milwaukee County Children's Court?"

Rylee nodded. "That's right, but my sister recommended you because you really helped her after she finally got pregnant with her last IVF."

"I see," the doctor said, a slight frown ruffling his eyebrows. "You would be our first court referral, Rylee," he said. "Looks like there's a lot of paperwork." He looked at Sam and raised one eyebrow, perplexed.

Sam nodded. What was there to say? Sorry that they'd had sex, and the state was piling on the paperwork?

The doctor cleared his throat and looked down. "Normally, we'd offer to walk you through the services that our center has to offer, including a birthing doula, wellness and nutritional classes, a birthing class, as well as prenatal and postnatal exercise classes to help you prepare for your child's birth and aftercare." He stopped to clear his throat again. "It looks like some of this will be covered by the mandatory parent training classes. I can give you our package information, but I'm not sure how much overlap there will be or how much your BadgerCare insurance will cover."

It was Rylee's turn to frown. "But I don't need BadgerCare," she told him. "I'm on my parents' insurance."

Dr. Zastrow shook his head. "The paperwork refers to BadgerCare, but you should be able to keep your regular insurance as a secondary insurance."

"I was hoping to get a doula. Chloe really liked hers," Rylee told him. Sam knew that sad pout. That doctor didn't stand a chance.

"Well . . . " the doctor said, looking a bit uncomfortable. "Why don't you talk with your caseworker to find out what is and is not covered," he finally told her. "We can always move the doula to your secondary insurance, or you can pay for it out-of-pocket, if you'd prefer. Going forward, I'll need to see you every four weeks until you're in your thirty-second week, so please get those scheduled before you leave."

He looked at Sam, then back to Rylee. "Do you have any questions or concerns to discuss today?"

Sam shook his head and looked at the tech standing next to the door. She took a hint and moved aside.

"Okay then," the doctor said. He stood up and handed Rylee a folder. "Please let the nurse know if you have any questions. See you in four weeks."

And, with that, they were gone.

Sam looked at Rylee. "Now, what?" he asked.

"That's easy," Rylee answered, her face relaxing into a soft smile. "Let's go shopping!"

As he eased his car onto I-43, Rylee insisted that now was the time for her to look at maternity clothes. "Winter stuff has been out for weeks," she told him, sounding like she was trying to make herself sound excited. "There might be some great stuff on sale!"

"You're only nine weeks pregnant," Sam reminded her, annoyed.

"I know, but it doesn't hurt to start getting ideas," she replied. "I have no idea what I should be wearing."

"Okay." Sam shook his head. Better to just agree with her than listen to the inevitable meltdown.

That seemed to settle her down a bit. Rylee pulled out her phone and started a running dialog as she scrolled through Instagram. Maternity jeans, hospital bags, breastfeeding shirts, underwear. Once upon a time, Rylee's need to just hear herself talk had been cute. Now, it just grated on his nerves.

Their exit was coming up. Sam merged onto the exit ramp. *Almost over*, he told himself. A few more minutes and he could drop her off at home.

They were almost to the exit when Rylee looked up. "What are you doing?" she asked accusingly.

"Dropping you off at home so you can go shopping," Sam told her.

"Uh, no," Rylee responded sharply. "You have to come with me."

Sam sighed. "No, Rylee. I'm not taking you shopping. Period."

"I need you to come with me!" she scolded him. He could hear the tears creeping into her voice.

"Rylee—"

"No, Sam. I mean it. I need you to come with me."

That was it. He jerked the wheel sharply to pull over on the ramp, slammed it into park, and hit the flashers. "Why?" he demanded as he turned to her. "Why do I have to come with you?"

"Because it's not fair!" she told him, her blue eyes dark with anger. "This was supposed to be my gap year. I was going to take some time to really relax before next year. To travel and maybe see what's out there before I spend the next four fucking years *networking my ass off* at Wellesley. I planned to spend my junior year overseas, Sam. An entire fucking year!"

Sam blinked. "You were?" *Where the hell was this coming from?* he thought. Rylee had always been a bit on the emotional side, but this was just a bit over the top.

"Yes, Sam. I was!"

"Okay," Sam drawled, unsure of what else to say.

A tear slid down Rylee's cheek. "So, if I don't get a choice about how I'm going to spend my gap year, you don't either!" And with that, she started bawling in loud, screaming sobs that seemed to echo in his small car.

Sam undid his seatbelt and scooted over just a bit in his seat so that he could reach over and pull her into an awkward hug. "I'm sorry, Rylee," he said. "I didn't know that you wanted to travel."

She leaned forward, pushing her forehead against his chest as she sobbed. "This is your baby, too! I can't do this alone, Sam. I just can't!"

Sam tucked his cheek against her head. There was no way he was going to win this one. "So, where do you want to go shopping?"

Rylee wiped her face against his shoulder. "Can we start at the By-The-Bay mall?" she asked, her voice muffled. "I don't remember if they have a maternity shop, but it would be good to just get out to walk around for a bit, you know?"

"Sure, Rylee," he said. "Let me turn around."

Sam gently pulled away and focused on getting his seatbelt on while she blew her nose. *It was going to be a long nine months*, he thought as he got the car in gear and eased his way back onto the ramp.

The mall was a bust, so Sam drove back to Mequon, which was just north of the city. Rylee insisted that they stop by some upscale maternity shop that carried a limited selection of designer clothes. She chattered about how her sister Chloe had told her to get started early and that she needed to fill her closet with comfortable clothes, with styles that were easy to coordinate. Not everything had to be designer.

Designer maternity clothes? Sam shook his head. *Of course, there had to be designer maternity clothes out there.*

Soon enough, he found the shop tucked in a small strip mall right off of Main Street. He let Rylee wander around while he stood outside to check his phone for messages.

There was just one. Northwestern's Financial Aid office. He skipped to the end of the voicemail and hit redial.

"Hello, this is Melanie Thomas. How can I help you?"

"Hi, Melanie," Sam replied. "This is Sam Maxwell. I received a call from the financial aid office about my scholarships, I believe."

"Ah, yes, Mr. Maxwell. Thank you for returning my call so quickly. We're pretty overloaded due to the start of the school year." She paused for a moment. "Let me pull up your file. One moment."

She put him on hold, and he spent a long moment listening to some mediocre soft rock. Then, "Thanks so much for waiting, Mr. Maxwell. Your file was flagged due to a change in enrollment. Looks like I need to confirm a few things before we make a final determination on your academic scholarship."

"That's fine," Sam said, feeling like his heart was going to jump right out of his chest.

"According to the plan approved by your adviser, you will be moving from full-time to part-time enrollment and from on-campus to remote learning this quarter," she said. "Can you confirm if you'll be back to full-time for the winter quarter?"

Sam looked out into the distance, past the cars streaming across Main Street. "I hope so, but I can't say for certain. I have a personal issue that I need to take care of."

He heard her sigh. "Okay," she said. "Your athletic scholarship for the 2028-2029 school year has been rescinded. That scholarship is only available for full-time students. You should receive a confirmation letter by mail within a week."

Sam's heart sank. "I understand."

"Now, as to your academic scholarship. In order to keep this, you must be a full-time student and maintain a minimum of 3.0 GPA. By dropping to part time, we will have to pull back your academic scholarship as well," she advised. "If you need to take a complete break, we always recommend that you send a request to place yourself in an 'inactive' status. That way you can file an appeal to request to have both scholarships reinstated when you return to campus full-time."

It was Sam's turn to sigh. "Okay," he whispered, then cleared his throat. "Anything else I need to know?"

"Once the Registrar's office has processed your updated academic plan, you will receive an updated bill from the Student Finance office," she patiently explained. "This will include changes to the mandatory enrollment fees and removal of the student health plan. Please review it and let me know if you have any questions, as any outstanding charges are due within fourteen days."

"I don't understand," Sam said. He swallowed past the sudden burning sensation in his throat. "I already paid this quarter's bill. How could I owe money if I just dropped two classes?"

"As I said, Mr. Maxwell," Melanie replied, her voice a soft drawl, hinting at just a bit of underlying sarcasm. "The loss of your scholarships may have some unexpected financial impact. It should take about a week for the Student Finance office to get this cleaned up as both were partial scholarships."

"Okay. Thanks for your help." Sam disconnected the call. How the hell was his tuition going to go up if he was going down to part-time? Wendy was going to stomp him under the carpet when she found out.

It took a few days, but he finally got up the nerve to call his attorney. He needed help and obviously no one at school was going to be able to give it to him.

"Olivia Davis." Sharp and to the point.

"Um, hi, Olivia," Sam stuttered. "This is Sam Maxwell."

"Ah, good morning, Sam," she said, her voice warming up. "How are you holding up?"

Sam sighed. "Not so good," he admitted, rubbing one hand across the side of his face.

There was a pause, and Sam heard her close the door to her office. "How can I help?"

Oh, boy. That probably meant that they were on the clock for billable minutes. "Since I can't go back to campus, I had to ramp down from full-time to part-time at school and I lost my scholarships."

"I'm sorry to hear that, Sam," she replied. "Hopefully, when this is over, the school will accept a hardship letter that outlines why you had to drop to part-time so that you can get your scholarships reinstated."

Sam walked over to his bedroom window and looked out over the backyard. "Maybe. I'm just not sure what to do right now. I need to find a way to get out of the lease for my off-campus housing and, without my scholarships to help with my expenses, I'm basically screwed."

"Well, I can help you with the off-campus housing issue, at least," she told Sam. "Send me the landlord's contact information and I'll see what I can do."

"That would really help, Olivia." Sam felt relieved. Just one less thing on his plate.

"I need just a bit more information," she said. "First, do you have a copy of the signed lease that you can send me via email? I need to confirm your specific liability."

Sam nodded. "Yeah, I can get you a copy," he replied. He had to have a copy of that lease around here some place, right?

"Good," she told him. "Next, I'll also need proof of security deposit and first month's rent. Is this an automatic payment, or do you use an online service?"

"The landlord required us to set up automatic payment," Sam told her. "We had to pay September upfront, plus the security deposit and last month's rent."

"Hmm . . ."

"Is that a problem?" he asked.

"I'm not familiar with Illinois rental property laws, so I'll need to validate if that's legal for off-campus housing," she told him. Sam could almost hear the frown in her voice. "I assume that you have roommates."

"Yes," he replied. "Four of us rented a renovated condo not far from campus."

He could hear her typing in the background. "Got it," she told him. "Last question: did each of you sign a separate lease or a single lease with all of your names on it?"

"A separate lease," he replied. "Why? Is that important?"

"Well, that could be good news or bad news," she told him. "On the one hand, it means that your landlord will not expect your friends to make up the difference if they let you out of the lease."

Sam took a deep breath and let it out slowly. "And on the other hand?"

"Well—" she drawled. "That means your friends might need to get another roommate as soon as possible to minimize the landlord's financial loss."

"Do I need to start advertising for a sublet?" he asked.

"Let me take a look at the lease first," she advised. "As for the rest? You're going to have to be patient, Sam," she said. "I know it must be incredibly frustrating to have to scale back on your class load this late in the game. And I understand how painful it is to lose both scholarships. But unless Rylee miscarries—and there was no foul play—you are going to have to accept that there isn't a lot that we can do at the moment."

"I know," Sam muttered.

"My best advice is for you to focus on your schoolwork and keep a low profile for now," she said. "And remember, if you aren't the biological father of Rylee's baby, this is just a small speed bump in your life. You will get that money back."

Whoa. "I didn't know that," he breathed.

"Yup," Olivia said. "You will receive a refund from the state and the actual father has to repay it. It's a win-win situation."

"Well, that's a relief!"

"We can talk again once you've had your first meeting with your case manager and had time to sign up for the mandatory parental training courses," Olivia told him. "Our next step is to review all of the court documents so that you understand your rights and responsibilities under the current law."

Sam looked down. "We have a meeting with the social worker later this week," he told her.

"Good!" she replied. "I'll set up a meeting for the end of next week."

"I'll let my dad know," Sam said. "Thanks." He stabbed the icon on his phone to end the call.

He sat on the edge of his bed and buried his face in his hands for a moment. It was as if his entire life was a giant Jenga tower about ready to topple over. One bad move and it was all over. What the hell was he going to do?

He laid back on his bed for a moment. *One step at a time*, he told himself. *Now, get up off your dead ass and find that lease!*

The next morning was more of the same. He barely had time to grab a bowl for his granola before his dad started in.

"Sam, we need to talk," his dad told him, his disappointment evident as he looked up from the document he was reading. "Olivia called yesterday afternoon to advise that she had reviewed the lease for the Northbrook condo and would be reaching out to the landlord." He gave Sam a frown. "Next time, I'd like to hear it from you, not our attorney."

Dammit. Sam closed his eyes for a moment. "Sorry, Dad," he said. "I forgot. There's just a lot going on right now." He walked over to the far side of the kitchen to grab some coffee, then brought his breakfast to the kitchen table.

"I know," his dad replied. "I should have checked in with you earlier. I'm sorry, I know it's been a struggle. And it's probably best to leave your mom out of this for now." He paused, then gently slid the document across the table. "Just so you know, Olivia may have to file an emergency petition with the Court so that they send an official request to the landlord to terminate your lease agreement. I know, different state, different expectations, but it's the best we can do for now."

Sam gave the document a cursory glance, not sure what he was really looking at. "Thanks, Dad. I was going to call and see if they would let me sublet it, but it made more sense to have the lawyer do it."

His dad nodded. "We'll figure this out, Sam. I promise. In the meantime, have you given any thought to getting a part-time job? Olivia was very firm on the amount of money that we'd be able to give you for the pregnancy-related expenses."

"Yeah," Sam said, looking down at his bowl. "I figure something like DoorDash might be a good place to start. I can set my own hours around school and stuff."

"I'm glad to hear it," his dad said, looking relieved. "This is the part where I'm supposed to remind you that schoolwork comes first, but you're old enough to know how important it is to balance things, right?"

Sam nodded and ate a spoonful of his granola. Two online classes, that stupid parenting program, and trying to pull as many hours as he could in between things. *What could go wrong*, he thought ruefully.

Crap. His tuition bill. "One more thing, Dad," Sam said. "I had to drop to part-time because two of my classes were not offered remotely."

His dad looked up from the document he was reviewing. "Weren't you able to substitute different classes?" he asked.

Sam shook his head. "I reached out to my adviser," he told his dad, "But most of my major courses require in-person instruction."

"Which means that you will have to take classes over the summer to catch up," his dad responded. "That's okay."

Sam set his spoon down. "No, it's not, Dad." He took a deep breath, struggling to say the words. "I—I lost my scholarships."

"Because you dropped to part-time status for one quarter?" his dad asked, incredulous.

Sam nodded. "I should be able to reapply for both of them when I'm back on campus," he said. "Problem is, the tennis scholarship depends on me being able to attend off-campus tennis matches."

"Ah," his dad replied. "Makes sense." He paused for a sip of coffee. "Lost your place on the team?"

Sam looked down at his bowl. "Probably."

"I'm sorry to hear that, Sam," his dad said. "Have they updated your bill yet?" Sam shook his head. "Once they do, we can take a look at the impact and reassess your financial plan. Sound good?"

Sam nodded and took a tentative spoonful of granola. *Maybe it was going to be okay*, he thought.

Maybe.

Lucas texted him that evening. *SMH. OG is poppn, we need to talk!*

Sam rolled his eyes. Of course, the rumor mill was in full swing. Between the church's young adult program and his friends from the old robotics team, Sam was mildly surprised that it had taken this long for people to jump in. He had no doubt everyone had a theory . . . and an opinion.

Whatever, he texted back. *Hungry?*

Starving, Lucas responded.

That settled it. Sam grabbed his keys and headed out. *OMW*, he texted Lucas. At least he still had one friend that he could count on.

As Sam drove to Lucas's off-campus apartment, he couldn't shake the feeling that this was all just a bad dream. It just didn't seem real. He should be back on campus, with Rylee just a soon-to-be forgotten mistake. He should be settling down in the condo, checking out all of those fresh faces, and figuring out which of them might be interesting enough to ask out.

Instead, he was stuck at home. Most of his old friends were spread out across several Midwest college campuses, except for a small handful that attended the Milwaukee School of Engineering. Lucas was the only one that he was close to, though.

They went through the drive-thru to grab a bite and drove to Doctors Park to eat. Close enough to the lake to appreciate the cooler breeze and far enough away that no one would intrude.

They found a picnic table near the parking lot. While they ate, Lucas insisted that Sam go over the entire incident, from the time he was served, to the talk with the attorney, to almost a step-by-step walk-through of what happened during court.

"Day-am," he breathed. "How the hell did that happen?"

Sam looked at his friend but couldn't restrain that sarcastic comeback. "I think it's a bit late for the 'birds and the bees' talk, don't you?"

Lucas snorted. "Yeah, probably."

"So, the attorney tells me to play nice in the sandbox for now. It's not that I don't want to help Rylee out . . ." he trailed off.

"It's just that it's not really your problem," Lucas finished for him.

"Exactly!"

"So, what do you do now?" Lucas asked.

Sam looked across the way. A couple slowly walked along the trail leading into the forest reserve, holding hands.

"I guess I'm stuck with Rylee for now, unless she has a miscarriage."

Lucas leaned forward. "Seems awfully convenient, doesn't it?" he asked. "I mean, you broke up, she came back, and—"

"We got back together," Sam responded.

"And just after you broke up the last time, what happened?"

"She got pregnant."

"Awfully convenient, that," Lucas said, slowly nodding his head. He looked down at his burger.

Sam thought about how many times they'd had sex in that month before the last break-up. Just remembering the feel of her as he pounded into her luscious body got him going. That hungry look on her face. The urgency. Her demands to have sex in potentially compromising places. On the beach. The church coat room. Robotics' storage room. It was almost as if the thrill of being discovered drove her.

Unlike other girls, Rylee hated condoms. She was on the Pill, so what difference did it make?

Sam straightened up and looked out into the distance. Wait. She had been on the Pill, right? He vaguely remembered seeing the pill pack in her purse. Plus, her smart watch tracked her cycle because she didn't like to have sex while she was bleeding.

Her cycle. It seemed very important to her at the time. Sam tried to remember that conversation, but couldn't quite pull it in. Something about her sister or a family friend using an app to get pregnant. Or to avoid getting pregnant.

Eh. It would come to him eventually. Might be something to talk over with the attorney.

"I asked Rylee to find out if a friend of hers could run down to Illinois to pick up abortion pills for her," Sam confessed.

Lucas frowned. "Was she able to get them?"

"No," Sam picked up a few fries, "she's too scared to try. Apparently, her attorney told her that she'd be investigated for premeditated murder if she miscarries."

"Day-am."

They sat in silence for a while, listening to the birds as they settled down for the evening.

"So, what's your next move, man?" Lucas finally asked.

Sam mentally went over the list of appointments on Rylee's calendar. "We have an appointment with our case manager coming up and a few in-person parenting classes to sign up for. And then there's Rylee's doctor appointments that I have to go to." Sam sighed. "I know one thing's for certain. I ain't driving her around. I don't even think that baby's mine!"

"I hear ya," Lucas said, a telltale smirk on his face. "Want me to ask around? See if there's a missing baby daddy out there?"

Sam nodded. Maybe Wendy was right, and Rylee had slept with another guy. It wasn't like they'd spent every waking minute together, so it just made sense that someone else might be responsible for that embryo. He wasn't willing to play nice in the sandbox if this was just a way for her to keep him around. Nope. Not going to happen.

Chapter Six

S am looked up from his phone, scanning the packed lobby again. It was as if all of Milwaukee County had an appointment with a social worker today. Kids ran around, shrieking, as they played some form of tag that included tossing small stuffed animals around. Older women, probably their parents, filled out paperwork on identical clipboards while they socialized. The crowd was sprinkled with just a few folks, like him, who looked a bit dazed that they had been called in for a serious talk with social services.

Rylee stirred, her knee brushing his. She leaned forward as if the mere touch of the plastic chair was going to give her a rash. "Didn't we have a 10:30 appointment?" she asked, almost as if Sam had any control over when they would be called back.

Sam nodded. Of course, they did. It was obvious that the county was understaffed. The woman at the front desk had said as much when they had checked in.

"Maybe we should ask how much longer," Rylee said, scrunching her nose. "I mean, that's what you're supposed to do when your doctor is running late, right?"

Sam shook his head in disgust. *Whatever, Rylee*, he thought. *They'll get to us when they get to us.* He already had a pile of homework to get done. Just because his courses were self-paced did not mean he was going to let himself fall behind.

There wasn't a lot that he could do about that, so he opened Substack and started scrolling through trending news.

Rylee brushed up against him as she stood, her purse hitting his shoulder. "Fine," she said with an icy pout. "I'll go ask."

Sam ignored her. He didn't want to be here anymore than Rylee, but throwing a fit wasn't going to help.

"Rylee Williams and Sam Maxwell?"

Sam looked up. An older woman, her dark hair randomly streaked with warm blond highlights, stood by the reception desk. She held a rather large folder up against her chest with both hands, as if it could protect her from the crowd.

"Finally!" Rylee breathed. She took a few steps, then looked back over her shoulder. "You coming?"

Sam stood up and tucked his phone into his back pocket. Then, he walked past her and approached the caseworker.

"I'm Sam," he told her.

"Hi," Rylee said a bit breathlessly as she caught up. "I'm Rylee. And you are . . . ?"

The caseworker smiled, pushing a stray hair back behind her ear. "Beth Hoffman. I've been assigned to be your caseworker to help you navigate the Wisconsin Individual Family Education program." She gestured. "If you'll follow me to my office, we can get started."

The hallway echoed with half-heard conversations as they made their way to Beth's office. The faded linoleum was cracked in places, Sam noticed. He idly wondered just how old this building was.

Beth stopped at one of the partially open doors and waved them in. It was a small room, with two mismatched guest chairs crammed between the door and a worn desk. A small bookshelf sat directly under the window against the far side of the room, books randomly piled on the shelves.

Sam took the seat closest to the wall, carefully easing the chair as close to the wall as he could. After a short pause, Rylee sat next to him. Beth closed the door and moved around them to sit behind the battered desk.

"Alright," Beth said as she pulled a pile of documents from the folder. "It looks like you've already been assigned a guardian ad litem and had your first court date." She ignored Rylee's scoff. "Our next step is to provide an overview of the parenting preparation program, make sure you've validated your Badger-Care account with updated contact information, and talk you through the program requirements."

"Why do we have to go through this?" Rylee asked. "Isn't it bad enough that I can't go anywhere without permission? We're being treated like criminals!" She pointed at her ankle. The GPS anklet peeked out from under her conservatively tailored pants.

"I understand your concern, Ms. Williams, and I share it," Beth calmly replied. "However, the State of Wisconsin has a vested interest in ensuring that all of our citizens have a right to a fulfilling life, even the unborn."

Sounds like something you'd say in front of the cameras, Sam noted.

"Then why am I under house arrest?" Rylee demanded. He found himself leaning up against the wall. He did not want to be in the flood zone when the waterworks started.

Beth gave Rylee a tired smile. "Ms. Williams, you are not under house arrest. The state is monitoring your movements because, under current statutes, we are required to ensure that you carry your embryo to term."

At that, Sam stirred. "What about me?" he asked. "I'm not pregnant!"

Beth looked at him. "No, you're not, Mr. Maxwell," she said, with a slight frown. "Unmarried fathers-to-be are considered an automatic flight risk. And, as such, we need to ensure that you fully participate in all aspects of your child's gestation and birth." She paused, looking at Rylee for a moment.

"So, that being said, let's get started, shall we?" she asked brightly. She pulled out two packets from the pile in front of her and pushed a copy to each of them. "Here is an overview of the parenting prep classes you're required to take," Beth told them with a smile, almost as if she was a used car salesperson and really needed to close the deal. "The Court provided you a link, but we've found this guide to be particularly helpful for our new clients. There are several programs to choose from based on your current home addresses. As you can see, the first trimester has a total of eight courses, four of which can be taken online . . ."

Sam found himself tuning her out as she walked them through the courses. He still didn't understand how he was a flight risk. It really bothered him because the judge had said the same thing.

Flight risk. What the *hell* did that even mean? Of course, he was going to step up if it turned out that he really was the dad. It's not like he was going to flee the country. He just needed to be allowed to leave the state so that he could get back on campus!

He stirred as Beth started to review the next set of forms with them. "As you can see, the program includes automatic enrollment for BadgerCare medical as well as short-term disability insurance."

Rylee, of course, objected. "I already have insurance. Why do I need this?"

"BadgerCare is required for all program participants," Beth told her. "This allows Wisconsin to standardize maternal care across the entire state. But," she held up a hand to prevent the next outburst, "you can retain your current plan as a form of secondary insurance, if needed. Keep in mind the short-term disability insurance, which is also a part of BadgerCare, will cover time off from work for up to twelve weeks of pay, although some participants receive this coverage through their employer."

Rylee pouted. "I'm on my gap year. I don't need a job!"

Beth nodded, pursing her lips as if she wanted to say something biting. "I understand, Ms. Williams." She turned to Sam. "We also offer BadgerCare for fathers-to-be," she told him. He nodded, and she handed the form to him. "However, this coverage is optional, as most men already have some sort of insurance coverage through their current job. You must make less than 200 percent of the federal poverty level to qualify.

"Last item. Here is some information about your mandatory support group meetings," Beth told them as she handed them even more paperwork. "These are scheduled to start the first week of October. You'll want to sign up as quickly as possible as these groups tend to fill up fast. They're small, usually less than ten people, and each group is assigned a mentor who can act as a liaison between yourself and social services."

Sam looked down at the stack of brochures and small flipbooks. "Exactly how much is this going to cost?" he asked suspiciously.

"Good question, Sam," she said. "Some of the courses are free as they are a part of BadgerCare. Others are means tested and you'll have to provide information regarding your annual income."

"Does that apply to my personal income or to my family's income?" Sam asked. "I'm a college student. I don't really have an income."

Rylee snorted, shaking her head. "Neither do I."

Beth looked at them, blinking a bit. *Probably not her usual client*, Sam thought ruefully.

"Contact the program sponsors for the courses that you're interested in. I'm sure that they can advise you as to how they determine annual income," she finally said. "Make sense?"

She didn't wait for them to respond. She stood. "Do either of you have any questions?" she asked, already moving to open the door. "If not, I suggest you get started on this paperwork. You can complete them here and turn them in at the front desk. Or, if you'd rather sign up online, there are websites listed at the bottom of each form. Please remember that these are due to be completed one week from today." And with that, Sam found himself being ushered down the worn hallway and out into the reception area.

Sam looked at Rylee. "Now, what?" he asked.

"Lunch, then the program overview course," Rylee answered, a smug but determined look on her face.

"How did you—" Sam started to sort through the brochures, looking for the class information.

"I signed us up for the first trimester in-person parenting classes over the weekend," Rylee told him. "It's in the baby calendar. I thought you knew that."

Sam looked up at the ceiling and sighed. Of course, Rylee signed them up without checking with him. It's not like he had a life, or any commitments that he needed to take care of, right?

She put her hand on his arm. "I'd rather get this over with as quickly as possible. It's the introductory course, and it's only a few hours."

"Fine." Just one less thing that he had to keep track of.

Sam slouched in his seat, wishing that he could pull out his phone and just disappear for a while. But no. All electronic devices had been exchanged for binders packed with worksheets at the classroom door. This 'parenthood' class sucked.

He looked around the room. It was a mostly young crowd, almost evenly split between the professionals in their interesting mix of hipster and casual business attire and the service/manufacturing folks.

A few were older and looked completely out of place with their 'I'm already a parent' vibe. Sam vaguely remembered that parents going through a divorce had to go through the program, but that didn't really make any sense. They already knew how to handle kids, right?

The instructor had the group sit in a large circle that spanned the small room. She reminded him of his first-grade teacher with her frizzy gray hair and randomized glare. The chairs, probably leftovers from some ancient company's closure, were incredibly uncomfortable and designed for one purpose: to keep you awake.

Despite the chairs, Sam had problems staying focused, and he knew that he was not alone. Everyone seemed to be struggling this afternoon. The woman's voice droned on, rising and falling at random intervals as she read the worksheets to them, word-for-word. She reminded him of a chubby dog yapping at a squirrel.

The instructor held up the next worksheet. "Next, we're going to review updates to the State of Wisconsin FMLA statute," she told them.

The guy across from him groaned, juggling the binder on his knees. "Why do we need to know this? Federal FMLA supersedes anything that the state has put out there," he asked. A few people nodded.

"Not true," the instructor barked, brushing uneven bangs out of her eyes. "State and Federal FMLA may run concurrently, but our state has several 'buckets' of FMLA coverage, and eligibility criteria is completely different. If you'll turn to page three of the FMLA section . . . "

There was some paper rustling amid scattered groans and sighs. "As you can see, the State of Wisconsin recently updated state FMLA law so that both parents are allowed up to eight weeks for unpaid family leave time. This includes the birth of a newborn," she intoned. "Please note that there is an important difference between federal and state FMLA. Serious health conditions now include prenatal care appointments for both parents in the state of Wisconsin."

"Which is fine, if I really wanted to go," the guy next to Sam breathed.

"I know," Sam responded, lips barely moving as he tried to keep his voice low. *It's a fucking doctor's visit*, he thought. *Why should I care?*

The trainer glared in their direction. "It's important to remember that, in order to qualify for state FMLA, you must have worked for the same employer for more than fifty-two consecutive weeks *and* been on payroll for at least one thousand hours in the rolling fifty-two-week period."

One of the women across from Sam nervously raised her hand. "What about pay?" she asked in a quiet voice. "My boss told me that I can take off as much time as I need, but he doesn't have to pay me for time not worked."

"That's correct," the instructor said, her lips pursed with disapproval. "However, BadgerCare does include short-term disability insurance to help defray some of your lost wages. You should have received a copy from your social worker, but I've included a copy of the form in the back of your binder. You only have a few days left to sign up."

"Yo!" another guy called out. "What if I can't afford to take all of this time off? How the hell am I supposed to have money to eat and a place to live?"

The guy next to Sam muttered, "Sounds like this is just pro-birth, not pro-life!"

There was a muted gasp, and several of the girls glared in their direction. Sam held up a hand in protest. *Wasn't me*, he thought. Besides, the guy had a point. It sounded like each couple was on their own.

The instructor frowned. She pawed through the binder, looking for a specific page to show them. "I believe that there's information about financial support in the appendix," she said as she looked. "Ah. Here we are." She shifted the binder so that it sat open on her lap for them to see. "In addition to community-based assistance and means-tested grants, each set of grandparents may provide up to $15,000 per year to support their child as they transition into parenthood."

He glanced over at Rylee, and she shook her head. Looked like that was news to her, too. The social worker hadn't mentioned that!

"My parents can't afford to give me $15, let alone $15,000!" one girl blurted out.

"Yeah!" said the guy across from her. "I can't afford this!"

The instructor glared around the room, mouth pursed, as she tried to make eye contact with the offenders. Slowly, the room quieted down.

"Parenthood is costly," she told them. "No ifs, ands, or buts about it." Her expression softened as she looked down, almost sad. "You should have all met with your caseworker prior to this class to get an overview of what the state can do to help you with your next steps. The good news is that this program includes an appointment with a financial adviser, who will help you assess your financial resources in the next few weeks. By the end of October, you will have a good start on creating an individual plan to support your child."

She paused for a moment to let that sink in, ignoring the muttering around her. "Part of the program includes helping each couple determine if they are ready to raise a child." She held up a hand to try to stop the conversation before it got out of hand. "There are a number of options, including sharing post-delivery expenses, even if you don't live together. One parent may decide to give up their parental rights in exchange for paying all expenses until their child is twenty-one. Or, both parents can agree to give their child up for adoption and will only be responsible for costs up to childbirth."

Sam straightened up. Adoption?

One look at Rylee and he knew that it was off the table. She glared at him over imaginary glasses; head tilted to one side. Her face was flushed, lips clenched. *If looks could kill*, he thought.

The instructor sighed. "Quiet down," she told them, her loud voice cutting through the conversation around her. "I know that this can be overwhelming, but we're here to help. Please turn to page three of the FMLA section so that we can review your rights and responsibilities under state and federal laws."

During the break, Sam grabbed a soda from the small cooler at the front of the room and headed out to the hallway. They hadn't been given their phones back, but he desperately needed something to get his mind off of this bullshit.

The guy who had been sitting next to him in class walked over. He was a tall Asian, and his black jacket made him look like he'd just ducked out of a business meeting. "I can't believe that they're making us do this," he said as he leaned up against the wall, brushing at a slight crease in his sleeve. He looked over at Sam. "I'm Mike, by the way."

"Sam," Sam replied. He slouched against the wall next to Mike. "I don't care what my attorney says, this can't be legal."

"I know, right?" Mike said, irritated. "My cousin's girlfriend got pregnant and a quick trip out of state was all it took to get it fix!"

Sam nodded, taking a gulp of soda. "I have no idea how I'm going to take these stupid parenting classes, handle my regular course load, and try to find some way to pay for all of this," he growled.

"That sucks, man." Mike brought his right leg up so that his ankle crossed over his left knee, then tapped the ankle bracelet. "I feel like a goddamn criminal. I can't even imagine the conversation that I'm going to have with HR over this!"

Mike turned to look down the hallway where a small group of girls were huddled together, giggling as they compared bellies, then turned away in disgust. "So, you're in college?" he asked.

Sam glanced at the girls, then back to Mike. "Yeah," Sam replied. "Northwestern University."

Mike nodded, taking a sip of water from the bottle he held. "I take it that you didn't have to drop this semester. Remote learning?"

Sam grimaced. "Yup."

"Oof," Mike groaned in sympathy. "Remote learning sucks!"

"Tell me about it," Sam grumbled. "I had to drop two classes this quarter."

They stood there for a moment in a comfortable silence.

Mike asked, "So, your partner. How far along is she?"

Sam took another gulp of soda. "Rylee's about ten weeks pregnant," he replied. "Or so they say. It looked like a blob on the ultrasound."

Mike chuckled. "I hear ya," he replied. "Jennifer is almost thirteen weeks along. Our social worker actually yelled at us for 'shirking our responsibilities as parents' by ignoring a potential pregnancy for so long."

It was Sam's turn to laugh. "Ignoring your responsibilities?" he asked. "What the hell, dude!"

"I know," Mike exclaimed. "Being forced into parenthood wasn't exactly on either of our minds. To be honest," he added, "it really feels like it's time to move on. Too much baggage, you know?"

Sam nodded. He definitely understood.

"Break's over," the instructor announced as she walked down the hallway. Her hands fluttered in a vague shooing motion as she tried to get people moving.

Sam drained his can of soda and chucked it into the garbage, then turned to Mike. "Looks like I could use a wingman, Mike."

"Yeah, I got your back," Mike replied with a tight smile. He sauntered down the hall.

Sam grinned, feeling a small part of him relax as he followed Mike back to the classroom. It was nice to finally meet someone who understood exactly what he was going through.

By the end of the session, the class had been separated by pregnancy trimester and loaded up with so much random information that it was difficult to digest. But the worst was yet to come. Over the next four weeks, they had to complete four online courses, meet with their financial counselor, and sign up for the mandatory support groups. Sam consoled himself that his load was just a bit lighter than Mike's. Rylee didn't hit her second trimester for a few more weeks.

"Remember, your course load is based on your trimester," the instructor said before she dismissed them. "For those of you that are in your second trimester, I strongly encourage you to schedule the rest of the first trimester courses immediately before moving on to the required second trimester courses. I've also included some optional reading for those of you who are first-time parents. Have a lovely weekend!"

"Lovely weekend," Mike muttered as they slowly filed past her desk to pick up their phones. "I don't think she knows what those words actually mean!"

Sam laughed. When you're right, you're right.

They got back out to the hallway, moving away from the crowd. Sam unlocked his phone and waited for it to boot back up.

"You up for a beer?" Mike asked, slyly looking at the instructor as she waddled past them.

Sam looked up. "Nah. I'm not legal for a few more weeks," he told him.

"I know a place that doesn't card," Mike said with a smile. "I'm friends with one of the owners. There won't be a problem."

Sam thought about it for a moment. It would be nice to be able to go out and not feel like he was under house arrest. He knew that the fine for underaged drinking was just a few hundred dollars, but it just didn't feel right. There was a difference between stopping by an off-campus party where he knew people and going down to a bar that *might* not card him.

Besides, he still wasn't entirely sure about going out to the bars. The judge had told him it wasn't allowed, but he hadn't seen anything in the program that said he couldn't. Probably not worth the risk until after his birthday.

"Sorry, dude," he said, shaking his head. "I've got enough shit going on that I can't give my parents any more ammo to throw in my direction. Maybe next time."

Mike shrugged. "No worries. I'll be at Deuces if you change your mind." He walked over to the gaggle of girls and claimed his baby momma. "Time to go, Jen," he said.

"There you are!" Rylee squealed as she grabbed his arm. "I really need to get home, Sam."

Sam sighed and tried to gently pull his arm away without upsetting her. Maybe he should have taken Mike up on that offer. He was going to turn twenty-one soon anyhow. Some rules are meant to be broken. Maybe this was one of them.

It had been a day. Sam slouched down over his laptop, going through his German Literature homework list just one more time. Two chapters. Three recorded lectures. A quiz. And, of course, a paper due in two weeks. Perfect. Just perfect.

There was a tap on his door, then his dad poked his head in. "Are you interruptible?" he asked as he let himself in.

Sam nodded. *Now was as good a time as any*, he thought.

His dad sat down on his bed. "I talked to Olivia today," he told Sam, grimacing as if he'd tasted something bitter. "I have some updates to go over with you."

Sam closed his laptop and turned fully around. He knew that expression well. It never meant good news.

"Olivia lost our appeal to allow you to move back on campus," he told Sam. "I'm sorry, but that means you'll have to continue with remote classes for the entire year."

Sam couldn't suppress a groan. "Figures. I had been hoping that Rylee's medical appointments could be scheduled Monday mornings or Friday afternoons so that I could move back on campus," he admitted.

His dad nodded. "That would have been a great compromise," his dad replied. "But maybe it's for the best."

"How so?" Sam asked. All he could think of was how much Rylee's pregnancy had cost him. His scholarships. His life. Everything.

"I know that you probably don't want to hear this, Sam, but being closer to home might help with the situation," his dad shared, pursing his lips in sympathy.

Sam frowned. "The situation?" It wasn't like his dad to dance around the subject.

"Rylee," his dad said, vaguely waving his hands around. "It might be better for you to be closer to family after the baby's born, not to mention that you have an opportunity to really be involved in Rylee's prenatal care."

Sam ground his teeth. Closer to family? With all of the crap that Wendy was putting him through? *Really, Dad*, he thought. *Really?*

His dad held up his hands in defeat. "Okay," he said. "Too soon. I get it. But the good news is that your landlord has agreed to let you out of your lease, effective October first."

"That's great, Dad," Sam replied, although he wasn't sure how happy his roommates were going to be. "Do I need to do anything?"

"No, the landlord is going to list it as a sublet."

Sam sighed. "I figured that would happen." He glanced at his laptop. "Anything else?"

Sam's dad stood, brushing his hands against his shirt. "No, that's it for now," he told Sam. "Your tuition has been sorted out and paid. Your off-campus housing cleared up. I can't think of anything else that we need to talk through."

"Thanks, Dad," Sam said as he turned back to his desk and opened his laptop. He ignored the door closing behind him. He had a couple of lectures to watch.

Chapter Seven

S am grimaced as he jockeyed for parking downtown. The mentoring meetings were held in a nondescript office building just a few blocks from Cathedral Square and surrounded by restaurants and bars. It was Friday night, which meant that it was almost impossible to find street parking anywhere near the building.

He gave up and pulled into the parking structure across the street. $15 for the evening. *Great*, he thought. *More money I shouldn't have to spend*. He inserted his card and found a space on the second floor. Didn't want to miss his first meeting.

It was only the first week of October, but it was hard to believe that Rylee was already twelve weeks pregnant. The crisp air reminded him that he should be on campus. It was homecoming week. The campus was crawling with alumni, families, and local business leaders—and he was missing it.

He waited until the electric streetcar rolled past to cross the street. The Hop ran from downtown all the way to the Historic Third Ward neighborhood. As he walked across the street, he saw Mike and jogged to catch up. They entered the squat brown building together and made their way down the hallway to the only room that had lights on.

An old biker, complete with tats, a worn leather jacket carelessly heaped on a nearby table, and a weathered attitude that told you to pay attention, manned the door. He nodded at them as he handed them name tags to fill out. "I'm Theo," he said. When you're done, take a seat."

It wasn't a large group, just seven of them clustered in a circle like an AA meeting. Sam grabbed a seat next to Mike. He nodded to two other familiar faces from the introductory parenthood class as they took their seats. Most of the guys appeared to be around his own age, but one stood out. He was an older African American, with white threads beginning to make their way through his conservative haircut and a tightly trimmed beard.

At least the chairs were more comfortable than in the parenting class, he told himself.

"Alright," Theo growled as he walked into the circle and took a seat. "You're here because the state decided that not only does life start at conception, but so do your responsibilities as fathers. Since you couldn't keep it in your pants, you're going to do what the State of Wisconsin legislature says is necessary for you to step up to that role. Think of it as a shotgun wedding, only the government is the one holding the gun to your back, not her daddy."

A few snickers broke the silence.

"My job is to make sure that each and every one of you avoids mandatory prison time," Theo said, sweeping the group with his gaze.

Mandatory prison time? Sam looked over at Mike, confirming that he hadn't been told that either. From the low murmur around them, it sounded like this was news to everyone.

Theo frowned. "Looks like a few of you hadn't heard that." He nodded. "Here's what you need to know. You are required to fully participate in the court-ordered prenatal medical visits. You will complete *all* of the court-assigned coursework. You will cohabitate with your partner starting in the third trimester so that you're there for your kid's delivery. All of that is to help prepare you to be an active father for the next twenty-one years of that kid's life."

A guy across from Sam raised his hand tentatively. "What if you've already agreed to an open adoption?"

Theo nodded. "Great question," he said as he leaned forward to try and read the name tag, "Noah. You're stuck with your partner until your kid is handed over to foster care prior to the adoption."

Noah looked confused. "But—"

"Sometimes, all it takes is spending a small amount of time with that baby to make you change your mind," Theo told him. His rough voice was soft. "You still need to meet all of the program requirements."

Noah scrubbed his face with both hands and then looked away. "Whatever," he muttered.

The older African American man leaned forward. "What about me?" he demanded. "I'm getting a divorce. Why am I here?"

Theo looked over and crossed his arms. "Matthew, right?"

Matthew nodded. "Look, we already have a kid and we've been separated for so long that I don't think this one is mine. I shouldn't be here."

"Things have changed," Theo told him. "It doesn't matter if this was a one-night stand, if you're in a relationship, or you're in the middle of a divorce. Once upon a time, you could get away with handing your ex-wife a small percentage of your income. And there was very little consequence if you just walked away."

"And if it's not mine?" Matthew demanded.

"Then, the Court will refund any and all of the money you spent during the pregnancy," Theo said. "But you are still responsible for half of your other child's reasonable expenses. The law is the law and you're not going to win."

Matthew turned away in disgust. "Unbelievable."

Theo studied Matthew for a moment, then he leaned forward, his forearms on his upper thighs, hands steepled together almost in prayer. "Tonight's an open forum. I know you all must have a million questions. My job is to answer them." He paused. "Who wants to go first?"

Sam looked around at the group, at a loss as for what to say. No one made eye contact within the group.

"I got all night." Theo sat back in his chair, almost slouching as he glared at the floor. It was almost as if he was daring someone to speak.

"This fucking sucks!" the guy across from Theo snarled. "A friend of mine got his girl pregnant and all he has to do is give her $350 a month! He didn't have to take no classes or move in with her!"

Sam sat back and looked around the room. There was a pause, like the entire group wasn't sure if they should agree or not. A small smile puckered one side of Theo's mouth, but he said nothing as he continued to study the faded carpet squares in the center of the circle.

Finally, Mike jumped in. "Yeah! Why the hell is the government punishing us because some bitch got pregnant?!"

Sam nodded. *Why in the hell was it anyone else's business,* he thought angrily.

The muttering got louder. Theo smiled a bit more, nodding as the outbursts grew louder.

"She was supposed to be on the Pill. Why am I being punished because she forgot to take it?"

"Yeah, I hate condoms, so I pulled it off. So what?"

"I told her to get that IUD before they became illegal in our state!"

"She should have gone to fucking Illinois and gotten that abortion instead of crying to her mom about it!"

Sam was about to open his mouth, ready to add his issue with Rylee when Theo stood up. "Enough!" he yelled. "You all should hear yourselves." He began to mimic them in a whining baby voice. "She forgot to take the Pill. I hate condoms. She should have gone out of state to get that IUD like I told her. Whine, whine, *whinewhinewhine*!"

He moved to the center of the circle, hands on hips as he glared down at them. "If you didn't want the responsibilities that come with being a parent, you should have just rubbed one out and been done with it!"

Sam found himself slouching low in his seat as he tried to avoid Theo's rage. He didn't really understand why Theo was so angry, but he really did *not* want to become a target.

Theo slowly turned, looking at each of them individually until, one by one, they dropped their gaze to stare at the floor like errant children. "Obviously your own dads didn't teach you a lick of common sense," he told them. "So, rule number one for this group is to take personal responsibility for your own actions. Each and every one of you made a choice to have unprotected sex with the woman carrying your baby. It's time to grow a pair!"

Sam opened his mouth to protest, but nothing came out. Yeah, they'd had unprotected sex, but this couldn't be his fault. Rylee was on the Pill, dammit!

Theo moved back to his chair and slouched down, one hand in his front pocket. "We're going to go around this room and hear everyone's story." He overrode the collective groan with a growl. "Starting with my own!"

That got everyone's attention.

"My dad left when I was young," he told them. "Mom worked two jobs, and there was never enough money to go around. When I was seventeen, I scored a job working on motorcycles at a place that was cool hiring a high school dropout. A few years later, I hooked up with a sweet girl who loved motorcycles almost as much as I did. It didn't matter that I didn't have a GED or much money. What mattered was how much we loved each other. Until she started throwing up every morning."

He paused. "Sound familiar? Turned out she was nine weeks pregnant." He sat up, suddenly looking much older. "What did I do? Did I step up and act like a man? Hell, no! I ran, like some stupid asshole who didn't give a fuck about anyone but myself. I left Hannah to deal with all of that crap, all by herself, because I wasn't man enough to handle it." He frowned and looked around the circle. "I eventually got my shit together, but I will never forgive myself for being such an asshole. Neither will Hannah, or Ginny, my daughter.

"So, I'm here to make sure that you don't make the most stupid ass decision of your life," Theo growled. "Who's next?" He pointed to the guy on his right. "You. What's your story?"

The guy next to him ducked, almost like he was expecting Theo to follow up with a gut punch. He straightened up and looked around. "I'm Jacob. My girl's Emily. We live in River West. I have no idea why I'm here except that she's pregnant. We were thinking about getting married, maybe."

Theo looked over, eyebrow arched. "Married, maybe?"

Jacob gave a sardonic smile. "Yeah. It would make her mom happy, I think, and if it doesn't work out, we can always go our own way later, right?"

"You mean 'get a divorce'?" Theo asked with a small smile.

"Maybe," Jacob said, with a slight shrug of his left shoulder. "If I move out of state, what are they going to do? They can't force me to pay child support if I'm not here, right?" He shot a knowing look at Matthew, who leaned back in disgust.

Theo snorted. "Man, you really didn't read 'Your Rights and Responsibilities', did you?"

"What do you mean?" Jacob demanded.

"You think that all of this is going to go away just because you married your baby momma?" Theo responded, shaking his head in mock disappointment. "*Vlákas*," he growled. "There's no loophole in the law, man. Walk away or get divorced, they will hunt you down and make your life a living hell until you step up and accept your responsibility. And that includes issuing a warrant for your arrest and extraditing you from whatever shithole you try to hide in because you committed a felony by running away from your legal obligations."

He looked around, moving from face to face as if he could see every secret they collectively hid from the world. "You probably don't keep up with the news, so let me give it to you straight: You are in the system. Every single one of you. You do not have the option to walk away from your financial and personal responsibilities for that baby and every other baby you help make from now on."

Sam felt a stab of rage. *What the absolute hell?* He moved around in his chair, not quite sure of what to do or say.

Next to him, Mike finally broke the silence. "What does that mean?" he demanded.

Theo turned to him, looking from Mike to Sam and back again as if sizing them up. "It means that gone are the days of getting a girl knocked up and letting social services pick up the tab or paying a few hundred dollars a month to make it go away," he told them. "No. Free. Pass. Period."

"And another thing," he added as he looked around the circle. "Once the DNA confirms that you're a dad, it doesn't matter how many kids you help make or if you get a divorce a decade from now. You are responsible for providing financial and personal support for all of your kids. Even the ones you don't know about until you get served."

"What about the ones that were born before the law went into effect?" asked a Hispanic guy across from Sam. "Are they going to come after me for them, too?"

"Do you have a court-ordered child support agreement in place, Max?" Theo asked, almost gently. Max shook his head. "If not, you're fair game. If you do, then you might want to take a second look at the agreement language. If you're in default . . ."

Theo let that hang for a moment. He shot a look at Jacob. "Anything else to add, Jacob?"

Jacob flushed, slumping back into his chair as if he didn't have any energy left to fight with. "Whatever."

Theo turned to the next guy, and they went around the room. Each of them seemed to have a version of the same story: Boy meets girl. Boy and girl have sex. Girl gets pregnant, and suddenly the government is hauling your ass into court to pay for maybe twenty minutes of action.

As they wrapped up, Theo reminded them about the 'no alcohol' rule. "Probation means no alcohol, period. If your baby momma can't have a beer, neither can you. So, no bars, no liquor stores. Don't even have a few at your family's tailgate party."

Someone sniggered. "It's not a joke," he told the group. "I don't want to have to move this meeting to county lockup because you think you don't need to follow the rule. Peesh?"

As they headed out of the building, Mike groused about the no-alcohol rule. "Dude, there is no way that I'm going to make it through this without some serious drinking. Come on, let's hit Deuces. I told you, I know the owners."

Sam thought about it for a moment. So many people had warned them about how drinking was against the rules, but he really had a hard time believing that it was something that could be enforced. Frankly, he was getting tired of it.

"What the hell," Sam replied with a grimace. "My birthday was a week ago. Maybe it's time to celebrate in style." *Besides, one drink wouldn't hurt, right?*

"Happy birthday, man!" Mike said, and Sam pumped his fist. "First rounds on me."

Sam got in his car and waited for Mike to get moving so he could follow. One beer. Not a big deal, right? Besides, things couldn't get any worse, could they?

Finding parking in the Third Ward was close to impossible on a Friday night, so Sam followed Mike to the parking lot across the street from Deuces. $20 seemed excessive, but it was the Third Ward so they could charge whatever they wanted.

He could hear the live band playing as they crossed the street. They dodged a few cars, but traffic was lighter than Sam expected. He let Mike take the lead as they approached the open door. A bouncer sat on a bar stool, periodically looking up from his phone.

"Hey, Bill!" Mike called out. "Long time no talk to, eh?"

The bouncer, Bill, stood up, sliding his phone into the front pocket of his shirt with a practiced gesture. "Hey, Mike. Where you been, man?"

"Well, you know," Mike said, evasively. "Things with Jen are strange right now."

"I hear ya," Bill said. He turned to Sam. "Hey, man."

Sam nodded at him. "I'm Sam." He put his hand on his back pocket, already anticipating the request to see his ID. He prayed that the new driver's license wouldn't make that much of a difference.

Mike clapped Sam on the shoulder. "Sam and I just stopped down for a quick drink, Bill. Apparently, *someone* has homework!"

"Oh, yeah?" Bill looked him over. "Where do you go to school?"

"Northwestern," Sam told him. "I'm studying environmental engineering there."

Bill nodded with a grin. "Great weekend for a visit. The Invisibles are playing later tonight. Go right in," he said, waving them in as another group walked up. "Lemme see some IDs, ladies!"

Mike walked into the darkened bar, Sam just a few steps behind. The bar was packed, but Mike quickly made his way through the tightly packed groups of people until he was up against the bar. He waved a hand to get the bartender's attention, then stepped on the foot bar so that he could hoist himself up and snag two bottles from an ice bin on the stainless-steel counter.

He stepped down, handed them to Sam with a flourish, and pulled out his wallet. He handed a $20 bill to the woman, then pulled out his keys from his front pocket to find his bottle opener. A short time later, both of them were threading their way closer to the stage, cold beers in hand.

Mike led him past the stage, where a band was playing noise rock, and out to the beer garden between the buildings. It was only slightly quieter, but there was a free table in the patio's corner. Most of the couples were either dancing on the other side of the patio or actively making out.

"So, what do you think?" Mike asked as he sat down.

Sam looked around, taking in the lights hanging from the pergola that covered the patio. "Nice place," Sam told him.

Mike laughed. "No, I meant Theo."

"Ah," Sam paused to take a long swallow of beer. The craft brew tasted like freedom. "I donno. They call him our 'mentor,' but he seems more like our parole officer, you know?"

"Yeah, I'm not sure what to make of him," Mike said. "What the hell is a . . . what did he call Jacob? A 'vuhlacuss'?

Sam laughed. "Sounds about right. I have no idea what it means!"

Mike traced the label on his bottle with an idle hand. "You're lucky that you're still in college. Had the strangest meeting with my boss and HR last week. It felt like a disciplinary meeting, but without the PIP, you know?"

Sam leaned forward, curious. "What's a 'pip'?"

Mike took a quick drink. "Personal Improvement Plan," he told him. "That's a disciplinary letter that gives you 30 or 60 days to get your act together before they fire your ass for 'not meeting expectations.'"

"Huh," Sam replied. "So, they tried to discipline you because Jen's pregnant?" He thought back to the FMLA overview class. "That doesn't sound legal."

Mike smiled ruefully. "It's not. HR spent a lot of time going over the corporate attendance, FMLA, corporate leave and vacation policies, just to make sure they covered all the bases," he told Sam. "My boss painstakingly went over my annual goals and insisted that we meet weekly to make sure that I'm on track. They even sent me the meeting notes afterward. For my own records, I'm told." He took another drink. "It feels like they're building a case to fire me."

"Sounds like," Sam agreed. "But why would they do that?" he wondered.

Mike shrugged, sitting back in his chair. "I might not be a model employee, but I get the job done," he said. "Problem is that Jen has a bit of a temper. She's called me a few times at work, and we fought. It's an open office, so even if I go into the back hallway, people can hear us."

"Oof," Sam grimaced in sympathy.

"I have to turn off my personal cell phone at work," Mike told him, frowning as he looked across the patio. "I was forced to block her number on my company cell phone. Some time, I should let you hear the voicemails she leaves me."

"Did it start before she knew . . . " Sam's voice trailed off. "I mean, sorry, dude. TMI."

Mike waved a hand. "No worries," he said. "Jen's always been a bit of a bitch, but things really ramped up after she got pregnant. It's like the bitch switch got stuck in the on position!"

Sam nodded. They sat in silence, taking the occasional swig of beer and listening to the band as they belted out a new song.

At length, Mike leaned forward. "I'm ready for the next round."

Sam drained his bottle and placed it on the table. "I'd like to stay, man, but I have a backlog of homework that I haven't even started thanks to Rylee." He stood and grabbed the bottles so he could drop them in the trash on his way out.

"Yeah, I hear ya," Mike responded, getting up to follow him back into the bar. "I want to grab one more before I hit the road. I probably need to take another look at that paperwork before I miss a deadline or something."

"See you next week!" Sam said, trying to make himself heard over the band.

Mike waved as he disappeared into the crowd.

Sam made his way to the front door and nodded to Bill as he left the building. He was surprised at just how relaxed he felt. He liked Deuces. Sometimes you just need to find a space to call your own.

"That's not fair!" Rylee yelled, tossing her napkin on the dining room table as if it was a live grenade.

Sam jumped, but kept his gaze firmly on his plate. He gently pushed pieces of lemon chicken and roast potato around before taking a small bite. *Join us for lunch after worship service*, he'd been told. *There are things we need to discuss.* Uh huh.

"Rylee, there's a legal limit to what we can do," Rylee's dad told her, his voice deepening as he tried, once again, to get through to her.

"Don't you tell me that!" Rylee shrieked. "I am allowed to move furniture and my belongings from my home to this new apartment." Her father started to object, but she overrode him. "All I want is a few pieces for the bedroom, kitchen, and living room! Why is that too much to ask?!"

Rylee's mom threw her napkin on the table as well. It landed close enough to Sam's plate that he flinched as he looked up. Her mom leaned toward Rylee, hands almost strangling the dining room chair's arms. "You should have asked before you bought that kitchen set, Rylee!" she spat, outrage etched into puckering cheeks. "Our lawyer has repeatedly told you that your credit cards are a part of court records. That means that you just ate into the small amount of money that we can give you!"

"I have my own money, Mom!" Rylee spit out. "I can spend it any way I want!"

"And where are you going to store that kitchen set until you find an apartment?" Rylee's mom demanded.

Rylee threw up her hands. "I don't know, Mom. Maybe I'll just rent a heated storage locker!"

"We are not renting you a heated storage locker, young lady!" Rylee's mom replied, apparently seething at the idea. "Every single penny you spend must be reported to the Court. We are not wasting one penny on storage!"

"What?" Rylee shrieked. "Since when have you ever worried about wasting money?" She gestured around the room as if to point out the lavishly decorated dining room. She jabbed an accusing finger at a piece of furniture across the room. "That sideboard was imported from Italy!" she yelled, then spread her fingers over the table. "And this china? Gucci Herbarium doesn't come cheap!"

Rylee's dad cleared his throat. "Rylee, you need to understand the position we're in," he told her as he tried to cut through the raw argument. "We are—"

"Pillars of the community," Rylee growled. "Yeah, I got that. That's all I am, someone who is supposed to set the best example for others to follow!"

Rylee's dad covered his eyes with one hand. "Sweetheart," he finally said. "We need to be very careful about our next step, that's all."

"We're already in the spotlight, thanks to Sam—" Rylee's mom interjected.

"Mom!" Rylee gasped.

Sam pushed away from the table and stood, swaying from the sudden movement. "Sorry," he mumbled as he dropped his napkin on the chair. "I should go."

"See what you've done?" Rylee hissed. Then, she stood and moved around the table. "Sam, you don't need to leave," she gently told him. "We can figure this out."

Sam quietly pushed his chair in, then looked around, carefully avoiding eye contact with Rylee's parents. "Thanks for having me over."

As he retreated, his phone buzzed. It was Lucas. "Hey, man," Sam said, ducking through the kitchen and out the door that led to the driveway. "Can I call you back in a bit? I'm just about to leave Rylee's."

"Sure, man," Lucas said. "No worries. I'll be here."

Sam walked outside, carefully closing the door behind him. He vaguely knew Wendy and Rylee's mom didn't really like each other. It wasn't so much that Rylee's family had more money than most of the folks they worshiped with at New Covenant. No, Wendy didn't like the way that Rylee's mom, Ashley, used the money in a game of one-upmanship that Wendy was always going to lose, and that included volunteer work.

Wendy made cookies for the robotics team during the competition season? Ashley had lunch for the entire team delivered the next weekend. Sam's family went on a skiing vacation to Colorado? The Williams family rented a private villa in Switzerland for their entire extended family.

Sam got into his car and slowly drove the long and winding driveway past the family compound until he hit the main road that snaked its way through the estates. Once he was back on the main road, he hit redial and put it on speakerphone. Lucas picked up on the first ring.

"Hey, Lucas," he said. "What's up?"

"Just checking in," Lucas told him. "Did Rylee change her mind about getting those pills from a friend?"

"No," Sam told him, scanning the traffic ahead. It was early afternoon and traffic was starting to pick up. "She's not even willing to talk about adoption, either."

"Oh, man," Lucas breathed. "That sucks. Did you see that a bunch of premed students were arrested in Oklahoma? The police said that they were suspected of being a part of the Jane 'menstrual extraction' network."

"Really? I hadn't seen that."

"Yeah, apparently the police got a tip based on a few videos posted online. Might not stick, but who knew?" Lucas told him. "Anyhow, can you meet me at Culvers? I think we need to talk."

"Sure." Sam took a deep breath as he hung up. That blob was getting bigger. He tapped on the steering wheel with an idle finger, trying to tease out what else they could do. Rylee was almost thirteen weeks pregnant. Can't travel more than 50 miles from home and a surgical abortion wasn't an option unless Rylee was actually dying.

Think. Think, think, think! There had to be a solution.

Open a PO Box and try to get the pills delivered from over-seas? Nah. Too easy to track and Rylee wouldn't take them anyway. Try to find some over-the-counter meds or herbal supplements that might cause her to miscarry? He sighed. Probably not his best idea. For all he knew, anything that might cause a miscarriage would require him to show his driver's license, like that time he had to buy Wendy some head cold medicine.

Yep, any way you looked at it, he was screwed. He pounded the steering wheel in frustration.

Sam spotted Lucas sitting in the outdoor dining area as he drove into Culver's parking lot. He waved and pulled into a nearby parking space. They went inside, placed their order, and had a seat near the back of the restaurant to eat when their food was ready.

Sam pushed ketchup around with some fries. He wasn't really hungry.

"So," Lucas said, picking up his burger and shaking it a bit to let some of the extra lettuce drop to the table. "I heard a rumor about Rylee. I'm not sure if it's true or not, but I figured that you really want to know." He took a bite, waiting for Sam to respond.

Sam dropped the fries, wiping his hand on a napkin. "What kind of rumor?"

Lucas quickly swallowed. "Rumor is that Rylee got pregnant on purpose."

"What?" Sam snapped. "Says who?" He could feel the acid pouring into his stomach, and fumbled for the small container of antacids he kept in his jacket pocket.

"I went to a party last weekend," Lucas said as he put down his burger. "There are a few folks at church who heard what happened with Rylee. See, you're the first person we know who is going through this shit and everyone has questions."

"I'll bet." Sam popped a few of the chewable tablets in his mouth. He pushed away the fries as he chewed. Fruit flavored. Yum. He picked up his soda to try and wash away the taste, then grimaced. The two didn't mix well at all.

"Yeah, so anyhow. From what I heard, Rylee spent a lot of time crying when you broke up. Both times," Lucas told him. "Saying that she needed you. That it wasn't right for you to dump her. That she would find a way to keep you in her life, no matter what."

Sam set his soda down, feeling like Lucas had just sucker punched him. "' . . . keep me in her life, no matter what?' Dude. She dumped me!"

Lucas nodded. "I know. But it sounds creepy, doesn't it? Like she had motive."

"Motive to get pregnant." Sam thought about it for a moment. "I don't know, man. She's always been a bit emotional, but I can't believe that she'd get pregnant just to try and throw her hooks into me. I mean, she's really pissed that she's missing her gap year." He paused for a moment. "Not to mention how pissed her parents are."

Lucas snorted. "Yeah, getting knocked up will do that. Especially when your dad is a billionaire."

Sam smiled sardonically. He didn't think that the Williams had that much money, but they sure did act like it.

"There is one other thing, though," Lucas told him. "According to her friend, Rylee was hyper-focused on tracking when you two had sex. Made a big deal about it, from what I heard. It was almost like she *wanted* to get pregnant. Like she was focused on making it happen."

Sam sighed, then looked up at the white ceiling. No way. He refused to believe it. "She was on the Pill so she couldn't get pregnant!"

"Okay," Lucas said as he picked up his burger. "There might be another reason for her being so interested in tracking her period. Only know what I was told." He took another bite, slowly chewing it.

Sam gingerly picked up a few fries and popped them into his mouth. *No way Rylee wanted to get pregnant*, he thought. It didn't make any sense. Obviously, the rumor mill was wrong.

Chapter Eight

"Oh, for heaven's sake, Rylee, we can't live on the East Side!" Sam yelled, almost dropping his phone on his bedroom floor. "You're already in your second trimester and we have to get moving on this. Have you even looked at the apartments I sent you?"

"Sam, please don't yell at me," Rylee said in a surprisingly calm voice. "Of course, I looked at the listings. Not one of them has enough room or amenities that we'll need when the baby is born."

Sam raked his free hand through his hair. "Look, we can only afford so much per month."

Rylee sighed. "I know that you're working on that budget for that 'financial class,'" she finally said. Sam could almost see the air-quotes in her voice. "But we don't have to live in actual poverty. We have options."

"Really, Rylee?" Sam growled. "I know you have some money of your own, but we're only allowed to get $15,000 a year from each of our parents. So, unless you're sitting on a pile of money that I don't know about, we're going to have to stay on budget."

"Well, in theory, I do have money . . ." Rylee trailed off, sounding incredibly pleased with herself.

"Really."

"Sam, it's no secret that my family put away money for me when I was a child," Rylee told him, her tone oozing condescension. "I mean, that's how it's done."

Yeah. And some of us weren't born with a silver spoon shoved up our ass, Sam thought. "Get to the point, Rylee."

"Under normal circumstances, I wouldn't have access to my trust fund until I graduated from Wellesley. But I'm working with our family attorney to find a way to legally get access to the money after the baby's born." She laughed ironically. "According to my financial adviser, this should constitute a 'significant life event', so he should be able to free up some money to cover expenses."

"How much?"

"That depends on the attorney," Rylee told him. "I should have an update in a few weeks."

"Rylee, this changes nothing," Sam told her.

"Why not?" she asked with a pout.

"Because, unlike you, I don't have a trust fund to draw from," Sam told her, struggling with the urge to yell. "We have to divide our living expenses equally between the two of us. That means, we can only spend as much as I can afford. Period."

"Well, no one has to know," Rylee crooned. "Our actual budget is no one's business."

"Oh. My. God! Rylee, haven't you been paying attention at all?" he growled.

"What do you mean?" she asked coyly.

"Didn't you listen to your dad?" he demanded. "All of our documentation has to be submitted to the Court. That includes the apartment lease!"

"I know that," Rylee snapped back. "We just need to turn in some of our receipts. It's not like anyone's going to actually do the math!"

"Right," Sam growled. He closed his eyes, stretching his neck as he tried to think. "So, if you pick out a place that costs $3,000 per month, no one's going to look at my paycheck and figure out that I can't afford my half. With my schedule, DoorDash doesn't pay anywhere near enough!"

"It doesn't?" Rylee sounded genuinely confused. "I thought that made good money."

Sam bent his head until his forehead was firmly planted on his desk, eyes screwed shut. "For some drivers, sure. But I'm trying to get through my regular classes, take these stupid mandatory parenting classes, and squeeze in time to make myself available for deliveries during prime time. I'm not making a whole lot here."

"Well, I've been busy, too, you know," she shot back. "Pregnancy is a lot of hard work and I'm trying to get us ready for when this baby is born!"

Sam screwed his eyes shut. *Pregnancy is hard*, he thought. She eats. She sleeps. She goes to weekly spa visits and does a lot of yoga. Oh, and buys a lot of stuff that probably won't fit into the average apartment.

After a pause, he finally found his voice. "Rylee, unless you find something that's within our *actual* budget, one that has two bedrooms and is affordable, it's going to be a hard pass."

"I'm absolutely positive that there's a way around this," she told him.

She sounded so confident, Sam thought. "Rylee, you've got to meet me halfway on this," he finally told her. "We need to keep looking. Think about the near east side of Milwaukee, or lower east side."

"Why not Mequon or Bayside? Those are much closer to home."

"Because the rents are closer to $1,500 a month, and we need to keep it under a thousand."

"But a thousand dollars is nothing!" Rylee exclaimed.

Sam sat up. "I know," he told her. "But we have other bills to cover, and this is the best we can do for now."

"Fine," Rylee said with a sniff. "But I won't settle for living there for more than a few months. I just can't!"

"Fine," Sam retorted. "We'll keep looking, okay?"

"Yes, we will," she responded with an icy jab. The connection dropped, leaving Sam with an uneasy feeling. He was working his butt off with school, these stupid parenting classes, and his side job. What the hell was he supposed to do?

A few days later, Sam found himself back in that cramped exam room again. Rylee stood in front of the mirror, looking at her profile and running a hand across her belly.

"Oh, my God," she breathed happily. "I think I'm starting to show!"

Yeah, Sam thought. *You're starting to get fat. Woohoo.*

There was a knock on the door, followed almost immediately by the technician. "Why don't we get a quick look at that baby?" she chirped.

Rylee scrambled up onto the exam bed. The tech pushed Rylee's skirt up higher and squirted some of that medical gel on her stomach. Then, she pushed the flat-head wand across Rylee's stomach, hunting for that elusive blob.

For a moment, he almost thought that he was off the hook, but nope, she finally found it. "There we are!" Both women laughed as they stared intensely at the screen.

Dammit. He shook his head in frustration. From what Sam could see, that blob was starting to resemble an actual baby.

The tech rattled off some facts that made Rylee giggle, like the baby was able to open and close their fingers and curl their toes. And that the nose and fingernails were starting to form.

"And here's the heartbeat," she told them. The filaments seemed to have resolved into a single spot on the screen, flickering rapidly. "Would you like to hear it?"

"Oh, yes," Rylee breathed. Sam rolled his eyes. Of course, she did.

The tech picked up another wand and coated it with gel. Then, she moved the wand around Rylee's belly, hunting for the heartbeat. After a long while, she pulled the wand away.

"What's wrong?" Rylee demanded.

"You're in your fifteenth week, so it might be just a bit too soon for the Doppler to find it," the tech told her. "Your baby is fine. We should be able to pick up the heartbeat at your next visit." She quickly cleaned the Doppler wand and set it aside. Then, she grabbed the original wand, added a dab of gel and rolled it across Rylee's baby bump.

Rylee glared at the tech. Sam held up a hand. "It's okay, Rylee," he told her. "You saw the heartbeat on the screen, right?"

"When will I be able to feel the baby move?" Rylee asked petulantly, ignoring him.

"Well," the tech said. "You should start feeling the baby move when you're in your twentieth week, so you've got a bit of time." She fiddled with a control and zoomed in on the blob's back.

"Let me get a quick measurement of the baby's neck and we'll be done."

Dr. Zastrow came in at that moment and looked over the tech's shoulder as she continued to take screenshots of the blob. Sam slouched in his chair. He made appropriate noises from time to time as they worked. He couldn't share Rylee's momentary excitement. It was just too much.

Another place, another time, definitely another woman, maybe he could be happy. Maybe. He knew that he should feel guilty about not feeling . . . anything . . . about Rylee's pregnancy, but in reality, it was *her* pregnancy. Her baby. Not his. Not *theirs*. He was just another nameless drone in #TeamRylee that was expected to step up and make things happen.

"Alright," the doctor finally said. "Let's go ahead and get you cleaned up." He stepped back, and the tech handed Rylee a rag to wipe the goop off. Then, she cleaned up the wand and left the room.

Rylee finally sat up and pulled her skirt down protectively over her small bump.

"Let's get started," Dr. Zastrow said as he moved to his seat at the desk. "We're seeing healthy development, Rylee, and the ultrasound confirms that you are fifteen weeks pregnant."

Rylee nodded, silently taking it in.

"Your risk of miscarriage will continue to go down the further along you are," he told her. "Preliminary ultrasound doesn't show signs of a chromosomal disorder, but we'll be following up with a blood test to determine if you have risk."

Sam stirred. "Meaning what?"

"Prenatal screening cannot diagnose any specific condition," the doctor told him. "A fetus with a buildup of fluid at the base of their neck is at increased risk of having a chromosomal problem, such as Down's Syndrome." He looked at Rylee. "You need to keep in mind that we can only assess the risk, Rylee. We'll need to follow up with a blood test but, as of right now, things look very positive."

"Hang on a minute," Sam replied. "At our court hearing, we were told that you couldn't test for this stuff until later." He frantically tried to recall the exact words. "I think it was called amnio?"

"Ah. Yes, amniocentesis can be performed at about fifteen weeks' pregnant to analyze fetal chromosomes for abnormalities," the doctor replied. "We insert a needle into the mother's uterus—"

"Um, no!" Rylee interjected, her hands protectively covering the micro baby bump.

"—however, this is only done if we determine that there is a significant risk of genetic abnormality."

"But you'd also be able to verify paternity, right?" Sam asked, looking at Rylee. She looked crestfallen.

"We could," the doctor slowly replied, "but given the circumstances, we'd need approval from the Court to run a paternity test if we need to proceed with amniocentesis."

Sam took a deep breath and nodded. Didn't hurt to ask, right?

Dr. Zastrow looked down, then cleared his throat before he began to pepper Rylee with questions like how her appetite was, did she still feel nauseous in the mornings, did she find herself needing a nap or to rest throughout the day, had she experienced any dizziness or fainting. The list went on and on.

Sam tuned out most of it. Every once in a while, Dr. Zastrow would look to Sam for confirmation on something, and Sam would just nod. The only time he actually spent with Rylee was taking the parenting classes that had to be in the classroom or during these mandatory doctor visits. He even avoided her family at worship services. How the hell would he know if she was still sick in the morning? And, more importantly, why should he care?

Enough, already. Sam pulled out his phone to check the time. "Um, I hate to interrupt, but I need to leave soon," he told them. "I have a test today. It's a third of my grade, so I can't miss it." It was a lie, of course. They didn't need to know that his courses were asynchronous, and he had until the end of the week to take the test.

The doctor stood. "That's fine," he said with a disapproving look. He turned to Rylee. "Please touch base with our billing department. I believe that we may have gotten approval for your doula." He looked back at Sam. "I'll see you again in four weeks."

He left the room, closing the door firmly open behind him. Sam looked at Rylee. "What did I do?" he asked.

Rylee gave a small shrug and picked up her purse. "Doesn't matter," she finally told him. "You're going to be late for your test."

It was beginning to feel like Sam would never get anything right. Both of their parents were pissed at him. The doctor expected him to keep tabs on Rylee, even though they rarely saw each other. And now, Theo was yelling at him in the mentoring meeting.

"Listen, I know that most of you are just starting the second trimester, but you all need to be looking for an affordable apartment now," Theo told them as he glared at Sam. "You absolutely must pass your home visit before the start of the third trimester."

Sam looked away. As if he hadn't been trying. You would think that someone as organized as Rylee would be all in. But no. She was oblivious to how much living by themselves would actually cost. Considering that Rylee was a week into her second trimester, he felt like he had a bit of time.

Jacob stood up and moved behind his chair, gripping it tightly with both hands as he leaned forward. "Don't we have a couple of months on that?"

"You all realize that the third trimester starts at the twenty-seventh week, right?" Theo looked around. "It's not enough to have just signed the lease. You have to be completely moved in prior to the home inspection. That means that you have furniture, that your driver's license is updated with your new address, that you've started working on the baby's room . . . " he trailed off as the collective groan filled the air.

Theo overrode the noise. "Look, failure to pass this inspection means more than just a fine, guys. You'll also spend a few sleepless nights in detention until you come up with a plan—and a court-approved timeline—on how to get this done. And that means both of you will be locked up."

Sam blinked. *Detention? Was Rylee getting the same information from her mentor*, he wondered.

"I've been looking, Theo," Tyler said, pushing back the hat that hid his short dreadlocks. "But everything out there is way too expensive!"

Theo nodded. "The market's pretty tight right now," he told him. "Let me know if I need to work with you on finding something you can afford. If necessary, we can check with the housing authority to get you on a waiting list for rental assistance."

"Waiting list?" Ethan asked. "I thought we were top priority?"

"For some things, yes," Theo confirmed. "Problem is that there's about a six month wait for affordable housing. But we might be able to get the housing authority to provide emergency vouchers if they can't get you into public housing."

Jacob sat down in his chair, slouching down until his shoulders were firmly planted against the chair's back, feet widely spread. "And, even if we can't find a two-bedroom place, we're still not allowed to move in with a relative, right?"

"No," Theo confirmed. "The law is very clear: each child deserves to have two parents raising them. Not family members. Not grandparents." Theo got up. "Let me see if we have any housing authority flyers here." He crossed the room and sorted through the stacks of flyers on the back table.

Jacob groaned. "Emily's grandparents live in Sussex. They have a small house behind theirs and they've offered to let us live there."

Theo didn't look back. "Two bedrooms?" he asked as he continued his search.

"Just the one bedroom, but we might be able to create a bedroom for us down in the basement," Jacob said.

Theo grunted as he brought a stack of flyers with him. "Yeah, that probably won't pass inspection. Depends on the house, of course, and how far away it is from her grandparents." He started handing out the flyers. "If it's one of those mid-century mother-in-law houses that they used to build in the backyard, you definitely will not pass inspection. Too close to family."

Sam took a quick look at the flyer before jamming it into his back pocket. It seemed simple enough. Joint income couldn't exceed $60,000 per year. Applicants had to pass a credit report, criminal history check, and provide the last three years of rental history.

He was positive that Rylee's trust fund would make them ineligible for any assistance, even though she couldn't access it right now. *An asset is an asset*, he thought.

Sam looked at Mike. Every single time he thought that he was finally ahead of the curve, this happened. He leaned over to the side. "I think I need a drink," he quietly told Mike.

Mike smiled. "Cool. Meet me in the parking lot."

A dull roar greeted them as they walked into the packed bar. Couches and chairs clustered around the large screen TVs that dotted the walls. One of the teams playing must have scored because a large cheer went around the room and some popcorn was tossed at the ceiling by a rambunctious fan.

They pushed their way through the crowd until they were up against the bar. Mike waved a hand, and one of the bartenders came over.

"Mike," the bartender yelled over the background noise. "Long time, no see!"

Mike nodded. "Give us two Black Cows, Greg."

The bartender nodded and grabbed two bottles out of the under-counter refrigerator. Sam pushed a couple of bills across the counter. "No change," he told Greg.

Sam and Mike moved away from the bar and tried to find a quiet place away from the TVs. They settled down at a small table in the far corner, away from the noise. They could still hear the crowd, but it was manageable.

"So, what do you think?" Sam asked. "I can't believe they're forcing us to move in with the girls."

Mike laughed. "According to Jennifer, this is all a plot to increase Wisconsin's birth rate."

Sam took a swig from the bottle, then shook his head. "No way. Where'd she get that from?"

"I have no idea," Mike said. "She swears that it's an evangelical conspiracy to make white people have more babies. Apparently, abortion was legal and legit before evangelicals got their undies in a bundle about the 'Great Replacement Theory'. Now, it doesn't matter if a preteen is raped by their stepdad. All that matters is that women are walking baby machines." He shook his head, then tipped the bottle back for a long drink. "It's got to be the hormones talking," he said.

Sam took a swig of beer and sat back. "Probably," he told him. He thought for a moment. Wendy was always grousing about how marginalized their community was; how secular society had become. It wasn't that she had fully embraced the idea that the United States was a Christian nation. More like she missed the days when people were not surprised that she was a stay-at-home mom and proud of it!

They sat together for a moment, each lost in their own thoughts.

Sam finished his beer and glanced at his phone. "I gotta get going," he told Mike. "We're walking through a few apartments tomorrow morning."

"Yeah?" Mike said. "Jen and I need to get started on that. Where are you looking?"

"The River West neighborhood," Sam said. "I want to be as close to the east side as possible, but we can't really afford much."

"Don't Jacob and Emily live out that way?" Mike asked. "I thought he said that there weren't a lot of available two-bedroom apartments in the area?"

Sam shrugged. "A lot of what I'm seeing in our price-range are small and not something I'd want to live in long-term, but you gotta take what you can get, right?" Sam told him. "My only problem is convincing Rylee that she can survive a whole nine months outside of the east side."

"I hear you," Mike said. "I have to move out of the condo that I'm renting in Brewer's Hill because we need a two-bedroom place."

"That sucks. Are they letting you out of the lease?"

"Court ordered, man," Mike said, with a rueful smile. "Landlord is arranging for someone to sublet."

Sam stood, grabbing his empty bottle. "See you next week," he said. "Lemme know if you find a place. We can compare notes."

Chapter Nine

The next day was brutal. Finding parking on the east side was difficult most of the time, but Sam had expected it to be a bit easier in the River West neighborhood.

Rylee had provided him with a list of what she considered to be acceptable rental units, but he'd had to cross most of them off the list because of the expense. Personally, he'd have loved to grab that unit at the Water Complex, but the rent for a two-bedroom place was over $2,000, and Rylee was already burning through the money that their parents had given them toward their living expenses.

They had looked at a number of places already. Some had no parking. Others were crowded with college students, and neither of them really wanted that reminder. They had finally settled on looking for something that allowed a month-to-month lease, with a sixty-day notice. That way, they weren't locked into the place and could just focus on getting through the next few months.

Sam thought that the place on Humboldt had potential, although it didn't look like much from the street. The place had started out as a single-family house, with a small yard, but at some point, the owner had carved two small apartments out of the house.

"This place is about as big as my bedroom," Rylee muttered as they dutifully followed the apartment manager around. "I can't believe you're suggesting that we live in such a dump!"

"Well, if you hadn't spent so much on maternity clothes, and your urgent 'spa time,' we might have been able to afford more!" Sam retorted, flexing his fingers to keep from clenching them into fists. "We need to save some money!"

"Well, excuse me for being pregnant and needing deep tissue back massages!" Rylee protested. "This baby of yours is starting to push my back out of place and I can't take anything for the pain! Besides, if we're running out of money, maybe you should, you know, work more hours!"

"Yeah, that would work, wouldn't it, Rylee?" Sam snapped back. "Maybe I should just drop out of school so that I can give you money for more massages! Besides, why don't you use your own money?"

"Because you and my father have made it *very apparent* that I have to turn *every single receipt* into the Court, Sam!" she snarled. "Which means my parents can't cover my bills anymore. It's not like I can walk into any business, and they'd just hire me!"

Unbelievable. He spared a quick glance at the apartment manager before ducking into the bathroom for a look. Rylee followed him, but he ignored her as he focused on the details. Small. Shower/tub combo with just a pedestal sink.

"Look," he said, lowering his voice. "We really need to get a place, and this one will do until we find something better. It's only $950 a month."

Rylee looked over the sink, giving it a critical eye before turning to him. "I don't like this. There's no room for my make-up or anything."

"We can get a small cabinet or some shelves or something," Sam told her. "There's plenty of room against that wall." He held up a hand to stall the next outburst. "As it is, this place doesn't become available until January first. We don't have a lot of options and are running out of time."

She gave him a long look. "Point. I just need this to be over."

"You and me, both."

They continued to walk around the small space. The living room was barely large enough to fit the current tenant's couch, coffee table, and entertainment center. The kitchen was tiny, with barely enough room for the appliances. A small kitchen table was jammed into the far corner.

Both bedrooms were about the same size, but Sam realized that none of the furniture either of them currently had would fit. Maybe a full bed, two nightstands and a small dresser, but that was about it. Obviously, Rylee would claim the closet for herself.

Well, the living room had a rather large closet that he could use. And, if they got a futon couch, he could sleep out there.

"Would you like to check out the backyard?" the manager asked. She pursed her lips together in a tight smile. Sam wondered just how much of the conversation she had overheard. The walls in this place were pretty thin.

"Sure," he said, dutifully following her through the kitchen, down the back stairs, and outside.

She explained that there was only room for one car in the garage. Street parking was an option but it was difficult to predict availability, especially during the winter months when parking restrictions went into effect.

Sam walked around the small yard. A tired, paint peeled picnic table. An old grill. A rusted fire bowl. A few folding lawn chairs propped up against the side of the house.

"I'll leave the two of you alone to decide," the manager told them. "I'll be upstairs if you need me."

He had a seat at the old picnic table and gestured for Rylee to join him. After a moment, she carefully sat down across from him, looking around with disgust before settling her hand on the least objectionable part in front of her. He reached over the table for her hand.

She hesitated, then settled her hand against his. He absently rubbed his thumb against the back of her hand. A few short months ago, they would have sat on the same side of the table, comfortably spooning as they sat together. Now, it took a lot of effort just to have a conversation without sniping at each other.

"This is the least expensive place that we've seen, Rylee," he told her. "We need to pick a place so that we can check this off the list." He shook his head to stop whatever she was going to say. "It's only temporary until we can find another place that we can afford," he reminded her.

Rylee sighed, leaning forward. She looked down at the weather-worn table, a bleak look in her blue eyes. "Okay," she said. "We can take this place for now as long as we can keep looking."

Sam nodded, pulling out his wallet as he stood up. Time to find the apartment manager and get the credit check done. Once they cleared that hurdle, they'd have to pay the first month and last month's rent, and security deposit. They should be able to move in at the start of the new year, well ahead of the court-ordered deadline.

Sam trailed after Rylee as she shopped at yet another maternity boutique. He was holding a pile of stuff that Rylee wanted to try on with no end in sight. Seriously, how many of these stores were there in Southeastern Wisconsin? They must have hit every single one of them. Rylee might be sixteen weeks along, but she seemed to be stockpiling enough clothes to never wear the same outfit twice!

Time to make the move, Sam thought. He cleared his throat, then plunged in. "Did you hear that Tyler and Devi have decided to put their baby up for adoption? Makes me wonder—"

"Stop it, Sam," Rylee snapped. "Adoption is not on the table and never will be!"

"Why not?" Sam demanded. "Don't you want to get your life back when this is over?"

Rylee stopped and pulled yet another dress out of the clothes rack. She shook her head and put it back. "I do, Sam," she said. "But giving this child up for adoption is not an option."

"Can you at least tell me why?" Sam asked.

"This baby is a miracle," she told him as she moved deeper into the boutique. "An actual gift from God. I shouldn't have been able to get pregnant and I am not giving up this baby."

Sam blinked. This was new. "Why couldn't you get pregnant?" he asked, ducking around the shelves so that he could look directly at Rylee.

"Because I have fibroids and my ovaries don't really work," she told him as she pushed another piece of clothing at him to hold. "Same as Chloe. Which means this may be my only chance of becoming a mom. I have to take it, whether I'm ready or not."

Fibroids? Sam thought. *Ovaries don't work? What the hell did that even mean?*

"What about me?" he growled. "I'm not ready for any of this shit!"

"Neither am I, obviously," she snapped, throwing another piece of clothing at him. "But we have to make this work."

Sam caught the shirt and glared at her. "How?" he demanded. "I've given up tennis. My scholarships. I'm not going to graduate on time. I even got a side job to help pay for all of this. It's not enough, Rylee. How are we going to make this work?"

Rylee grabbed the pile of clothes and glared up at him. "We will find a way," she snapped. "Just because you've given up doesn't mean that I will!" And, with that, she stalked toward the changing room.

Sam looked around until he found a seat nearby. Several women glared at him. Obviously, they'd overheard at least part of the conversation.

He pulled out his phone and tried to log into the remote learning portal. Maybe he could review a few of his classmates' projects while he waited.

It was late Thursday night when he received an email from the property manager that indicated they'd gotten the apartment. There had been little doubt in his mind that they would pass the credit check. Both of them had credit cards in their own names, and Sam had a verifiable income. Besides that, he was sure that the names of every single couple in the Wisconsin Individual Family Education program were in the system, somehow.

Now all he had to do was arrange to pay first and last month's rent and security deposit. He checked his calendar. Yeah, next Friday was a good day to stop by the rental office to drop off the check. He typed up a quick reply and put down his iPad.

Sam had spent the last few days avoiding Rylee. Refused to answer her texts. Ignored her emails. He'd even periodically turned off his phone because he didn't really want to talk to anyone. Besides, he needed to focus. That German literature class was kicking his ass!

So was Wendy. The church ladies seemed evenly split on who was to blame for Rylee's pregnancy. Some quietly rallied behind Rylee's mom, treating Rylee like she was some sort of virgin princess who would never have thought of having sex if it hadn't been for him. Others looked at Rylee's 'known indiscretions' and silently joined #TeamWendy. And, since Wendy's life revolved around the work that she did for the congregation, Sam spent most of his time either holed up in his room or at the local library when he wasn't out making deliveries. He had no idea when the war was going to break out.

He had just settled down to try another crack at his current assignment, *Die Horen* by Friedrich Schiller, when his phone rang. Josh. Right on time.

He put the call on speakerphone. "Hey, Josh," he said.

"Hey, Sam," Josh replied. "How're you holding up?"

Sam sighed. "I guess I'm okay. Rylee's baby bump is really starting to show and, as you can imagine, the church ladies are really starting to talk."

"Yeah," Josh drawled. "I can imagine. She's what? Fourteen weeks along now?"

"Sixteen weeks," Sam reminded him. "Sixteen weeks of pure hell."

Josh grunted. Then, he asked the most important question: "How's Wendy taking it?"

"She's not," Sam told him. "She's trying to ignore the whispers, but at some point, someone is going to confront her. It's only a matter of time."

"Yeah." It was Josh's turn to sigh. "How are your classes going?"

Sam closed his laptop. "Remote classes suck!"

"I hear ya," Josh said. There was a long pause as both of them tried to find something else to talk about. "What are you hearing about the protests in Madison?"

Sam pressed his phone to his ear. "What protests?" he asked.

"The forced birth protests," Josh told him. "At Capitol Square." He paused. "Don't you watch the news?"

"No," Sam sputtered. "I've got enough on my plate right now. I barely have enough time to get my homework done. What are you seeing?"

"Hang on. Lemme pull up the BBC article," Josh said. His voice sounded a bit muffled as he put him on speakerphone. "'Six people were arrested after several hundred people descended on the state capitol to protest what participants are calling the "forced birth movement." Police stated that the opposing sides were separated on either side of State Street, a usually peaceful pedestrian mall that runs through the downtown area. Several businesses were vandalized as tempers ran hot near the end of the evening.'"

"Wow," Sam said. "No. I hadn't heard anything about it."

"Well, it looks like things are heating up," Josh told him. "From what I've seen, it looks like several other states are going to adopt Wisconsin's policies. Florida, Mississippi, Idaho, Tennessee."

Great, Sam thought. "This is the point where I'd say something about maybe I should move to Germany, like you, but they took my passport."

"They took your passport?" Josh asked, incredulous. "For how long?"

"I have no idea," Sam told him. "Probably until after we finalize the financial and placement plans."

"I have some vacation time saved up," Josh said. "I could come home for a few weeks."

Sam looked out the window, studying the moonlit backyard. As awesome as it would be to have Josh home for a while, he really didn't want to cause any more drama. Every time that Josh came home for a visit, Wendy got emotional when it was time for him to leave. "Nah," he finally said. "I'm good."

"Okay," Josh replied, sounding doubtful. "Call me if you need me."

"Will do," Sam said.

After they hung up, Sam sat for a long time. He would never admit it, but his world felt just a bit smaller.

Sam slowly walked into the doctor's office, trailing after Rylee like an apprehensive child. Yes, he was supposed to go with her to every single doctor's visit because that's what the law said. Going with her for a simple blood draw was going a bit too far, in his opinion. He was beginning to feel like he was just her driver.

He immediately grabbed a chair in the waiting room and turned on his iPad. He half-heard Rylee answer a few questions as she checked in. Yes, she was currently seventeen weeks. Yes, she had a follow-up appointment to review her test results next week.

Right now, the only important thing was to try and get through this next lecture. He popped his earbuds in and tried to focus.

His German literature course was killing him. It should have been easy enough. He had taken two years of German in high school and another year in college. Problem was, the course was taught entirely in German and, as a remote student, Sam knew he was missing a lot. He basically had to transcribe the audio lectures into English so that it made sense, only to have to reverse the process to submit his homework.

Rylee sat down next to him and started babbling. He tried to ignore it, but the standard complaint about how much she hated needles bled past the audio.

"I just don't understand why they have to keep taking blood," she complained. She brushed her hands against her thighs. "It's not like I'm taking drugs or anything!"

Sam nodded absently. They kept telling him that everything that applied to moms-to-be applied to their partners. It was probably only a matter of time before they were required to have matching his-and-her blood work.

They called Rylee's name, and she started to walk away. She turned and looked at him. "Aren't you coming?" she demanded.

Sam paused the video and pulled the earbud out of his right ear. "Is this just blood work or are you seeing the doctor, too?" he asked. He kept his eyes on the screen.

"It's just blood work," she replied. "But I hate needles. You should come with me."

He shook his head. "I'll be here when you're done," he told her.

Rylee huffed, then followed the nurse back.

Sam started to put the earbuds back in, but the audio from the TV in the corner caught his attention. "Thanks to the Wisconsin Individual Family Education program, I have access to a whole community of support."

He looked up. The video showed a young woman in a very familiar classroom, with an older woman leading the class. The group laughed at something the moderator said, then cut to the same young woman in a mentoring meeting, listening intently as the facilitator gave some sort of advice.

Sam pulled out his other earbud and slammed his iPad case closed. "My partner and I have taken classes to prepare for childbirth and parenting," the woman said in the commercial, a bright smile on her face. "I've met with other parents who understand what I'm going through. We've even gotten educational resources to help us prepare financially for our child."

He stood up and walked closer to the TV, eyeing the screen, clenching his jaw in rage to keep from screaming. The video cut to her sitting on a park bench, holding a newborn baby in her arms.

"Sonofabitch," Sam breathed.

The woman looked at the camera. "Thanks to the Wisconsin Individual Family Education program, I feel confident and ready to take on this new chapter of my life."

The screen faded to black. 'Empowering new parents, building strong families' appeared in white, superimposed over the all-too-familiar WIFE program logo.

Sam turned away in disgust. What the fuck? An entire commercial that glamorized forcing people into parenthood? And people believed it?

He looked around the waiting room. Mostly younger women, with a small number of guys. A few of them made eye contact as he scanned the room, but no one seemed to have watched the commercial.

Sam sighed and moved back to his seat. No one seemed to care. It was just background noise to them.

And that was part of the problem, he thought bitterly. Until the state made it his problem, Sam had been in the same place.

Rylee came through the door, a band aid covering the inside of one elbow. "Ready to go?" she asked. She stopped and looked at him. "What's wrong?"

Sam gathered up his iPad. "Doesn't matter," he told her. "I have a paper to write. Let's get going."

Another week, another stupid-assed mentoring group session, Sam thought as he found a seat. The last few weeks had crawled by so slowly that it had felt like time was standing still.

"All right, settle down," Theo said as he claimed the last open chair in the circle. "We have a lot to talk about tonight."

Sam quickly scanned the circle as the muttering faded, trying to figure out if he was the only one struggling. As usual, Mike looked like he was in a bad mood, but that could have been something at work or Jen. No way to tell. Most of the group was slouched down in their chairs. Hunter was the only one who actually seemed to be in a good mood.

Theo got right to the point. "Now that all of your baby mommas are in their second trimester, the courses that you're required to attend will be significantly reduced," he told them. "But, from here on in, everything will be a bit more challenging."

He paused for a moment to let that sink in. "Up until now, the program has been about the basics: insurance, FMLA, simple budgets, prenatal and parenting overviews, nutrition . . ."

Theo's voice trailed off as he rubbed the back of his neck. "The next few months will include negotiating your child placement plan, finalizing your financial support plan, and even a section on grandparent rights and responsibilities."

Matthew groaned. "Theo, this is a total waste of my time."

Theo looked over. "Just because you're in the middle of a divorce doesn't mean that you get a free pass, Matthew," he told him.

"Look," Matthew said, throwing his hands up in the air. "I already have both sets of grandparents in my face almost every single week. And my so-called 'child' placement and financial support plans are being worked on by our divorce mediator. Enough already!"

"You can send a request to the Court asking for a course waiver," Theo said. "But your wife may need to do the same or the judge can deny it."

Mathew looked down. "Of course, he will," he muttered.

Theo looked over at him for a moment, then looked around the room. "Based on what I've seen so far, I have recommended that an additional course be added to your third trimester coursework: partner empathy," he told them. He overrode the collective groans. "I haven't seen any ounce of understanding as to what your partners are going through."

"Hey, at least I already live with Abigail," Hunter blurted out. "That's gotta count for something!" A few guys chuckled at that.

Theo went around the room, asking each of them for an update in their turn. Sam only half-listened. *Partner empathy?* he thought. Every single conversation that he had with Rylee seemed to revolve around how horrible it was to miss out on her gap year. That this was just the beginning of so many things that needed to be adjusted in her life, and how Sam was going to have to step it up.

If anything, Wendy seemed to echo Rylee's complaints. How horrible her life was now that the entire congregation knew that he had had *sex* with Rylee. That because of this heinous act he was going to make her a grandmother before he was even married! And don't even get her started on how this set Sam's graduation date back, possibly *for years*!

"Sam?" Theo grumbled. "You there, man?"

Sam looked up. "Sorry, what?"

"Any updates you'd like to share with the group?" Theo asked.

"Not really," Sam told him. "I'm still trying to adjust to remote learning. My literature class is kicking my ass. I'm working as many hours as I can, and we have an apartment lined up for January."

Theo smiled. "That's good to hear, Sam," he told him. "Anything else?"

"No, I'm good," Sam replied.

"Well, unless anyone has anything else to add, we're done," Theo told the group. "See you next week!"

There was general muttering as the group got up and started to disband. Theo stood and started folding up his chair to put it away, then turned back to the group.

"Sam," he called. "Can I talk to you for a minute?"

Mike smirked at him. "Uh-oh," he crooned. "Looks like you got detention, dude!"

Sam glared at him. "Shut up, man!" he snarled. Then, he turned around and marched back into the room.

"What's up, Theo?" he asked.

"We need to talk," Theo told him. "Why don't you help me put away the chairs. It won't take long."

Sam grabbed the nearest chair, folded it up, and walked over to the chair rack. "Now what did I do wrong?" he demanded. "Rylee say something?"

Theo paused and leaned against the chair he had been sitting on. "No," he told him. "Why would you think that Rylee complained about something?"

Sam looked down. "Because she's always complaining about something," he told Theo.

Theo chuckled and folded the chair up. "She's what, eighteen weeks now?"

"Nineteen," Sam corrected him. "But who's counting?"

"So, nineteen weeks," Theo repeated. "She's almost half-way through her pregnancy, Sam. Those hormones are pumpin'. Stomach muscles are getting stretched. Hips are taking a beating. I'll bet she's even getting leg cramps."

Sam put the chair into the rack and went back for another. "Your point is . . . "

"My point is that you need to cut her some slack," Theo told him. "She might say or do things that may not seem exactly normal for her." He paused and grabbed the last chair from their circle. "You need to cut yourself some slack, too. Right now, you're leaning in so far that you don't know if you're coming or going."

Sam sighed. "Yeah," he admitted. "I'm really having trouble focusing. There is just so much that needs to get done and not enough hours in the day to do it all."

"How are things at home, otherwise?" Theo asked, as he put the chair away. "Parents coming around to the fact that they're going to be grandparents?"

Sam snorted. "Are you kidding?" he asked sarcastically. "The only thing that Wendy cares about is how badly this is going to affect her standing in our community."

Theo looked at him as he started to gather up the flyers and assorted support packets that he put out for every meeting. "Her reputation?" he asked.

"Yeah." Sam gave him a sad smile and sighed. "She's very involved in our congregation. Sometimes, I swear Pastor Chapman can't plan a sermon without her help."

"What about your dad?" Theo prodded. "Siblings?"

Sam shook his head. "My dad is an attorney and isn't home a lot. He tries to play defense when Wendy gets out of control but there's only so much he can do, you know?" He shrugged. "My brother Josh works in Germany. We talk but . . . " his voice trailed off.

"How are your grades?" Theo gently asked. "I know that you're finding the remote stuff harder than you expected."

"Yeah." Sam gathered his coat and backpack. He'd never admit this to Theo, but his grades had fallen, and he was considering dropping his literature class so he could just focus on Uncertainty Analysis.

Theo came over and clapped him on the shoulder. "Hang in there, Sam," he told him. "Things will get better once you move into the apartment. Let's get outta here."

Sam followed Theo out of the room and watched him lock up. "You think so?" he asked.

Theo smiled. "Absolutely," he assured him. "You'll be able to focus on just one woman in your life at a time!"

Sam hadn't been sure that he wanted to go to the football party that Lucas was hosting that Sunday. Finals were coming up and none of his friends were home for winter break yet.

The Packers were playing the Bears, but neither team was especially interesting. It was early in the second quarter, but it was pretty clear that the Bears were going to lose. He hugged the back of the room, nibbling on a hot wing, watching people as they watched the game.

Here and there, he spotted someone he knew, but most of them were Lucas's college friends. Sam walked into the kitchen and looked over the bottles poking out of the ice in the sink. Almost everyone was drinking beer and here he was with a can of soda. But, before he could make up his mind, Lucas walked over.

"Gotta minute?" he asked. "We need to talk."

Sam nodded and set his plate on the kitchen table. Then, he followed Lucas into one of the bedrooms.

"What's up?" Sam finally asked. Lucas had a rather somber look on his face, as if someone had died or something.

"I've been talking to folks, you know. Trying to figure things out," Lucas told him.

"What are you hearing?" Sam asked.

"You remember Kathryn, right?" Lucas asked.

Sam nodded. "Of course," he told Lucas. "Why?" In high school, it had been an open secret that she was gay. Things had come to a head about a year ago and Kathryn had left their congregation because she had decided to be openly and unapologetically gay. Wendy had embraced the whole 'hate the sin, love the sinner' trope, but it got old real fast.

"I don't know how to tell you this, Sam," Lucas hesitantly said, slowly walking across the room to the window. "Kathryn stopped by the robotics lab last weekend to check in with her little brother and we got to talking." He looked outside at the snowy parking lot. "Apparently, Rylee stopped taking her birth control pills right after Christmas last year."

Sam searched Lucas's face as he tried to understand. He felt like he was missing something. "Wait. That doesn't make any sense," he breathed. "Rylee stopped taking the Pill after we broke up?"

"Sounds like," Lucas replied. "All I know is what Kathryn told me. The story is that Rylee stopped taking the Pill because she dumped you. Rylee was absolutely convinced that you were sleeping around when you were at out-of-state tennis competitions. You were completely out of her life, so why bother taking them?"

"Yeah, like I had time for that!" Sam retorted. He vividly remembered the late night screamfests even after they broke up. "And didn't Katheryn and Rylee hook up after that?"

Lucas smiled. "That's what it looked like," he drawled. "Kathryn denied it, though. Said that they are just close friends." He picked at his lip, looking down at the carpet.

"I know that look," Sam growled. "What else?"

"You remember her sister, Chloe?" Lucas asked. "The one who just had a baby?"

" . . . yeah . . . " Sam gestured for him to continue.

"Kathryn told me that Rylee told her that she was so happy for Chloe," Lucas said. "That she was so excited Chloe had finally gotten pregnant, and she couldn't wait to start a family of her own."

"Okay . . . " Sam drawled. "Not sure I know where you're going with this."

"Think about it, man," Lucas said intently. "The two of you break up. Her sister just happens to get pregnant, and Rylee starts telling people that she wants a baby of her own. She stops taking the Pill, gets back together with you, and bam! A few months later, she's pregnant!"

Sam scoffed. "I can't believe she planned this!"

"Why else would she have stopped taking birth control pills?" Lucas asked. "They're so hard to get in the first place!" After a moment, he added, "Don't know what to believe. I mean, she was leaving for college next fall, right? Maybe she was planning to take the baby with her?"

Sam shook his head with a grunt. "None of this makes sense, Lucas," he said. He sank onto the messy bed, considering his options. Confront her? Nah. He could just imagine the screaming fight that would follow. He always came out as the bad guy, no matter who started it. Talk to his lawyer? Nah. He could hear the whole 'hearsay' lecture now.

Finally, he looked over at Lucas. "Can we keep this between us for now? I don't know why she did this, but the only way to find out is to keep an eye on her. Something will slip out. And then I might have something concrete that I can take to the lawyer."

"Sure, man," Lucas mumbled. "Just thought you should know."

He nodded to himself. The acid in his stomach felt like he'd taken a ground stroke to the gut. He didn't know what to believe anymore. Did Rylee lie to him about being on the Pill just so that she could get pregnant? If he could just get her to admit that, it might be a way to get out of this.

Maybe.

Chapter Ten

Sam was silent on the drive to their new place, but Rylee barely noticed. She chattered to him with random updates. How she'd finally started working with her doula, Diana. How unfair it was that she had to skip her annual trip to Cancun with her friends this year. How unreal it was that they were forced to live in such a horrible, tiny apartment.

He sighed but kept his eyes on the road. Parking was at a premium in this part of the city, so the cars that crowded either side of the street made navigating the narrow streets especially treacherous after the recent snowfall.

It was hard to believe that Rylee was twenty-five weeks pregnant. Of course, it didn't help that she insisted on pulling every single dress or shirt up under her belly to show off that baby bump. Everything that came out of her mouth was a complaint and yet every single time she had the opportunity to show off her pregnancy, she took advantage of it.

He pulled into the alley behind the apartment and parked the car alongside the garage so that they could unload items directly into the backyard. He opened the trunk and grabbed a box before stomping into the yard, trying to clear a path. Rylee moved to stand against the chain link fence and watched him as he trudged back to the car for the first load.

He swiped at the pile of snow that covered the picnic table with an elbow, then dropped the first box on the table. He turned and looked over at Rylee. "Aren't you going to help?" he asked.

"You know that I'm not supposed to lift anything heavy!" she reminded him with a grimace.

"Good thing that these are small boxes and weigh less than five pounds!" he called over mockingly. "Wouldn't want you to strain anything."

"Fine, I'll help!" She pouted as she slowly minced across the slushy snow. "But if I fall, it's your fault!"

Sam followed her back to the car, seething as he stomped the muddy sludge from his boots. "Well, maybe you should have told me before you stopped taking your birth control pills so that I could've gloved up!" he snapped. He glared at the pile of boxes in the trunk, waiting to be taken in.

Rylee opened the backseat door and picked up a few shoe boxes from the top of the pile. "Sam, we've already gone over this," she told him, that telltale whine creeping into her voice. "I have a medical condition. I wasn't supposed to be able to get pregnant without help."

"Bullshit!" Sam snapped, trying to ignore the corrosive jab in his stomach. "Obviously, you could—and did!—get pregnant!" He moved around the back of the car to glare at her.

Rylee clutched the shoe boxes to her chest. "Don't you re-member the problems that Chloe had getting pregnant?" she asked, that sharp tone grating on his nerves.

"Why would I?" he demanded.

"Because she's my sister, Sam!" Rylee told him, pushing away from the car to glare at him. "She had to go through IVF and even that wasn't easy!"

Sam wanted to grab his knit hat off the top of his head and pull the damn thing apart. "What does that have to do with you?" he demanded.

"Every single woman in my family has struggled to get pregnant, Sam!" she screamed, glaring up at him. "Did you ever wonder why there is a four-year gap between Chloe and Mackenzie and a three-year gap between Mackenzie and me? No? Well, apparently my parents had problems having kids, too!"

Sam stared at her. "So?"

"So, why should I take pills every single day that mess me up, when I only have my period two or three times a year because I can't ovulate!" she shrieked.

"Don't ovulate, huh?" Sam barked with laughter. "Seems like you managed to squeeze an egg out, didn't you?" he growled. "You should have told me you had stopped taking the Pill. I could have picked up a box of condoms and we wouldn't be here!"

Rylee slid into the backseat of the car, crying as she let the boxes fall to the ground, spilling the shoes onto the muddy asphalt.

Sam turned around and went back to the trunk. "When you're done, I'll be upstairs," he told her. Then, he picked up the top box, marched across the yard, and through the back door. It was going to be a long afternoon.

He was putting dishes in the cabinet by the stove when Rylee finally came in from outside. He ignored her and just kept working. If he was lucky, he'd have time to grab another load before making himself available for evening food deliveries.

He heard her open the window in the living room, letting in a blast of cold air that cut through the dull reek of fresh paint.

"What are you doing?" he demanded, walking across the kitchen and into the small living room. "It's thirty degrees out there!"

"Airing this place out," she told him with a haughty expression. "Paint fumes are bad for the baby. It's bad enough that we already had some furniture delivered, so everything picks up that horrible smell." She walked past him and into the kitchen. She opened that window, as well.

Sam shook his head, then went to the thermostat and turned off the heat. No sense wasting the money while the windows were open.

He walked back into the kitchen, grabbed another box off the floor, and placed it on the counter. "You going to help or what?" he asked.

"Sure," she sniped. She stepped past him and started to unpack the cups and assorted silverware. "I can't believe you're okay with the smell."

"It's just paint, Rylee," he told her, still irritated by her temper tantrum. "Give it a few days and it will be fine. Besides, we don't have to officially move in for a few weeks. All we have to do is get it ready for the inspection."

He picked up his empty box and set it next to the back door. Then, he wandered back to look over the fridge and stove. Old appliances, but it seemed like everything worked. Of course, he wasn't happy about the electric stove, but they could put up with it for now, right?

Sam grabbed the empty boxes off the floor and headed back outside. He could use them to pack up some of his stuff tonight.

He placed them on the picnic table, grabbed a couple more boxes from the car, and headed back in.

He slowly climbed the steep stairs up to the second-story apartment, hearing the floorboards creak a bit as he went up. The carpeting was worn and coming apart in a few places, but he was sure a bit of duct tape might help. He pushed open the door to the kitchen and put the boxes on the counter.

He opened a box and sorted through the few pots and pans that he'd gotten at Goodwill. Even though Wendy had plenty of surplus kitchenware, she'd refused to part with even one piece of her collection. She'd given him enough money to buy a cheap futon couch, a cabinet, and a small TV, but insisted that he use the $15,000 allowed by the Court and any money he might make from DoorDash for the rest. He'd checked the prices at a few places before deciding that used was just as good as new.

" . . . don't like this place very much, Kathryn," Rylee said. He glanced into the living room and saw her standing next to the windows, looking out over the street. "It's such a dump. The carpet is old. It smells, and it's so small! I just want to go home!"

Kathryn, huh? he thought, half-listening to the conversation as he started to put the pots away. The rumor mill said that Rylee and Kathryn probably hooked up when she'd broken up with Sam. Then, after a few months, Rylee wanted him back, only to break up with him again.

A horrible thought occurred to him. Had the girls planned to raise the baby by themselves? Was he just a glorified sperm donor that the state had roped in to pay half of the expenses because same-sex marriage had been banned?

Sam put the last pot in the cabinet and braced himself against the counter. *No way,* he thought. The first thing Rylee had done when she found out she was pregnant was try to get back together with him. She wouldn't have done that if she had wanted to be in a relationship with Kathryn.

He stood up and looked into the living room. Rylee had moved from one side of the windows to the other. "No, Sam says it's fine," she complained. "Yeah, I know. He doesn't understand what it's like to have to climb two flights of stairs just to get to the bedroom with a baby growing inside of you!" She paused for a moment. "I gotta let you go. It's freezing in here and I need to turn the furnace back on."

She put her cell phone down on the windowsill and started across the room to the thermostat.

Sam moved to head her off. "Close the windows first, Rylee."

Rylee turned to him, her lips drawn into that familiar pout that said, 'But I don't wanna!' "It's cold in here, Sam," she said.

"That's because you had to open up all of the windows," he told her. "It's winter, for chrissake!"

The pout turned into a frown as she placed a protective hand over the slight swell that peeked out against her winter jacket. "But it still smells in here!"

"If you're worried about the baby, go home," he told her. "I can finish unpacking and close things up before I leave."

"But you drove us here," she protested.

"So, call Kathryn back. Call your mom. Hell, call an Uber if you want to," he shot back. "Or you can help me put things away so we can get going sooner."

"Fine. I'll help," she told him. "Those back stairs are pretty steep, though. If I break an ankle, it will be your fault!"

Sam closed his eyes for a moment. Of course, it would be his fault. Everything was always his fault, one way or another. It was going to be a long ten months until they were allowed to separate. He definitely needed a beer.

Sam only scored three deliveries before he called it quits for the night. Midweek traffic was either incredibly busy or spotty. Besides, he was tired from moving boxes and deserved a bit of a break.

He didn't remember much of the drive down into the Third Ward or even where he parked his car. He found himself walking on the sidewalk a few blocks away from Deuces, hands stuffed in his pocket from the cold. *I deserve this*, Sam thought. Just a bit of a break from the craziness that life had thrown his way.

Sam could hear the music before he got to the door. Sounded like a great playlist tonight.

Bill looked up as he came into the vestibule. "Sam, great to see you!" he said, straightening up on the barstool that was set in the corner. "Where's Mike?"

Sam shrugged. "I haven't talked to him for a few days," he told the bouncer. "It's been a day. I just need a beer."

Bill smirked and waved him in. "Have a great night!"

"Thanks, man," Sam said as he opened the inner door, letting the sound wash over him for a moment. Then, he moved to the bar on the left side of the room.

Greg saw him coming and pulled a bottle out of the ice bin with a quick tug. He popped the cap off in a practiced gesture and set it on the bar just as Sam closed the distance. "You look like hell, man!" he yelled over the noise.

Sam grabbed the bottle and took a long drink. "Thanks," he yelled. "I really needed this!" He grabbed the $20 out of his pocket and slid it across the bar. "Keep the change."

Greg nodded and grabbed the bill. Then, he moved to the group of girls that crowded the other end of the bar.

Sam scanned the crowd to see if he recognized anyone. It was his first time here alone. This was Mike's playground, and he didn't want to piss him off by going nuts tonight.

Maybe just one beer and he'd go home. Or maybe back to the apartment. Rylee's mattress had been delivered before he'd left, so that was an option.

He noticed a lone DJ sat in the booth that overlooked the nearly empty dance floor as he worked his way across the room. The bar wasn't quite as crowded as usual, so he was able to settle into an empty couch near one of the big screen TVs.

He took a long gulp of beer, then another. He still couldn't believe that Rylee had stopped taking the Pill because she thought that she couldn't get pregnant. Sam snorted. *That's what happens when you leave sex education up to the Internet*, he thought.

Sam laid his head back against the couch and stared at the random college football game that was playing on TV. The sound was muted, but the closed caption kept up a random monologue running with play highlights.

He closed his eyes for a moment to think. Rylee. Somehow, it always came back to her.

At Weston Prep, Rylee had been an amusing addition to the robotics team. In theory, she was a member of the five-person drive team. Problem was that, as a freshman, Rylee was more likely to be found flirting with the build team instead of practicing during the simulations running up to competition. The team learned the hard way to keep her sidelined than at the controls.

Very little had changed during Sam's senior year. Rylee, now a sophomore, had agreed to move from the drive team to the public relations/corporate sponsorship committee. The good news was that she was able to bring in significant corporate donations from the community. The bad news was that she moved from flirting with the build team to flirting with team sponsors, local media, and even members of their congregation.

When Sam had left for Northwestern, he'd thought that he had left that chaos behind. True, he'd kept in touch with his old team and, since Rylee's family belonged to the same church, he knew that he was bound to run into her from time to time. By the time she reached her senior year, she'd grown from just pretty to rather beautiful, from flirty to sexy, and from being merely amusing to a force to be reckoned with.

He drained the bottle and got up to grab another beer. Greg saw him coming and opened a fresh bottle for him. "Bad day?" he asked.

Sam chuckled. "You could say that," he said as he slipped a $10 bill across the bar, nodding just in case Greg couldn't hear him over the music.

"Well, hopefully, things get better with the new year," Greg told him. With a smile and a nod, he moved over to a couple waiting for him.

Sam sipped at the fresh brew. A bit too hoppy for his taste, so he checked the label. Silver outline of a horse on a black background. A mid-grade IPA. *Okay, then*, he thought and took another swallow. *Maybe it would grow on me*, he mused as he made his way back to the couch.

A year ago, life had been so much simpler. Sitting in the back of a movie theater with Rylee's shirt unbuttoned, as she dared him to make love to her in public. Her excitement about the chance of getting caught as they had sex in the church coat room. That possessive glare at the annual robotics holiday party.

He hadn't been prepared for what happened after winter break. Demands that he come home every weekend. Fights over any mention of other girls on campus, including the TA that taught one of his classes. The harder he tried to make things work, the worse it got until she finally broke up with him over how much he was traveling for tennis competitions.

Shouldn't have gotten back together with her over the summer, he thought, taking another deep swallow of the IPA. It was obvious that they didn't have what it took to maintain a long-distance relationship. Rylee's pending move to the East Coast made it almost inevitable that they would break up again.

A group of girls at the far side of the bar caught his eye. They were giggling and dancing as they raised plastic champagne glasses in the air. The group parted for a moment. Sam saw that one of them, a tall brunette, wore a gold sash that read 'Bride to Be' in neon white lettering.

He grimaced. *Great. A bachelorette party.* Just what he needed tonight. A bunch of drunk girls making noise and flirting with every single guy in the bar. Maybe it was time to leave.

He got up and made his way across the bar. As he walked by, one of the girls grabbed him around his waist and pulled him close. Her bright green eyes, framed by soft purple glasses, looked up at him with distracted amusement, and her lips puckered as if she was looking for a kiss.

He looked down at her for a moment. So tempting. So very tempting.

He smiled ruefully and backed away with a smile. It was obvious that she was more than just a little drunk. Unlike his friends at Northwestern, he had to worry that she might get pregnant because a condom tore. He already had enough on his plate.

He waved at Greg on his way out. *Apartment or back to the house*, he thought while he wandered down the street in search of his car.

The apartment won out. It was closer, and it meant that he wouldn't need to deal with either Rylee or Wendy tonight. Definitely worth it.

Chapter Eleven

"Today, we're going to work on breathing," the instructor told the group. "I know, you're thinking 'why do I need to work on breathing? I do that every day, right?'"

The class laughed. Sam looked around the room at the other couples. The women were seated between their partner's legs, leaning up against them, and the men leaned back just a bit on their hands. Every single bump was front and center. Most of the women looked happy. The guys, not so much.

"We're going to learn three different breathing techniques today," she told them, settling down on the floor in front of them. "One is for active labor. One is for transition, which can be the most painful part of labor. And the last one you'll use is when you're ready to push."

One of the women raised a hand, nervously biting her lip.

"Yes, Julia?" the instructor asked.

"Should we be practicing that last one?" she asked. "I mean, I have six more weeks to go and don't want to go into preterm labor!"

"Good question," the instructor said, even though her expression said it was anything but. "Each of these exercises are designed to help you relax and work with your body when it's actually needed. It's perfectly safe to practice these in advance. In fact, we encourage it!"

She turned her attention back to the group. "Let's start this exercise with your hands on your belly," she told them. "This will help to remind you to breathe deeply into your diaphragm. You should feel your hand move as you breathe in and your belly expands."

She looked around the room. "Breathe in, ladies. Slowly let your breath expand beneath your hands." Rylee shifted position as she followed the directions. "Pause for a moment. Now, slowly release that breath. Good!"

"Now remember, when you are in active labor, that space that you're breathing from is where your baby is, so that's where you need to focus your energies," the instructor told them. "Let's try that again, ladies. We're going to focus on breathing in for four to six seconds. Slow and steady. Fill that tummy like it was a balloon and make sure that you are breathing only as deeply as is comfortable for you."

Sam rolled his eyes and shook his head slightly. He should have seen it coming. The instructor was obviously one of those New Agers. Breathe into the baby. Great . . . !

"Hold for just a moment," she continued. "Now quietly exhale through your mouth." She opened her eyes and looked around the room for confirmation. "This time, we're going to count it out. I need everyone to breathe with me, even you, dads! Expand that tummy as you inhale. Relax and breathe in one, two, three, four. Pause. Now exhale, breathing out all of that tension. And again . . . "

Sam's attention drifted away even as he followed along. This was a complete waste of his time. Rylee had already said that she was going to have an epidural as early as possible. Why did they need to learn how to breathe?

The instructor cut in. "We do this four times in a row because this will help you focus during your contractions, which last anywhere from forty-five to sixty seconds during active labor," she told them. "Once you are in transition, your contractions may last up to ninety seconds long and come about every two minutes. Breathing through them is very important as it will help your body relax and help the baby move down into the birth canal."

Rylee squirmed a bit, her butt brushing up against him. It reminded him of the time that she'd spent an entire evening shimmying up against him while they were working on the robotics team, during build season. He eased himself back a bit. He did not want to get a hard-on. Not with Rylee, and definitely not during this class!

"Our next breathwork is to help you resist the urge to push before you're completely dilated," the instructor told them. "These breaths are two short, shallow breaths." She demonstrated, breathing in two short breaths, followed by two sharp pants. It sounded a bit like she was sucking air in through a straw and then panting it out in two short but hard exhales. "Now, it may sound like you're hyperventilating, but you're taking two purposeful and shallow breaths, followed by two purposeful breaths out. Let's give it a try, everyone."

Sam followed the class as he took two rapid but shallow breaths, then panted them out twice. "Let's do that again, everyone," the instructor said.

Hard pass, Sam thought. We could have gotten this as an online class and been done with it.

"Great job, everyone!" the instructor said. "Our last exercise is breathing for the final stage of labor: the big push." She smiled as the group laughed. "Here's the thing: most women instinctively hold their breath while they try to push. But that may actually cause vaginal tears."

Rylee sagged against him as she listened. "We're going to start by breathing in deeply and comfortably. Expand your belly as you did in our first exercise. As you exhale, groan in the back of your throat as you tighten your abs. If it helps, try to envision that groan extending all the way down into your uterus, relaxing that birth canal to help your baby come into this world."

"Let's give it a try, shall we?" she said. "Breathe in . . . now exhale . . . "

Sam stifled a chuckle. They sounded like a bunch of cows mooing, especially the woman next to them. She might have been trying to growl in the back of her throat, but man, did she sound like a cow.

"Great job!" the instructor told them. "Just remember to tighten those abs and relax as you push all of that energy down and breathe that baby out!

"Last thing, ladies. Don't be afraid to practice this while you're sitting on the toilet." She grinned. "I know it sounds silly, but for those of you who have never given birth, pooping is the closest sensation to giving birth."

Sam sighed. Now every single time Rylee was in the bathroom, he was going to think of her mooing while she pooped. *Not cool, lady*, he thought. Then, he surreptitiously checked his watch. Another half-hour, followed by lunch and the last session of the day on partner empathy.

"I hope everyone had a great lunch," their instructor said, using that fake happy tone that warned you things were going to be bad. "This afternoon, we're going to take your pregnancy support to the next level. You'll be wearing a pregnancy simulation vest for the next twenty-four hours!"

A collective groan went through the room. "Seriously?" someone muttered.

She cocked her head to one side and gazed over her glasses, her brown eyes blazing as she tried in vain to give them the 'mom death glare'. "We've talked about how difficult it is for men to really empathize about how strenuous pregnancy can be, right?" She paused but didn't wait for a response as she gestured to the boxes carefully piled next to her desk. "These pregnancy simulation vests are designed to give you a small glimpse into what your partners may be going through."

Sam looked down at the floor in disgust. *Seriously?*

He looked up as she pulled a black vest with wide shoulder straps out of the top box and dragged it onto the desk at the front of the room. "As you can see, it fits over your shoulders and uses straps along the back to adjust the weight appropriately. This model is just over twenty-five pounds."

"Why do we have to do this?" Mike demanded. "I mean, a full twenty-four hours? How the hell am I supposed to work tomorrow? I can't wear that back to the office!"

Theo stirred from where he stood next to the door.

"I hear ya, Mike," he responded. "But this is a mandatory part of your empathy training. No one gets a free pass just because they have to work."

Another groan filled the air.

"Look, it's just a single day out of your life," Theo told them. "One day and it's done." He looked around the room, listening to the backbiting for a moment. "What, you're not man enough to handle what your partners are dealing with every single day? Really?

"Fine," Theo said as he took the vest from the instructor and pulled it on over his t-shirt. "I guess I'm alone, then." The trainer moved behind him to adjust the straps along the back and side.

Theo turned around to look at the group. He looked ridiculous with cantaloupe-shaped boob bags and a black beach ball hanging off the front of the vest.

Sam looked at Mike, then Tyler, rolling his eyes. Looked like they had no choice but to accept the challenge. If an old biker dude had no problems being seen in public dressed like that, what choice did any of them have?

The trainer smiled. "I need everyone to grab a box so we can get started."

Noah got up and grabbed a box, dragging it back to his seat before he started tearing into the packaging. Mike shook his head in disgust, then grabbed his box, struggling to pick up the package before taking it over to his seat. Sam followed his lead, but the box was heavier than he expected, so he ended up dragging it across the room like Noah. The rest of the class followed suit.

The instructor walked around the room, stopping to help adjust the straps so that the boobs and baby bulge were in the right place as she lectured.

"This vest is designed to reproduce what an eight-month pregnancy feels like," she told them as she wiggled Noah's baby bulge so it was just a bit higher on him. "This will include pressure on your chest, bladder, stomach, and even your lungs."

She moved on to Mike to help him with the side straps. "It will also force you a small tilt in your pelvis, so you might waddle just a bit. You'll even feel fetal movement from time to time due to the steel ball that will simulate the baby's movement when you move."

Sam pulled the vest out of the box and gave it a small shake. It was bulky and didn't look at all like something that was supposed to 'simulate' pregnancy. He gently squeezed one of the boobs, feeling it squish between his fingers. He shrugged. Must be some kind of plastic gel.

He pulled it over his head, struggling to get it in place. "The straps need to be loosened," Theo told him. "Lemme help." He felt a bit of slack and then Theo gave a sharp tug on the side hems to pull it into place.

Sam doubled over. His back muscles screamed in sudden agony as all twenty-five pounds settled in front and made it hard to breathe.

He forced himself to slowly straighten, feeling the sudden pressure on his ribs and bladder. "What the hell?" he wheezed.

"Yeah, the first time is always the worst," Theo told him.

"You've done this before?" Sam asked, incredulously. Why would anyone voluntarily do this to themselves?

Theo studied him for a moment. "Every single mentoring group," he admitted. "Almost two years now."

"Alright, I need everyone to take their seats," the instructor called out. She moved around them, collecting boxes and packing materials, as they slowly returned to their seats.

Sam carefully eased himself into his chair, bracing himself with one hand. There was no way that this was what pregnancy felt like. No way was the blob this heavy. It had to be a scare tactic.

The instructor moved to the front of the room. "I'm sure you're all wondering why the simulation suit is so heavy." She looked around the room. "By the time that your partners are in their eighth month of pregnancy, your baby will only account for a small portion of the weight you're feeling. Amniotic fluids make up just over two pounds of weight. There's also about four pounds of additional blood volume, two pounds of added breast tissue, an increase in uterine tissue, the placenta, as well as additional weight gain needed to support a healthy pregnancy."

Mike stirred in the seat next to him. "Great. Just great!"

Theo moved to his spot next to the door, leaning up against the wall. "Alright, everyone," he said. "Time to go. Remember, this is a full twenty-four-hour exercise, so you will not be able to remove this until tomorrow night's meeting. So, skip your morning shower."

"Oh, that reminds me," the instructor said, holding up a hand to get their attention. "Each vest has a security tag that will keep the vest locked until you return tomorrow afternoon. Any attempts to open the tag and remove the vest will rupture the tag and release indelible ink."

Sam turned around and tried to look over his shoulder. Mike grabbed him by the arm and traced a line across his back. "I see it," he told Sam. "Looks like a pair of scissors won't fix it." He turned around and showed Sam his back. He could see a small, flat piece of plastic that hung between the back straps.

"Damn," he said.

"Yeah," Mike said. "As much as I want to call out sick, I can't. I have a deck to present for my staff meeting. Tomorrow's going to be a hoot," he growled. "What about you?"

"Me?" Sam paused as they walked out into the hallway. "I have homework to do. Normally, I'd try to get a few deliveries done this evening to pick up a bit of cash, but there's no way I'm going out like this!"

At that moment, the girls burst out of their classroom, giggling and pointing as they got closer.

"Oh, my God!" Rylee squealed as she walked over. "They didn't tell us that we'd be twins for the day!"

Sam scrubbed at his face in frustration. "Rylee, just leave it be for once."

"But it's awesome that you get to feel what I'm going through, even if it doesn't include the heartburn and cravings!" she told him. "Speaking of which . . . " she trailed off suggestively, tracing a delicate finger across her belly.

"No," Sam told her. "I'm not taking you out for custard. Not today. We're going back to the apartment and I'm going to get some homework done and watch a little TV. Period." Rylee started to protest, but he shut her down. "For once in your life, can you just think about someone else for a change?"

Rylee glared at him. "I am thinking about someone else, Sam," she told him. "I'm thinking about your baby. You know, the one that I'm currently carrying?"

Sam shook his head and started to walk gingerly down the hallway. They weren't kidding about that fake 'fetal movement'. Every single step he took caused that metal ball to bump up against his bladder.

"Dammit," he swore under his breath. "Bathroom first. Then, we're going back to the apartment."

He picked up his pace, trying to ignore the giggling behind him.

Later that evening, Rylee carefully eased herself down into the rocking chair next to the living room windows, one hand covering her belly. "We need to talk, Sam."

Sam stared at the small TV screen. It had been an exhausting day, and he really wanted to just focus on the movie he'd rented. "I don't have anything to say, Rylee. I'm tired and I just need to relax for a bit." He leaned back against the couch as he tried to get into a comfortable position, resting his forearms against the vest's bulge.

Rylee rubbed at her baby bump. "Oh, she's really moving around in there. I think we might have a future gymnast on our hands!" She paused, waiting for him to respond. The silence stretched between them, punctuated by the occasional sound of explosions and gunfire from the movie.

She sighed. "My mom helped me work through the list of potential nannies so we can set up a few interviews for next week. I really need your help deciding—"

"What?" Sam barked, tearing his gaze away from the screen as a group of soldiers went down under a hail of bullets. He struggled to sit up.

"Well, you know. A nanny. We're going to need some help when the baby's born," Rylee said in a singsong tone, as if she was stating the obvious. "I mean, we could go with an au pair, if you'd like, but then we'll still need an extra bedroom."

Sam threw down the remote control, watching as it bounced off the coffee table and skittered onto the carpet. "A nanny," he repeated, seething. "What makes you think we can afford a fucking nanny?"

Out of the corner of his eye, he watched Rylee's hand make small rubbing motions against her belly. "There, there, Allison. I know Daddy's yelling, but that's just how he is."

Sam closed his eyes for a moment. Unbelievable. Not only had she already settled on a name for the baby, but she was already trying to get the kid to team up with her against him.

Rylee shifted so that she could put her feet up on the footstool. "My attorney says that it looks like I'll have access to my money once the baby comes; that way I can pay for things, Sam," she told him quietly. "We're going to be fine, just like I told you."

He turned to face her, his head starting to pound from rage. "What the hell, Rylee. We already talked about this. You know the rules. I have to be able to provide half of our budget. I can't afford a nanny. You know that. I'm barely hanging on as it is!"

Rylee smiled. "You worry too much," she told him. "Everything is open for negotiation, including the budget that needs to be approved by the Court. Things might be a bit tight until I'm allowed to liquidate a few things." She paused, giving him a sly look. "Besides, there's no way we can continue to live here after the baby's born. I start at Wellesley this fall and you know that means that we'll have to relocate to Massachusetts."

"What?" Sam clenched his eyes shut. *This is insane*, he thought. Why does she get to go to her dream college when he might have to drop out of Northwestern and start over? "There's no way we're moving to Massachusetts," he told her. "We can't afford it."

"Sure we can," Rylee assured him. "You'll have to change schools, but we can figure that out later. I've already started apartment hunting near the campus. There are a number of great condos within driving distance." She paused, pursing her lips in a fake frown. "I'm still not happy that I won't be able to live on campus for my first year. That's where all the fun is!"

Sam groaned, pushing his clenched fists into the futon cushion. Everything he'd been working for over the last two years was slowly being taken away from him. Northwestern. That internship he was supposed to get over the summer. Scoring an engineering job with an international firm. All of it, gone!

She ignored his distress. "We'll need a four-bedroom unit, obviously, because the nanny, or au pair, if you prefer, will need her own room," she told him, babbling as if repeating her demands would make him calm down. "Babies can be so messy, you know? My mom has her service stopping by to help around the place now, but after we move—"

"We're not moving cross-country, Rylee! Period," Sam ground out. "As it is, I'm going to have to take a few classes this summer to catch up, and we need to stay close to home for now."

"Why?" Rylee demanded. "Neither of our parents are allowed to help much after the baby's born! There's nothing that ties us to this state, Sam."

He scrubbed his face. *Don't go there*, he silently screamed. *Just don't.* He dropped his hands to his lap and said the words that needed to be said. "Rylee, I am not moving out east. I don't make enough money to pay half of a nanny's salary, and I've been told—repeatedly—that there's no wiggle room in the way the law is written. We each have to pay for half of that baby's expenses!"

She pursed her lips, rapidly shaking her head in denial. "Sam. Stop," she replied. "My lawyer has already drafted the financial means document that will outline to the Court what needs to be done for us to move. Once the guardian ad litem signs off on it, we're all set."

"What? Why did you do this?" he exclaimed. It was like she was trying to piss him off on purpose. "I have rights, you know!"

"Because I can't live poor, Sam," she quietly told him, her lips quivering as she looked down at her hands. "I just can't. We deserve better." She looked up, a fake smile lighting up her face. "So, I'll pay for the nanny until you've graduated. You can pay for the next few years until we're even. Or, if you can't afford it right out of college, then you can just pay Allison's tuition for a few years. After I graduate, we can move to New York, and there are some really great private schools—"

"I'm not moving to New York, Rylee!" he stated, his voice flat. "Period."

"Well, I am!" Rylee told him, struggling to stand up. She managed to push herself up, wobbling for a moment, hands splayed until she got her balance, then turned to glare at him. "Every opportunity is waiting for me to make this move. Don't forget, you're the one who got me pregnant, Sam. You're the one with the super swimmers and didn't wear a condom!"

What the hell? Sam opened his mouth, but Rylee wouldn't stop this time. "I'm not your mom!" she yelled. "I will never be a stay-at-home mom," she screamed at him. "I *will* have a decent place to live, and I *will* hire a nanny to take care of your baby until I'm *actually* ready to become a mother, and there's nothing you can do to stop me!"

"You were supposed to be on the fucking pill, Rylee!" he yelled back.

"You know why I stopped taking the Pill," she whispered. "How many times do I have to tell you that I wasn't supposed to be able to get pregnant without medical intervention."

"Bullshit!"

"So, what, you're a gynecologist now?" she demanded. "You know everything about how women's bodies work?"

Sam stood, swaying as he tried to maintain his balance. "I'm out of here," he told her. "I can't deal with you right now!"

He grabbed his coat and headed for the door. Putting up with his mother for the evening was a small price to pay for the privilege of sleeping in his own bed for a change.

The next evening, complaints gave way to groans of relief as the group shed the extra weight of their simulation vests. Sam plopped his vest on the table that had been set up to sort, clean, and repackage the devices.

Theo walked across the room to help Mike as he struggled to shrug off the vest. "Great job, everyone," he told the group. "If you can all get back to your seats, we can get started."

Sam walked back to his seat, almost feeling lighter than air. He had barely slept last night. Between the extra weight that made him sleep on his side, the sudden poke against his bladder when he shifted his weight, and the general feeling of doom, it was almost impossible to get comfortable.

"I know it's been a struggle to stay on top of things, but you're doing a great job, guys," Theo told them. "I got the final update from social services. Everyone has passed the home inspections." He smiled, a rarity for the old biker.

There was a bit of rustling. "Hey, you're almost to the finish line. You did it!" Theo told them enthusiastically.

Max leaned forward. "It doesn't feel like it, Theo."

"What do you mean?"

"I still have a couple of classes to get through," Max reminded him. "Julia has been nagging me about them for weeks now."

Theo nodded. "Just a couple more online classes, Max," he told him. "And, no, you don't have to watch someone actually give birth. I promise!"

A chuckle went around the room. "Yeah, well, that breast-feeding class was a waste of time," Mike offered. "Jen wants nothing to do with it!"

"Oh, man!" Jacob exclaimed. "You are so lucky, man! Emily is so psyched up for it. She wants to co-sleep, so neither of us are going to get any sleep at all!"

"Babies are like that," Theo told them, a droll grin on his face. "Co-sleeping means that you have a shorter walk to pick them up when they're crying."

Jacob raked his hands across his face. "Dude," he said. "I'm so not ready for this."

"No one ever is," Theo reminded them. "Is everyone signed up for the postpartum support class?"

"Yup."

"Done."

"It's on my list, Theo!"

"Make sure that you sign into the Parenting Course portal and validate that you received credit for your work, including in-person classes," Theo told them. "I don't want to have to explain to a judge that you didn't log in and track your attendance! Deadline is next week." He looked around at the group. "Alright, break down your chairs and get outta here. We're done for the day."

As the rest of the group folded up their chairs and placed them in the rack before heading out of the door, Sam found himself standing in the back of the room, waiting for Theo to gather his things.

"Can I talk to you for a moment?" he asked.

"Sure," Theo said as he shrugged on his heavy leather jacket.

"I'm not sure how to talk about this, Theo," Sam admitted. He rubbed the back of his neck. "It's embarrassing and I honestly don't know what to do about it."

"Spit it out," Theo ordered. "Maybe I can help."

Before long, Sam found himself unloading everything on Theo. That Rylee didn't tell him she had stopped taking her birth control pill. That she'd broken up with him twice but demanded that they get back together. He even shared his suspicion that she secretly wanted to get pregnant so that he'd have to move to the East Coast with her.

Theo folded his arms against his chest, looking down at him like a judgmental parent. "Really?" he drawled. "That's the best you've got? She secretly wanted to get pregnant so you couldn't break up with her?"

"Seriously, if she had told me that she wanted to stop taking the Pill, I'd have worn a condom. It's not a big deal!"

Theo shook his head, his lips pursed with a small smile. "You know how many times I've heard that?" he asked.

"But it's true!" Sam threw back his head in frustration. "She claims that her sister had problems getting pregnant, and her mom did, too. She's trying to get me to buy into the idea that she can't ovulate because of some . . . medical disorder . . . and she thought that she couldn't get pregnant, so why bother taking the Pill? That has to be a lie! No one goes off birth control because they can't get pregnant. It's hard enough to get prescribed in the first place!"

"Or . . ." Theo held up a hand to stop Sam from interrupting him. "She stopped taking the Pill because it was causing other medical problems that are probably none of your business."

"But why didn't she tell me? Huh?" Sam demanded. "She hated how condoms felt and that we had to stop just so that I could put one on. She told me to stop buying them!"

"Did she?" Theo asked, his jaw jutting out with impatience. "Or did she say that to make you happy?"

What the hell, dude! Sam raked his fingers through his hair, pulling at it to keep from yelling. "Look, I only know what she told me!" he blurted out.

Much easier if we don't leave behind any evidence, she'd whispered at him the first time.

"Look, Sam, it sounds like the two of you need to talk this out," Theo said. "The state provides up to ten couple counseling sessions to help new parents adjust. I can get you on the calendar with one of them for next week. You know, someone who could act as a mediator and help you talk this out."

"And if she admits on record that she wanted to get pregnant?" Sam retorted. "Can I take it to the lawyer and get out of this?"

Theo looked at him closely. "Sam, any way you look at this, you're going to be a father. What's done is done. So, it's time to man up and stop looking for excuses, alright?"

Sam looked down. "Fine," he said. "See you next week."

He stomped away, barely listening as Theo called after him. He needed a drink.

The parking in the Third Ward was tight that evening, but Sam eventually found a place to park a few blocks from Deuces. The night was chilly, and he could feel the damp air through his jacket, but tonight he just didn't care. He couldn't take another moment.

He couldn't believe Theo wouldn't listen to him. Wasn't he supposed to be their mentor, their go-to guy who was supposed to help him sort this shit out?

He crossed the street, running the last few steps to beat the car that refused to slow down as it came around the corner. *Maybe I should talk to Dad*, Sam thought. If Rylee got pregnant on purpose, wasn't that entrapment and something the Court needed to know?

A distorted mix of guitar riffs, pounding drums, and intense vocals called to him as he got closer. Maybe he was in luck and a live band was playing. He quickened his steps, waving to the bouncer as he started to duck into the entrance. He really needed that beer.

"Whoa, whoa, whoa!" A hand came up and stopped him just past the vestibule. A tall, thin bouncer stood in his way. "I need to see some ID."

This was new. "Where's Bill?" Sam asked. "He knows me. I come here a lot."

The bouncer brushed his platinum and bright orange hair from his eyes. "He's off tonight," he replied. "Look, I don't care how often you come down here. I need to see your ID or I can't let you in."

Sam glared at the bouncer and then dug his wallet out of his pocket. "This is bullshit. I come here all the time. I just want to get a beer." He flipped his license up to show it to the bouncer. "See? I'm legal. Are we done here?"

The bouncer grabbed Sam's wallet in both hands to take a closer look in the dim light. "Hang on, let me see that. The birthday looks right, but that doesn't look like a normal driver's license to me . . . "

Sam grabbed his wallet back and shoved it into his back pocket. "I just got it. They changed the layout. Are you going to let me in or what?"

The bouncer lifted his hand and beckoned one of the servers over. "Can you watch the door, Jim? I need a minute."

"Sure." The server came over and settled on the stool in the corner of the vestibule. "Don't be too long, though. Stacy is running late, and orders are stacking up," he told the new guy.

The bouncer nodded. "I'm new here, so why don't we go back and talk to one of the owners. If he clears you, we're good." Sam nodded, and the bouncer casually grabbed Sam's upper arm as they pushed through the crowd.

"Steve!" the bouncer yelled, waving his other arm to get the bartender's attention. "Need a bit of help with an ID here!"

A dark-haired bartender that Sam had never seen before peered around the crowd. "Go ahead and take him to the office. I'll be right there," he yelled back, his voice almost drowned out by the band. Steve jerked his thumb to the right of the bar, then turned back to pull some microbrews from the ice bin.

The bouncer half-led, half-dragged Sam through the crowd to a small hallway. Bathrooms were on the right, an unmarked door on the left. A couple of girls spilled out of the bathroom, giggling, and almost ran into them before they flowed down the hall and back into the bar.

The bouncer opened the unmarked door, flipped on the light, and gestured to the guest chair on one side of the office. "Have a seat. I'm sure that Steve will get this sorted out. I gotta get back to work." He closed the door as he left.

Sam looked around, then had a seat. An oversized wooden desk dominated the small room. Two large black metal file cabinets were crowded into the far corner, random clutter and paperwork piled on top. The walls were covered with random posters of bands that had retired long before Sam had been born.

He sat in the room for a good five minutes, alternating between staring uneasily at his phone and at the closed door. He thought about just leaving, but couldn't make himself go. He was of legal age, he told himself repeatedly. Maybe the driver's license had a slightly different layout than a regular driver's license but, so what?

It didn't matter. He didn't care what that judge said. There was nothing wrong with him grabbing a drink. He'd been down to Deuces, what, three or four times now?

Finally, Steve came into the office, apologizing profusely for the delay. He was an older man, maybe his dad's age, wearing a white apron over his jeans. "You know how Friday nights are!" he said. "Short-staffed with Greg out of town. So, can I see your driver's license?"

"Sure," Sam said as he stood and pulled his wallet out of his back pocket. He pulled the license out and handed it to the older man. "Look, I'm over twenty-one and I've been down here several times. I don't understand what the problem is!"

Steve took the license and looked it over with a careful eye, brushing the license with a careful finger. "It says it's 'provisional'. Do you know what that means?" he asked so quietly that Sam could barely hear him over the band playing in the background.

Sam swallowed, acid starting to gnaw at his gut. "No, I don't know what that means," he replied. "I just came down here for a beer."

Steve looked a bit tired as he sat down on the edge of the old wooden desk. "It means that you're not allowed to legally buy alcohol," he slowly said.

"It has to be some kind of mistake," Sam told him, squirming a bit. "They must have given me the wrong kind of license. I'll have to go down to the DMV tomorrow and get it fixed." He stood up. Maybe it was time to leave.

Steve nodded, lips pursed like he wanted to say something. "Sure, that makes sense," he eventually said.

There was a knock on the door and a police officer poked his head in. Steve stood, but didn't give Sam his license back.

"What the hell?" Sam snarled. "You called the police?" Acid poured into the pit of his stomach. *Dammit, this could not be happening!*

Steve ignored Sam as he handed the license to the officer. "This might be a genuine mistake, officer, but I need to be sure."

The officer nodded. "Happens sometimes." He took the license, gave it a quick glance, and then used his shoulder radio to ask for officer assistance before pocketing Sam's license. "Good catch, sir," he told him. "That's a provisional license issued to those in the Wisconsin Individual Family Education program. He's not allowed to visit bars or buy alcohol." Another officer appeared behind him.

Steve hung his head for a moment. "Okay, then," he said. "I need to get back out there, officer." He moved past the officers and back toward the bar.

"Sir, please put your hands on the wall," he said as he took a pair of handcuffs out of his waist holder. "You have the right to remain silent. Everything you say . . . "

Chapter Twelve

It had been a very long weekend. Footsteps outside of his holding cell echoed in the hallway, slowly approaching with rhythmic, almost judgmental precision that made him want to flinch. He stood up, defiantly facing the cell bars. All he'd wanted was a fucking beer. That didn't make him a criminal, did it?

His attorney appeared, her dour face glaring at him from across the cell. "Did you have fun at the bar, Sam?" Olivia asked.

"I didn't get very far before the cops showed up," he spat. "I didn't do anything wrong."

She took a step closer to the bars, fingernails tapping the tablet she held against her waist. "Really?" she said. "Then why were you arrested for violating the terms of your probation?"

Sam glared back. "Probation for what? Getting a girl pregnant? That's not illegal—yet!" He moved closer to the bars. "It's a stupid rule and you know it! I'm twenty-one now and, if I want to go down to the bar and have a drink, I'm going to have a fucking drink!"

Olivia slowly shook her head, rolling her eyes as if he were a child that just got caught lying. "That's not what the law says, Sam," she told him. "According to the GPS log, this is not your first time going down to that bar. Four times, Sam."

"So?"

"So, there are consequences, Sam," she told him. "Not just for the bar, which faces a considerable fine." Sam winced. He hadn't thought of that. "At this rate, I don't know if we can avoid you doing some serious jail time."

"For what?" Sam demanded. "Look, I know my rights. At most, I could get a small fine, have my driver's license suspended, or maybe have to do some community service. It's not like I was pulled over for drunk driving!"

"This is different," Olivia told him firmly. "You violated the terms of your probation. The State of Wisconsin calls that a felony and is punishable by imprisonment up to two years in jail. Per offense."

Sam found himself backing up until he was sitting on the bed, feeling like he'd been sucker punched. "Two years per offense?" he breathed. This was unreal.

"Two years behind bars for each and every night out," Olivia repeated. "With supervised release for the birth and care of your child. I'm not here to bail you out. I'm here to represent you at today's hearing."

"Oh," Sam said, struggling to find the words. "What did my dad say?"

Olivia snorted. "He was livid, but it's your mom that you have to worry about."

Sam looked up, horrified. Wendy. She'd have worked her way into an absolute meltdown. "What—what did she say?" he asked, trying to stay calm.

"She said, and I quote, 'He can rot in hell, for all I care,'" Olivia told him. She shook her head. "You're lucky that she can't come down and yell at you in person, though. This will be a private hearing. That means you, me, the prosecutor, your mentor, and the guardian ad litem. Maybe a witness or two. No one else is allowed."

"Not even my dad?" he breathed.

Olivia shook her head. "You're an adult now, Sam. No parents."

Sam took a deep breath and blew it out. "Okay, so what do I do?"

"Try to stay out of trouble until they come to get you," Olivia told him. "Your dad sent a change of clothes for you."

"Okay," Sam said, hanging his head.

"Good," Olivia told him as she turned away. "I have some paperwork to file. I'll see you at the hearing."

"Wait!" Sam called.

Olivia turned, tapping her index finger against the tablet. "Something I need to know?"

Sam swallowed. "I think Rylee got pregnant on purpose," he admitted. "She told me that she stopped taking her birth control pills. On purpose," he repeated.

Olivia stepped closer to the bars, studying his face for a long moment. "Sam, that's a serious allegation to make."

Sam held his breath. Maybe Theo was wrong, and this was his way out.

"That being said, there's nothing in the current law that specifically addresses this," she told him. "The Court will look at domestic violence, incest, emotional abuse, all forms of rape, including sexual coercion, but unless Rylee made you have sex with her . . . "

Sam shook his head. "No. She didn't."

Olivia pursed her lips and thought for a moment. "Then, until the state legislature provides additional guidance, this may only apply to the financial and placement negotiations. I can't be certain, but the guardian ad litem might be open to reducing your commitments based on this information." She paused for a moment. "Or, maybe not," she told him. "I'm not sure how much wiggle room he'll have."

Sam opened his mouth, then closed it. What else was there to say?

"I'll see you in a few hours, Sam." And, with that, Olivia turned and walked away.

The bailiff led Sam into the courtroom and unlocked his cuffs so that he could take a seat at the table next to his attorney. The mid-morning sun cast a puddle of light on the floor. *Same courtroom,* Sam thought. *Same judge?*

Sam looked around as he sat. He recognized the guardian ad litem. *Attorney Mueller,* he thought as he nodded in his direction. He turned in his chair. Some corporate suits crowded around the table on his right where Rylee's family had sat during his last visit.

A flash of dark blue caught his eye as the trio sat down. He saw Theo sitting in the public gallery, leaning back in his chair with his arms crossed against his chest. Sam was mildly surprised to see him dressed in a jacket and nicer pants. He'd never seen him out of his typical biker gear: ripped jeans, faded shirt, and that worn leather jacket.

They made eye contact. Theo was pissed. Sam could almost hear the words 'what the absolute fuck, man?!' before Theo looked away, his three-day-old beard almost bristling as he clenched his jaw.

Sam turned back to his attorney. "Please tell me you have a plan," he begged.

Olivia looked at him out of the corner of her eye. "My contingencies have contingencies," she told him in a quiet voice. "Look remorseful. You and Rylee fight about everything and you had a huge argument about the baby, didn't you?" She waited for him to nod. "You know that you made a grave mistake. You knew it was wrong and you swear that if things get out of control again, you'll head home for the night to cool down." She paused and looked at him. "Right?"

Sam nodded. "Absolutely."

"All rise," the bailiff called out. "Court is now in session. The Honorable Judge Christina Olson presiding."

Everyone stood as the judge entered from the side door. She swept the room with a tired glance as she sat. "Everyone be seated," she finally said as she placed a folder on her desk.

Judge Olson sighed, opening the folder to read the documents. She carefully turned the pages as she read, stopping at one point to write a small note. She got to the end, picked up the documents, and carefully stacked them before closing the folder and pushing it away.

Sam found himself rubbing his hands against his pants in an effort to warm his clammy palms and tried to still his hand movement. But that seemed to transfer motion into his leg, and he found himself bouncing his knee rapidly under the table. His attorney looked at him and placed a firm hand on his arm to get him to stop.

"At 7:41 pm last night, you were arrested for attempting to patronize a bar called Deuces, in the Third Ward," the judge finally said, her dark brown eyes drilling into him. "Apparently, this wasn't the first time. The police ran your GPS tracker and determined that you'd violated probation multiple times. According to the police report, you consumed alcohol there three times in the past few months." She slowly blinked, annoyance dripping from her voice. "The bar owner has been ticketed and will receive a substantial fine for this."

Sam shrank into his seat. A substantial fine? He liked Deuces. It felt like a place where he could just be himself. Now, he could never go back.

"According to one of the owners"—she paused to review a page from the file—"Steve Warner, his staff told him that you had been to the bar several times in the company of one Mike Zheng, who is also in the Wisconsin Individual Family Education program. The GPS log corroborates this. Mr. Zheng may be of legal drinking age, but he has been arrested as well."

His attorney sat back in her chair and looked up at the ceiling. Sam cringed. This was bad. This was very, very bad.

"Your Honor—"

Judge Olson overrode his attorney. "Under normal circumstances, you probably wouldn't have been caught, just like hundreds of citizens out on probation that cross that line every single year," the judge continued, enunciating the last few words as she glared at Sam. "But times have changed, and we need to change with them."

She looked over at the prosecutor. "Mr. Spencer, does the District Attorney's office have anything to add?"

The assistant district attorney nodded and placed his hands firmly on the table in front of him as he stood. His voice was gravelly. "Your Honor, there is no question that the defendant violated the terms of his probation by drinking alcohol on three separate occasions. I would be well within my rights to request that we move this to criminal court and seek the maximum penalty of a two-year sentence per violation with a $1500 fine." He paused, dropping his gaze before looking up with an earnest expression. "However, it is our position that this will not serve Mr. Maxwell's child. Nor will it address the underlying problem of two highly immature young people being forced to live together."

The judge leaned forward; eyes narrowed. "What are you proposing, Mr. Spencer?"

The prosecutor sighed. "Your Honor, the city is willing to drop the charges and to consider his weekend detention as 'time served' for violating his probation if Mr. Maxwell will voluntarily submit to undergo a standard labor simulation."

"Interesting solution, Counselor," the judge said. She sat back, considering the recommendation. "Mr. Petropoulous, do you have anything to say?"

Theo stood up, slouching, as he placed his hands on the railing that separated the district attorney's table from the public gallery. "Your Honor, Sam is rather . . . *young* for his age. He appears to be caught between a passive-aggressive mother who cares only about her reputation in the community and an incredibly self-centered young woman with a severe case of affluenza."

Sam stared at Theo, his ears burning. *Passive-aggressive mother? Severe case of affluenza?*

"Affluenza?" the judge responded. "What do you base that observation on?" She pursed her lips in disapproval.

Theo looked over at Sam, then back to Judge Olson. "I had a concern, Your Honor," he said. "I hear it all. These kids tell me a whole lot about what is going on in their lives that led them to this mess. And, when I hear something that might lead them down the wrong path, I reach out to their partner's mentor to compare notes. You should have our analysis in your documentation."

Judge Olson looked down at the folder. "Can you summarize?"

Theo looked at Sam, a strange combination of sorrow and compassion lining his tired face, before he turned to the judge. "Sam is a follower, Your Honor," he said. "He's that kid in the middle of the classroom who doesn't raise his hand, even though he knows the answer. The one who will hang back and let other people yell at him because he doesn't want to make any waves. He's a good kid who made a very big mistake and is trying to do what is right to fix it."

Sam looked down at the table, shaking his head slightly. His eyes burned, and he blinked back tears. He didn't know what to think. Was that how people saw him?

"And his partner?" the judge asked, her voice a bit sharp.

Theo released the rail, hands rubbing his jeans. "Rylee Williams is a self-centered young woman whose self-worth is solely based on her financial status. She has trouble emotionally connecting with anyone and relies on manipulation to get what she wants. It's a classic case of a trust fund baby raising another trust fund baby leading to a severe case of affluenza."

The judge smiled. "Mr. Petropoulous, correct me if I'm wrong, but I believe that affluenza is not mentioned in the Diagnostic and Statistical Manual of Mental Disorders."

Theo smiled. "You're probably right, Your Honor. I'm just a counselor. My job is to help people adjust to difficult life transitions. Focus on their strengths. Understand societal pressures that have an impact on their situation. That's it."

"You do a good job, Mr. Petropoulous," the judge responded, matching Theo's smile with her own. "This Court values the work you do and your opinion in this matter. Thank you."

She turned to Sam. "Mr. Maxwell, do you have anything you'd like to say to this Court?"

Sam gulped, looked at his attorney, then back to the judge. "Your Honor," he said, his voice trembling with anxiety. "I'm sorry for what I did. I made a mistake and—and I take full responsibility for it."

Judge Olson studied him for a long moment, turning a pen over in her hand as she thought. "Thank you for that," she finally said, placing the pen next to the folder in front of her. "Mr. Maxwell, you have a decision to make. Either you voluntarily agree to undergo labor simulation, or you face significant time behind bars, with supervised release for the birth and care of your child, a large fine, and loss of driving privileges."

She held up a hand to stop him from interrupting. "If convicted, your incarceration will automatically be extended based on the number of days that you are released to care for your child. This means that you will serve your entire sentence in full. Labor simulation is a valid alternative."

"Your Honor, I must object!" his attorney protested, her voice almost squeaking in outrage. "Doesn't that fall under 'cruel and unusual punishment?'"

"Which is crueler, Counselor? Putting a twenty-one-year-old on trial for a felony offense and, if convicted, putting him behind bars for up to six years of his child's life or giving him the option of experiencing what childbirth feels like?" the judge said.

Sam looked from his attorney to the judge to Theo. Theo sat down, bowing his head as he dug his fingers into his scrunched-up forehead.

The judge cleared her throat. "Mr. Maxwell, I haven't got all day," she told him.

"Um," Sam stammered. He had a vague feeling that this was bad but drew a blank as to why. How could he experience childbirth? It wasn't physically possible. But it was either that or he could kiss his life goodbye. "The childbirth thing," he finally got out.

"Done," the judge said as she made a note on the file folder.

"Your Honor—"

"Counselor, one way or another, your client must be held accountable for his actions. Perhaps, if he experiences what women go through, it will help him to have a bit of empathy for his partner. We're done here." She ended the conversation with a quick bang of the gavel. "Case closed."

He found himself standing up as the bailiff returned to take him back to holding, mutely holding up his hands so that they could be placed in handcuffs. He ignored Olivia's babbling about trying to appeal the judge's decision. He couldn't really think.

Sam was placed in a holding cell for what felt like a few hours. At some point, they gave him a cheese sandwich and a small fruit cup for lunch, but the burning in his stomach made every minute he waited feel like an eternity.

Experience actual labor? How is that even possible? Simulated made it sound like it was just another exercise, like when he had to wear that pregnancy simulation vest.

Finally, he was taken outside to a police van with four other men. All of them had the same dazed look on their faces. He looked around, expecting to see Mike waiting for him. Instead, he saw Jacob sitting on the right-side bench, looking a bit like he was going to throw up. Sam sat down next to him.

"What happened, man?" Sam asked.

"I donno," Jacob said in a low voice. "I have a friend who's a mechanic. He said that he might be able to get this damn GPS thing off of me so that I could take a decent shower. How was I supposed to know that even a small break was illegal? I mean, he was going to put it back on. I didn't even leave the house!"

Sam shook his head. "Dude. You know that we weren't supposed to take it off." *Ironic*, he thought. They found out almost immediately that Jacob had taken off the tracking mechanism, but it took an actual bouncer to turn him in for them to find out he'd been going down to the bar.

"Yeah, well, I just can't take much more of this, Sam," Jacob whispered. "I feel like a fucking criminal."

Sam nodded. "Me, too."

They heard the door slam on the driver's side, and the van slowly started to roll forward. A short ride later, they found themselves outside of an office building downtown.

As the officers pulled them out onto the sidewalk, Sam asked one of them, "Where are we? Shouldn't we be going to a hospital?" That was where they took pregnant women when it was time to give birth, right?

The officer laughed. "You don't need to go to the hospital, my friend," he said. "You don't need surgery. They're just going to strap a TENS machine on you for a few hours so that you get to feel what it's like to have a baby. No big deal!"

"What's a . . . 'tens' machine?" Sam asked.

"Don't worry about it," he was told. "The doctor will explain everything. Now, let's get you upstairs!"

Chapter Thirteen

The police herded them into the elevator, exchanging smirks as they rode up. Sam felt queasy. That cheese sandwich he'd had for lunch wasn't settling well. *Maybe I should have just taken my chances in criminal court*, he thought. *The attorney could have appealed it, right?*

The elevator door opened. A woman wearing blue scrubs met them, a pink surgical mask dangling off one ear. She looked at one of the officers. "Is this them?" she asked.

The lead officer grunted in agreement and waved the group into the hallway so they could take off their handcuffs. The officers spread out and quickly uncuffed the group.

Sam tried to stay at the back of the small group, but ended up on the far end, far too visible for his own comfort. A surge of acid ripped into his stomach. Why did the nurse have a mask on? Was the officer wrong and they *were* they going to be operated on?

The nurse looped the other end of the mask back over her face, smoothing it across her nose with a practiced, quick pinch. "Alright, if you'll follow me, we'll get you prepped," she said, then started walking down the hall. The small group followed her, each of them escorted by an officer. He couldn't imagine anyone trying to run away, but obviously they weren't taking any chances.

The nurse opened a door on the left and gestured them in. "Go ahead and get changed. There's a hospital gown and disposable pants for each of you in the changing rooms. Once you're done, have a seat." She turned and walked through a door on the far side of the room.

The group hesitated. "Alright, you all. Get to it!" one of them barked.

Sam ducked into the first room on his right. Inside, the gown, paper pants, and hospital socks sat on a wide chair, waiting for him. He looked around. There was a small locker for his clothes and personal belongings. No lock, though.

Sam snorted. They hadn't given him back his wallet, cell phone, or keys. *Not that it would do me any good*, he thought as he started to undress. *Hell, the car had probably been towed already*.

He carefully peeled himself out of his sweat-stained clothes and stuffed them into the locker, then piled his shoes and socks on top. What the actual hell were they going to do to him? Surgically implant this TENS unit into him so that he could experience what it was like to have a c-section?

He felt himself starting to sweat. *This can't be legal*, he thought. *It just can't be*.

The pounding on his cubicle door startled him. "Hurry up in there," the officer yelled. "We don't have all day!"

"Almost done," Sam told him. He slowly pulled the paper pants up, then put the hospital gown on. He opened the door and stared at Jacob before realizing that he'd forgotten the socks. Before he could go back and get them, the officer grabbed him by the upper arm and yanked him toward the group. Collectively, they looked like they were being led to their execution.

The nurse popped her head into the room. "We're ready for you," she said, then backed up so they could follow her.

Sam stood there, frozen for a moment. He found himself staring at her, trying to translate what he was seeing. She was wearing surgical scrubs like he'd seen on TV, but that couldn't be right. Surgery would mean that she'd have gloves on, right? Maybe even one of those clear plastic facial shields.

Sam wondered if this was just a way of scaring them before they started to pretend like they were pregnant. Or, maybe they had some of those full-body tactical haptic suits waiting in the other room and were going to run this as a simulation in VR. He'd never tried one on, but he'd heard that they really made the game feel alive. You could actually feel it when you were shot.

"Come on, you lot," the head officer told them. "We need to get you strapped in."

Sam felt a hand on his shoulder, nudging him forward. They walked into a long but narrow room that looked like a surgical recovery space. There was just enough room for the five hospital beds that were lined up against one wall, each separated by a standard privacy curtain. He picked one and gingerly sat down on the bed, eying the strange device on the small table next to the bed. It looked like a small, black remote-control unit and was surrounded by round plastic discs with small pads underneath. No suit or VR gear in sight.

A doctor walked into the room and stood at the foot of one of the middle beds where everyone could see him. Sam eyed the white lab coat, faded blue scrubs, and blue surgical mask. No gloves, though. Maybe this labor simulation was just that: a simulation?

"Good afternoon, gentlemen," he said as he slowly made eye contact with one, then another of the group. "I'm Dr. Franks, an obstetrician with this clinic. According to the court order that our legal department just reviewed, you will be going through a labor simulation exercise to help you understand what active labor feels like when your partner gives birth. I'm here to walk you through what to expect and to monitor your progress."

Sam opened his mouth to ask why they were in hospital gowns, but the doctor held up his hand. "Please hold your questions until the end, understood?" He waited a moment, then continued. "This simulation will be done via a TENS unit." He held up a small device that was identical to the ones on each table. "This uses a low voltage electrical current to—" He stopped as the small room echoed with collective outrage.

"Electrocution?!"

"This is bullshit! I want my lawyer!"

"What the absolute *fuck*, man!"

"You're not putting that thing on me!"

"Shut up, all of you!" one of the officers bawled. "It's either this or I'm hauling you back to lockup. You waived your right to a trial by agreeing to this. So just suck it up!"

Dr. Franks shot the officer a startled look, then carefully looked around the room. "This procedure is generally safe. We will place the electrodes on your skin, here, here, and here," gesturing to show them on his lower abdomen. "The device will deliver electrical impulses that simulate the feeling of labor."

Sam raised his hand. The doctor nodded at him. "So, this is just something that you put on our skin? How does that make it feel like labor?"

The doctor nodded. "Good question," he said. "Without getting too scientific, a TENS unit sends a small, stimulating pulse along your skin. Your abdominal muscles will contract and this will cause your nerves to experience something similar to what women go through during delivery, except that it won't be as intense."

"Whatever, man," Jacob said with a snort. "Bring it on. I'm stronger than any woman."

Sam heard agreement from the other side of the room as he laid back on the bed and muttered something appropriate. He vaguely remembered that one of the childbirth classes had talked about how abdominal muscles contracted to help push the baby out. Muscle contractions. Sounded more like a leg cramp but for his abs.

Several women entered the room. They were dressed in pink scrubs similar to what the nurses wore at Rylee's ob-gyn doctor. All of them were masked. A tall brunette came over to Sam's bed.

"Hi," she said. "I'm Abby. I'm here to act as your doula."

"Hey, Abby," Sam responded. It sounded familiar. Rylee had demanded one, but he'd pretty much stayed out of it. "I know that I should probably know this, but . . . what's a doula?"

Abby sat in the chair next to him. Sam rolled over on his side so he could see her better. "A doula is someone who provides physical and emotional support during pregnancy, childbirth, and postpartum," she said. "My primary focus is usually on birth preparation. I've never been involved in a labor simulation."

Sam ruefully smiled. "First time for everything, right?"

The corners of Abby's eyes crinkled as she shook her head in agreement. "Absolutely." She handed him a blue surgical hair net.

He sat up and held it in his hands. "What's this for?" he asked.

"We're trying to make this as realistic as possible," she told him. "That's why we brought in delivery beds with stirrups."

"I'm sorry, what?" Sam asked, frantically looking around the bed. What the hell did they need something you use on a horse for?

Abby laughed and went to the end of the bed. She reached down and pulled out a metal bar with an attachment that looked like an oversized snow boot strapped to the other end. "Sorry," she said. "I should have explained that better. I meant lithotomy stirrups. They're used to support a patient's feet and lower legs during the episiotomy and delivery."

Sam laughed uneasily. Episiotomy. Another word he didn't recognize but should. "So, we're going to be strapped into those?" he asked as he put the surgical net over his hair.

"When we get to the second stage of labor, yes," Abby told him, carefully folding the stirrups back under the bed. "Although I'm not sure if we'll get that far. It all depends on what we hear back from the Court, I guess."

Sam laid back down, one fist pushing the thin pillow under his head. He didn't think that the judge would let them off too easily, but who knew? Maybe his lawyer was able to file some emergency request to get this down to just the basics.

Dr. Franks slowly walked along the back of the room. "Time to get started. Gentlemen, please open your gown so that we can get the devices attached."

Sam pulled the worn, green surgical gown open and tried to suck in his stomach. Between carting Rylee around, his college courses, the program requirements, and his mentoring circle, he hadn't had much time to work out. He definitely needed to reserve some court time at the athletic club in the near future.

Abby looked over at him, then reached for an alcohol prep wipe. She tore it open, then carefully swabbed his stomach. Sam tried not to flinch from the sudden chill, but she still noticed. "Sorry," she said as she moved the wipe to the other side of his stomach. "I know it's cold."

She fanned his stomach with her hands for a moment to encourage the alcohol to dry. Then, she picked up the black TENS unit. She spread the eight pads out in her other hand. The pads were interconnected with black wires and the wires attached to the controller.

"We're going to begin by asking you to flex your abdominal muscles so that we can locate the correct muscle groups," Dr. Franks told them. Sam managed what he thought was an acceptable flex, feeling the burn in his muscles. He knew he'd gotten flabby over the last few months, but this was ridiculous.

"The electrodes need to be placed along the right and left sides of the abdomen. Four pads per side," Dr. Franks said. "The bottom row should be right below the belly button. We'll start by applying a small amount of conductive gel to the electrode pads before placing them on the patients."

Sam shivered a bit as Abby squirted a small dab of gel on each pad and carefully arranged them on his stomach. Sam relaxed his stomach muscles as she stepped aside for the doctor to take a look at her placement.

"Not so wide, Abby," he said. "We need to fully engage the abdominal muscles all the way up." He carefully removed one of the pads and showed Abby exactly where to place them before moving on.

Abby moved the pads into the correct position, then snapped the electrodes to the fabric pads. "Sorry about that," she told him. "First time jitters."

"No worries," Sam said as he glanced down at the interconnected double line of pads that were lined up on either side of his belly button. The black wires were laced together to form a simple web over his skin.

"Next, you'll need to wrap an elastic bandage around the patient to keep the electrodes in place during the simulation," Dr. Franks told the doulas. "You will find rolls of non-adhesive tape in the top drawer."

Abby reached over and pulled out a thick roll of brown cloth tape. It was the same kind of wrap that Sam used when his wrist acted up. She quickly wrapped the tape around his abdomen, then used some medicinal adhesive tape to keep it firmly in place.

"Too tight?" she asked.

Sam wiggled around a bit. "Nope," he told her. "All good."

After the doctor had made sure that everyone was ready, he stood against the far wall so that everyone could see him. "To make this realistic, we're going to start with contractions five minutes apart," he told the group. "We'll be in active labor, with contractions lasting about forty-five seconds. The cervix should be dilated to four centimeters or so." He paused and looked around. "Does anyone have any questions before we begin?"

Jacob spoke up from the bed next to Sam. "How long will we be doing this?"

Dr. Franks grimaced and looked down. "On average, a normal labor can take anywhere between six and fourteen hours," he told them. "I'm hoping that we can end this sooner, but I haven't been given a clear direction by the Court yet."

Sam dropped his head back against the thin pillow. Fourteen hours sounded a bit long to him. But he seemed to remember something about not going to the hospital until the contractions were really close together, so maybe this included time before a woman went in to deliver the baby? He shook his head slightly and made a mental note to ask Abby later.

Jacob flopped back on the bed. "Whatever," he said. "Just get it over with, would ya?"

The doctor looked over at the clock on the left side of the room. "Alright," he said. "Doulas, please select 'endurance' from the main menu." He paused and waited until he had confirmation from each of them. "Begin with level one stimulation set at forty-five seconds. Time begins . . . now."

At first, Sam felt a strange tingling sensation. *Not bad*, he thought. But then the tingling gave way to a slight burning sensation as his muscles tensed. It felt like something was tugging directly on his stomach muscles.

Abby leaned over and caught his eye. "How do you feel?" she asked, studying him intently.

Sam breathed out. "It feels like a muscle cramp, you know?" he told her. "Like I just need to stretch it out." He winced and looked down, trying to see if his muscles were tightening up under the bandage. Not so bad. What the hell had he been worried about?

"Okay," Abby said. "Just try to relax your stomach. You're doing fine."

Sam tried to push his stomach muscles out as he took a deep breath. *It's just a muscle cramp*, he told himself.

He heard Jacob laugh. "This is labor?" he crowed. "This is nothing!"

"You're right," Dr. Franks said as he came to check Jacob's TENS setting. "Everyone experiences labor pain differently. One person's two is another person's five." He looked Jacob over carefully and turned to the doula. "Next contraction, let's increase his level by one point. If necessary, we can drop it back later."

Sam kept his focus on breathing, blowing out each breath slowly, just like they'd been told in that childbirth class. He counted nine total breaths before the burning sensation went away.

Sam looked at Abby. "That wasn't so bad," he said.

Abby shook her head, the corners of her eyes crinkling as she smiled beneath her mask. "The early part of labor can take hours," she told him. "If you were about to give birth, your pain level would gradually increase as the contractions got closer together."

Sam didn't know what to say. He finally nodded. He knew that, didn't he?

Dr. Franks walked along the back of the room, pacing as he continued his lecture. "During early labor, the contractions will get longer in duration, stronger, and closer together," he told them. "These contractions tend to be relatively mild and typically last no more than a minute. Once the contractions are about four minutes apart, it's time to go to the hospital because your partner is most likely in active labor. Speaking of which, next contraction."

Abby pressed a button on the remote. Again, it felt like a slight burning sensation as his abdominal muscles protested. He closed his eyes and focused on breathing.

"That's right," Abby told him in a soothing voice. "Just try to relax." He kept pushing his stomach muscles out, breathing slowly through his mouth. The burning sensation seemed to fade a bit as his muscles tried to relax.

This time, the contraction seemed to last longer. Twelve breaths. Sam relaxed against the bed. Jacob was right. This was nothing he couldn't handle.

"Doulas, we're going to move to four minutes between contractions now," Dr. Franks told the group as he walked from bed to bed to assess them. "Contractions should move one step higher in intensity and a full sixty seconds in length." He paused to look up at the clock. "Starting . . . now."

Chapter Fourteen

Time seemed to blur. He was curled up on his side, but there was no place to escape the stabbing pain that burned through his stomach muscles and into his back. He groaned, eyes clenched shut.

"Breathe, Sam," Abby told him, her gentle voice cutting under the yelling around them. "Count it out with me. Breathe in, Sam. Now, out! Woo! Woo! One. In again. Out! Woo! Woo! Two." He felt her hand push in beneath him, fingers digging in to try and ease his back spasms. "You can do this, Sam," she crooned.

He grunted and found himself on his back as he tried to roll from side to side in an unconscious effort to make the pain go away. His muscles were trying to tear themselves out from underneath his skin in waves.

He felt a cold, wet washcloth on his forehead and he blindly reached for Abby's hand. "Make it stop," he pleaded. "I don't care what you have to do. Please, just make it stop!"

"Fifteen seconds," Dr. Franks called out from the foot of the bed.

Abby squeezed his hand. "You're in transition now. It won't be much longer. I promise."

He heard one of the others start to gag, then the rancid smell of vomit filled the air. One of the police officers laughed. "Come on," he said. "My wife had two of them. Suck it up and be a man!"

"Officer, unless you'd like me to hook you up, I suggest you go back into the waiting room," Dr. Franks said, his voice sharp with disapproval. "Childbirth is one of the most intensely painful things that anyone can go through."

The officer's voice receded as he walked out of the room. "Yeah, but if my wife could pop our kids out without an epidural, these boys should be man enough to handle it." The door shut behind him.

Sam heard Dr. Franks walk across the room, his steps echoing against the walls. "Let's get him cleaned up, shall we? We're just about ready for the next stage."

The pain eased, but his muscles spasmed in outrage. "I can't," Sam moaned. "I just can't." He tried to wipe the sweat out of his eyes, but failed. The salt stung for a moment, but it was nothing like the agony in his stomach muscles.

Abby rolled him on his side and started rubbing his back with a long, gentle stroke of her hand. "I know," she said. "This is the hardest part of labor. Did you want to try changing positions again? Maybe getting on all fours will help."

Sam nodded. He tried rolling over onto his stomach and almost fell off the bed. Abby placed her hands under him and helped him off the bed. Then, he crawled back on, rocking back and forth as he waited for the next contraction.

He didn't have to wait long. Sam buried his face in the firm mattress, almost screaming in agony. He felt Abby's hands move to his back, her gentle fingers pressed against the fabric bandage in long sweeping motions.

He pushed up until he was sitting on his heels, back arched as he stared at the sterile drop ceiling tiles overhead. "I—okay, okay. Breathe," he panted. "Breathe." He leaned forward until he was able to rest his face and shoulders on the mattress again, teeth clenched as he tried to suppress his groans.

Her thumbs felt firm as she dug into his back muscles beneath the sweaty hospital gown and compression bandage. "Forty-five seconds," she told him, her voice almost lost in the rush of pain. He could barely hear her over the cacophony of agony around him.

His arms were underneath him, pushing against the pads on his stomach and feeling the long, interconnected cords. He clenched his fists, fighting the urge to reach under the gown and yank the compression bandage off so he could get at them. *Wouldn't do any good*, he told himself. *They'd just slap them back on.*

Abby touched his shoulder and helped him move to his side just as the contraction stopped. He curled up, feeling like a fool for crying, but the tears just wouldn't stop. If this is what women went through every time they gave birth, why did they keep having babies?!

"We are now at the delivery stage," Dr. Franks' voice pulled Sam back from the darkness. "Let's get them into position."

Sam clenched his eyes shut and felt warm hands rolling him onto his back. "We need to scoot him down a bit," Abby said. Carefully, the hands helped him move further down on the bed until his legs were bent at the knee and his legs dangled off the edge of the bed. One foot, then the other was gently lifted into a padded boot, then straps tightened to secure them.

"And up!" Abby said. Hands on either side grasped his own and pulled him into a reclined seated position. The bed moved up behind him, giving him firm support behind his back. His legs were pulled up into the air and spread wide enough that anyone could see his sweat-drenched crotch where it peeked out beneath his hospital gown.

Sam opened his eyes and pulled on one of the hands to bring Abby closer. "What's going on?"

"You're at the point where a woman would almost be ready to deliver," Abby whispered. "It won't be long now."

Another frenzied burst of pain hit him. "What does that mean?" he groaned.

Abby wiped the sweat from Sam's face with a gentle swipe of her cool washcloth. "It's just about time to push."

"Push?" That didn't make any sense.

"Yes," Dr. Franks said as he rolled over on a padded stool to sit between Sam's legs. Sam tried to focus on the doctor's dark eyes as he worked to make sense of the words, his face framed by Sam's splayed knees.

"I don't understand," Sam whined. "I'm not pregnant. There's nothing to push out!"

The doctor smoothed his mask with a gloved hand. "Focus on me, Sam. If you were pregnant, you would feel pressure in your lower abdomen and, with each contraction, we would need you to bear down."

The world blurred. "No!" Sam screamed, his back arched in agony as he squeezed the hands that held him upright against the mattress. "Make it stop," he begged. "Please, make it stop!"

"Turn the intensity down to level eight," he heard the doctor say. "Two minutes apart."

Sam barely heard Abby's response. The pain cut off abruptly, but his distressed muscles flared in continued misery.

"Sam," Dr. Franks said. "I know you're in a lot of pain right now, but we need to slow your breathing down. We're almost done."

In the bed next to him, Jacob started wailing. The doctor looked over, then said, "Prescott, trade places with me." A woman, fully masked and gowned as if she was in an operating room, moved between Sam's legs, and Dr. Franks scooted over to the next bed.

"I'm Doctor Prescott," the woman told him.

Abby rolled another stool close to him and placed her hand on his left shoulder. "Sam," she said. "Open your eyes and look at me." When Sam didn't respond, she touched his cheek with gentle fingers. "I need you to trust me, Sam."

Sam slowly opened his eyes, staring at Abby's blue-gray eyes. He nodded.

"With your next contraction, I'm going to need you to take a deep breath in through your nose," she told him. "Then, you need to empty your lungs in a slow and deep exhale. Do you understand? Deep, slow breath, long exhale."

Sam nodded.

"Okay, do it with me now," Abby commanded him. "Deep breath. Now exhale, slow and loud." She squeezed his hand. "Louder," she told him. "As loud as you want!"

On Abby's second exhalation, Sam managed to mirror her. Some small part of him recognized the breathing exercise from the birthing class. He managed a sound that was more of a deep, breathy groan that mirrored the agony in his stomach.

"Good job!" she told him.

Dr. Prescott touched his shin to get his attention. "Your contractions are going to slow down and be a bit less intense," she told him. "We're almost done. You're doing great."

The pain cut out in that moment, and Sam laid his head back against the sweat-stained mattress with a strangled sob. Then, he sucked in another breath and slowly pushed it out. *Please, Jesus*, he thought. *Let this be over soon.*

Abby grasped his right hand. "Almost done, Sam," she told him. "Just a few more contractions and we're done."

"Really?" he breathed, blinking sweat from his eyes.

"Really," she reassured him. "This is the last stage of delivery, the afterbirth."

He blinked. "Placenta, right?"

Abby smiled, and for the first time, he noticed that she had shed her mask. "That plus some," she told him.

The doctor lightly placed her hands on his sore abdomen muscles right above the electrodes. "Normally, I would massage or press right here to help things move along, but I can't do that right now because we can't remove the electrodes yet," she told him.

His overworked muscles began to clench again as the fire spread from his abdomen down into his lower back. Abby squeezed his hand tightly. "Breathe with me," she crooned. "Deep breath. Now exhale with me, slow and loud."

Sam did his best to comply, but he was so exhausted he could barely focus on Abby's face. "Woohh . . ." he responded weakly.

The pressure on his muscles eased, and Abby relaxed her grip. "Good job, Sam," she told him.

Sam found himself rolling his head from side to side. He knew that the contractions were easing, but his body didn't agree that the pain was any less intense. He just needed it to be over.

"Last one," Abby told him, renewing her hold on his hand. The next contraction gripped him, and it felt as if a ring of fire had engulfed around his midsection as his back muscles flared in sympathy.

"And we're done!" Abby told him. "Let's get you into a more comfortable position." The mattress moved beneath him. Hands gripped his and they eased him into a flat position on the bed. First one foot, then the other, was gently released from the boots. Sam struggled to move, but the sheet lifted him up and deposited him higher on the bed.

"Let's get those pants off of him," he heard Dr. Prescott say. "They're soaked." And before he could protest, gentle hands quickly removed the pants and a light blanket was tucked in around his legs.

The bed powered up slowly, pushing him up until he was in a semi-reclined position again. He found himself looking down as Abby gently cut the fabric wrap away. Then, she removed the electrodes and peeled the pads from his skin. He was surprised to see only the faintest outline left behind. His skin looked a bit red, but otherwise there was no sign of the agony he had endured.

"Would you like apple juice, fruit punch, or just some water?" Abby asked him.

"Apple juice," he managed to croak.

Sam looked around the narrow room. He watched as Dr. Franks moved from bed to bed, quickly validating that each of them was recovering as he moved.

"How are you feeling, Sam?" he asked.

"It feels like I pulled my groin muscle," Sam admitted, hissing as he tried to reposition his legs. "My back and stomach really hurt. Is that normal?"

The doctor pulled off his mask, frowning as he looked away for a moment. "That might be the closest analogy that I've heard to what women experience in childbirth," he admitted. "I know that you're in a good amount of pain right now, but it will subside over the next few days."

Abby brought a box of apple juice over and inserted a straw for him. Sam took a small sip, grimacing as he shifted position again. "Can you give me something for the pain?" he asked Dr. Franks.

The doctor looked away for a moment. "No, I'm afraid I can't," he admitted, pursing his lips.

"Why not?" Sam whispered. After all of that, they couldn't spare some overpriced Tylenol, or maybe give him something stronger?

"My role is only to oversee the simulation, not to act in my capacity as a physician," Dr. Franks replied. "I'm afraid I'm not authorized to prescribe anything for you at this time." He shook his head in disapproval. "Apply ice periodically to help reduce any inflammation and take an over-the-counter medication, as needed. Before you leave, we'll get you wrapped up with a compression belt so that you have a bit of support to help you walk." He started to move away, then turned back. "Good luck to you," he said.

"Alright, doulas," Dr. Franks announced as he made his way back to the front of the room. "I'm going to need each of you to help your clients into a compression belt. You'll find them in the drawer next to the bed."

"What?" one of the men protested. "I can't get out of this bed yet! You just tortured me!"

The door opened and the lead officer poked his head in. "We need to wrap this up, folks!"

Dr. Franks looked at the officer. Sam could see his fist clenched from across the room. "They're allowed twenty more minutes of rest before you can move them," he said.

"Doc, we're on a tight schedule," the officer told him. "I need to get them back to the station before 5 pm."

"And I'm the one in charge of this simulation, Officer," Dr. Franks snapped back. "I will decide when this group can be medically discharged."

"Fine, have it your way, Doc," the officer said with a sneer as he started to close the door. "It's not like they actually delivered babies!"

"Get out," the doctor ordered. He turned back to the group, studying each man in turn. "You have about fifteen minutes to get settled after the compression belt is put on. After that, I am required to release you."

"But, Doc," Sam said, "I don't think I can stand on my own."

"I know," the doctor said, sounding as wiped out as Sam felt. "But your partners will likely feel the same when they are released from the hospital. I have to treat you as equals in that regard." He looked around. "I don't make the rules, gentlemen. The courts do."

Abby held up a black abdominal support girdle. "Okay, Sam," she said with a small smile. "Let's get you wrapped up."

Chapter Fifteen

S am's dad picked him up from the downtown police station. He didn't say a word as they wound their way through side streets on their way back to Mequon to avoid the inevitable backup on the freeway.

Sam had expected a lecture, but his dad just focused on driving. *Cool*, Sam thought as he stared out the window. He really didn't want to talk anyhow.

He started to ask why Dad wasn't dropping him off at the apartment, but figured that it probably made more sense just to go home. He ached from head to toe and just wanted to climb into his own bed for once and get some sleep.

All too soon, they pulled up the driveway. Sam slowly pushed open the car door, his muscles screaming in protest. The frigid air punched through his light jacket, icing his arms and legs as he tried to get into the house as quickly as possible.

Wendy had other plans. She met them at the door, snarling, "What were you thinking?!"

Sam dropped his jacket on the entrance hall floor and looked around blearily. "Mom, it's been a long couple of days," he said. "Can't this wait until tomorrow?"

"No, it can't!" Wendy replied, arching her eyebrows as she looked from the jacket on the floor and back to him. "What the hell were you thinking going down to a bar?! I raised you better than that!"

Sam barely listened as he brushed by. *Water*, he thought as he walked to the kitchen. He was so thirsty. Probably dehydrated from the simulation.

Wendy stalked after him. "Samuel Kevin Maxwell, don't you dare ignore me!"

Sam opened the cabinet door and pulled out a glass, groaning as his muscles screamed in protest. He walked over to the fridge and tapped the water dispenser to fill his glass.

"Mom, I'm really tired," he finally told her. "Can't this wait until later?"

"I don't care how tired you are, young man," she snarled. "I want answers!"

Sam gulped down some water and then started to refill his glass. "What is there to say, Mom?" he asked, watching the glass slowly fill. "It's complicated. I just needed a break from Rylee, so yeah, I went out for a beer. I'm twenty-one now, and according to the State of Wisconsin, I'm legal."

"Except you're on probation and are not allowed to drink," Wendy retorted. "Do you have any idea what kind of trouble you're in?"

Sam pulled his glass away from the dispenser and turned around. Wendy was in high rage, face flushed, and her glare accentuated the deep wrinkles around her eyes. Her auburn hair threatened to escape her normally immaculate bun. One of her perfectly manicured nails was chipped from spending too much time tapping on the kitchen table.

Probation. Everyone used that word, but he hadn't been convicted of a crime. Somehow, just the act of getting Rylee pregnant had snowballed from a simple, civil matter into a huge legal liability that he still didn't understand.

"Did you talk to the lawyer?" Sam asked. He vaguely wondered where his father was. Probably hiding out in his office, waiting for the storm that was his wife to blow over.

"Of course, I did," Wendy shot back. "You were arrested for attempting to purchase alcohol, which violates your probation. And," she crowed, "you were charged with three additional counts!" She paused for dramatic effect. "What were you thinking?!"

He'd had just about enough of this bullshit. "I'll tell you what I was thinking," Sam growled. "I was thinking that I'm not ready to be a dad. I was thinking that what I really needed was help navigating this shit and *no one* in my life is stepping up. Not my parents, who supported this *stupid* law that made their son a *fucking* criminal. Not my friends. Not even the mentor appointed by the *fucking* Court."

He slammed the glass cup onto the granite countertop, splashing water over the rim. "I was thinking that if the *fucking* State of Wisconsin wants me to step up and be a man, no matter how Rylee got pregnant, then by God and by damn, I am entitled to have a goddamn drink like a man!" he shouted.

Wendy wilted, staring at him for a long time. "Language," she whispered.

"Did anyone tell you what my punishment was?" Part of Sam knew that he should just follow his dad's lead and hole up in his room until this blew over, but he was so tired of being bullied. His stomach and back muscles throbbed in protest, but he ignored the pain for the moment.

"You were in lock up all weekend," she replied, lifting her chin to glare at him.

Sam moved a few steps closer. "And after my court hearing? Did you even ask what happened after that?" he demanded.

Wendy looked away for a moment, flustered. "Well, obviously Olivia was able to work her magic—" she said, trying to regain control over the conversation.

Sam snorted. "Magic? What magic?" he demanded.

Wendy looked at him, a bit flabbergasted. "Well, obviously, she got you released because your dad was able to pick you up . . . " her voice trailed off in confusion.

"They sentenced you to labor simulation in lieu of referring it to criminal court," his dad said, hovering just outside the kitchen door. "I just got off the phone with Olivia. She filed a motion to suspend your sentence while an appeal was pending, but it was too late. I'm sorry, Sam. She tried to stop it."

Wendy cocked her head to one side. "Labor simulation?"

Sam grabbed his cup off the counter and took another gulp of water, mildly amazed that the glass hadn't shattered. With his free hand, he slowly pulled up his shirt until the compression band peeked out, grimacing as his muscles screamed in protest.

"I don't understand," Wendy said as she stared as if the black fabric was an alien appendage. She looked over at her husband, then back to Sam.

"They ran an electrical current through me to 'simulate' the feeling of being in labor," Sam told her as he pulled his shirt down. "Generally safe, I'm told, and painful as hell."

"What?" Wendy stepped closer. "They electrocuted you? Are you okay?"

Now, she asks! Sam thought. "I will be," he said. "I just need to lie down, alright?"

Wendy stood aside. "Fine," she said. "But we're not done with this, Samuel. I know that you forced Rylee to get pregnant, and we still need to talk about that!" He heard the words, but they seemed to be background noise.

Sam carefully placed his empty glass on the counter and pushed past her. "I don't even know what to say, Mom," he said as he left the room. He slowly made his way upstairs and crawled onto his bed, exhausted. He punched his pillow, trying to find a comfortable position so that the compression band didn't pinch as much. First Rylee, now Wendy.

He was almost on the verge of sleep when he realized that Wendy had accused him of forcing Rylee to get pregnant. *Where the hell did she get that idea?* he thought as he drifted off. She was wrong and when she found out that Rylee had stopped taking her birth control pills, all hell was going to break loose.

The next morning, Sam's stomach and back felt like an over-sized, deep bruise. He found his way down to the kitchen to grab some breakfast, feeling just a bit nauseous because he missed dinner the previous night. *Is this what Rylee said her morning sickness felt like*, he thought as he resisted the urge to rub at his stomach. Maybe some food would help.

His dad sat at the kitchen table, drinking coffee as he read through some legal documents, a plate with the remains of a bagel to one side. He didn't look up as Sam poured coffee into a mug and set it on the table.

Sam grabbed a bagel from the bag on the counter and popped it into the toaster. He moved cautiously to the refrigerator, struggling to open it as his inflamed muscles protested. He grabbed the strawberry cream cheese, a plate, and a clean knife while he waited for the bagel to toast.

"Your mother is quite upset," his dad told him without look-ing up.

"I know," Sam replied. "I'm not sure how she got the idea that I forced Rylee to get pregnant!"

"Apparently, someone at her Bible study group is a close friend with Rylee's family," his dad told him, pulling another page from the file he was reading. "This woman took your mother aside and told her that you made Rylee stop taking birth control pills so she would get pregnant with your baby."

Sam fumbled with his plate, almost dropping it as he tried to grab his bagel from the toaster. "What?" He turned to face his dad. "Dad, that's not true!"

His dad dropped the document he was reading and looked over. "It doesn't matter if it's true or not," he told Sam. "What matters is what people want to believe."

Sam grabbed his breakfast and moved to the table. He carefully set the plate down and braced himself as he slid into his seat. "I don't understand."

"We live in a binary world," his dad told him. "When it comes to an unexpected pregnancy, Rylee is either a victim or she's a whore. There's no middle ground. As long as it was consensual, I don't see a problem. But I'm in the minority, son."

Sam looked down at his plate, struggling to find the right words. "I had a huge fight with Rylee about this." He paused, then looked up. "She stopped taking the Pill because she has some kind of medical issue and thought she couldn't get pregnant. But, since she didn't tell me, isn't that some sort of entrapment?"

"Olivia told me your concerns with me, and I share them," his dad replied, pursing his lips. "However, the state doesn't currently recognize that as a legal defense." He held up a hand to stop Sam from protesting. "Yes, we could file a lawsuit, depose Rylee, her gynecologist, and even her closest friends, but it doesn't change the fact that you are going to be a father. The best you can hope for is a reduction in child support payments and child placement. This is as much your child as it is hers. Is this really what you want?"

Sam studied his father's face for a moment. Olivia had asked him that, too. "I don't know what I want, Dad," he finally said.

"Sam, even if we win, it will be years before this makes it through the court system," his dad told him. "A baby changes everything."

Sam nodded. "Thing is," he said. "I think that, deep down, Rylee wanted to get pregnant."

"Why do you think that?" his dad asked.

Sam sighed, studying his slightly burned bagel for a moment. "The way she's acting," he finally replied. "Always showing off that 'baby bump' wherever she goes. Telling people that this baby is a gift from God. A miracle baby. And she won't even consider adoption."

"If she changed her mind, would you agree to it?" his dad asked him gently.

"I don't know," Sam told him, dejectedly. "I don't think my opinion matters."

His dad nodded in sympathy. "I'm sorry, Sam."

Sam's mom entered the kitchen, almost gliding as she moved to the coffee maker. Her dark green sweater and black jeans stood out against the white kitchen cabinets. The colors seemed designed to draw attention to her as she moved.

She ignored both men as she poured herself a cup of coffee and crossed the room to the table. She pulled out the chair farthest away from Sam and carefully sat.

"Good morning, Wendy," his dad said, giving Sam a warning look. "How did you sleep?"

His mom sipped her coffee, grimacing at the hot liquid as she put it down on the table. "Not well," she admitted as she avoided eye contact. "I'm still trying to understand a few things."

"How can I help?" he asked patiently.

"I need to make sure that I understand this," she said in that sickeningly sweet voice that Sam had learned to dread as a child. It was the calm between the storms. "Rylee made the decision to stop taking her birth control pills on her own, right?" she asked.

Sam started to respond, but she held up her hand. "Don't talk," she said, not even looking in his direction.

Sam's dad licked his lip. "I believe that's a true state—" he started to respond, his brown eyes looking at her cautiously.

"And—I need to make sure that I have this right," Wendy overrode him, picking up her coffee mug and cradling it in both hands. "Sam didn't use any protection, even though the Pill is not one hundred percent effective. Meaning that even if this girl had been taking the Pill, there was still the possibility of getting pregnant." She took a small sip of coffee, finally meeting Sam's gaze. "Did I get that right?"

Sam felt himself blush, but refused to break eye contact. He nodded.

Wendy carefully placed her coffee mug back on the table. He could see the rage building in her eyes. "So, Rylee is pregnant with your child because you thought it was too much work to put on a condom?!"

Sam blinked. "Um," he said, trying to wrap his head around the fact that she had actually used the word 'condom' to describe a form of birth control. Her usual go-to word was 'protection' and she only used the word sparingly because the idea of her sons having sex was somehow embarrassing. "Mom, I didn't think I needed them because Rylee—"

His mom overrode him, her tone quiet and deceptively flat. "Rylee's mother has told our entire congregation you bullied her baby girl into getting pregnant with your child. She's not *quite* calling it rape, but people are making the assumption."

Sam gaped at her. The strange looks he'd gotten at worship. Not being asked to help out in the kitchen for the annual Advent by Candlelight potluck. Friends ghosting him online. Is that what people thought?

Wendy stared at him, letting the silence stretched between them as she waited for him to respond. "I swear to God that's not true, Mom!" he finally blurted out.

Wendy studied his face for a long moment, then picked up her coffee mug for a long sip. "I believe you," she finally told him. "However, I can't just sit back and let that whore's family ruin our reputation." She turned to Sam's dad. "I will talk to Olivia later today about suing the Williams family for defamation of character."

"Wendy, that's uncalled for!" his dad snapped.

Sam looked down at his uneaten bagel. Of course, Wendy was more worried about her reputation than her own son.

"Andrew," she said, the tone in her voice darkening. "You didn't hear what people were saying about us. About our son. About how we raised him."

"Wendy, anything you heard is considered to be hearsay," Sam's dad told her. "It's not admissible in court."

"I don't care, Andrew," Wendy retorted. "There must be a way to stop this nonsense, even if I have to sue Rylee personally." She turned to Sam. "As a part of that, we will not give you a single cent more, Samuel."

Sam looked up. "I'm sorry, what?"

"Wendy—"

"Enough, Andrew!" Wendy snapped. "I don't want another penny going to support that whore or her family! She's lying about our son. Her family is lying to our congregation. I'm done with this nonsense. Not one more penny!" And with that, Wendy picked up her coffee mug and stomped out of the kitchen.

Sam had had enough. "Unbelievable!" he yelled after her. "First you supported a law that made your own son a criminal and now you're writing off your first grandchild?!"

Sam looked at his dad, seething. "Does this mean you're not going to help with my tuition?" he quietly asked.

Sam's dad shook his head. "Your college fund is safe, but that only covers your tuition, not books or room and board. And, since you're enrolled in that WIFE program, I have to take a closer look at what we're legally able to assist with."

"But?"

"I'll do what I can, but don't expect your mother to approve of anything pregnancy related, not even fixing up the baby's room," he told him. "I'm sorry, son, but Rylee may have burned that bridge."

Sam picked up his knife and started to spread strawberry cream cheese on his now cold bagel. "Yeah," he muttered. "That's what she does, Dad. She burned down every bridge I had."

He nibbled at the bagel, hoping that it would settle his stomach. He wished he'd never asked Rylee out to begin with, let alone slept with her. He had no idea how he was going to be able to afford to go to college and support that baby.

After breakfast, Sam went with his dad to look for his car. Miraculously, it hadn't been towed or booted. There was a random chalk line on his front tire, but it looked like the police had not followed up with the towing company. Or maybe the towing company didn't work weekends.

Sam drove back to the apartment. He felt empty, as if every emotion had been ripped out of him until he was numb.

It wasn't just his mom. He was used to the judgmental rage that periodically reared its ugly head to mess up his life. It wasn't just Rylee. She had become just another Wendy in his world. It wasn't the way that this pregnancy had changed his life or the after-effects of that labor simulation, or even the fact that he'd been arrested. It was a combination of everything and nothing at all. It was as if he'd finally reached his limit and nothing more could touch him.

He eased the car into the alley and parked on his side of the garage, making sure that he left plenty of room between the cars. Then, he slowly walked through the backyard and up the stairs to the apartment. Every step creaked underfoot, his back and stomach muscles screaming in pain.

He unlocked the back door to the kitchen and let himself in. He could see Rylee looking out the window in the living room, talking on her phone.

"No, I don't know where he is, Mom," she complained. "No text, no call. Nothing. It's been three days. I'm really worried!"

Sam quietly closed the door. He shucked off his jacket and placed it on the hook on the back door. He turned, only to have his keys fall out of his coat pocket and hit the floor.

"Oh, he's home!" Rylee squealed. "Gotta go, Mom!" She pushed herself away from the window and waddled into the kitchen. "Where were you?" she demanded.

Sam scooped the keys up from the floor, then moved around her so that he could grab a soda from the fridge. "Does it matter?" he asked, idly wondering why no one from the Court had notified her. They were supposed to be a couple, right?

"Of course, it matters!"

"Why?"

"Because we missed you!" Rylee told him, rubbing a hand around her belly in a slow motion. "You're an important part of this, Sam."

"Really, Rylee?" Sam popped open the soda as he turned around to face her. "Did you know that someone in your family is telling people at church that I bullied you into getting pregnant!"

Rylee gaped at him. "Sam, you know that's not true—"

"Really, Rylee?" he snapped. "From what I hear, it was your mom who started that rumor!"

"My mom?" she cried. "Whoever told you that is lying!" She bit her lip in dismay.

"Not according to the woman who confronted Wendy!" he responded matter-of-factly. "Look, half of the rumor mill is saying that you got pregnant on purpose so that we couldn't break up. The other half is saying that I got you pregnant so that you would have to stay with me!"

"And you think that I have something to do with it?" she demanded in a tearful voice.

Great. Here come the waterworks. He took a deep gulp of soda, then wiped his mouth with the back of his hand. "That's the thing, Rylee. I have no idea."

"Sam, I had nothing—"

"I don't believe you, Rylee," Sam told her. He turned away, leaning against the counter, and stared off into space. "I've heard that your mom is telling people one story and that your friend Kathryn is telling the other." He looked over at her, frowning.

"In the end, it doesn't matter who started what rumor. People are going to believe what they want, and I know that, too. What I don't know is how this is going to work, Rylee."

She sat down at the table. "What do you mean?"

He could hear the panic in her voice, but he refused to back off. "I mean us, Rylee," he told her, hearing an edge in his voice that he really didn't feel. "How are we going to make this work so that we both have a life to get back to when this is over?"

"We'll move out east—"

"No, we won't, Rylee," Sam said, then drained the rest of the can and pitched it into the garbage. He turned to look her right in the eye. "I'm done taking orders. If we have to have the arbitrator decide, then that's what we'll do. Period."

Rylee flung her hair back from her face with a flick of her chin. "You don't mean that, Sam," she said earnestly. "We follow the plan—"

"Your plan," he interjected.

"—we move out east and start fresh. I am going to Wellesley. You can transfer to another college nearby, or finish your senior year at Northwestern before you join us." She paused, looking for any kind of reassurance that he was listening. "After I graduate, maybe you will find a job overseas like Josh and we can move to Europe. That works, doesn't it?"

He stared at her for a moment, drawing it out until she looked uncomfortable. "No, it doesn't, Rylee," he finally told her. "I'm not moving out east. Period." He paused and looked out the kitchen window for a moment. "It's been a long couple of days. I'm going to grab a shower and then dig into my homework."

Later that night, after Rylee had gone to bed, Sam pulled up his transfer application for Marquette University. He stared at the screen, trying to make up his mind on whether he should make the move.

Problem was, he loved Northwestern. It wasn't just the campus culture or the challenging course load. It was the way that the academic calendar helped him feel. Every quarter was like a sprint instead of a 16-week marathon. And, the school even gave him a small scholarship that let him play the sport he loved!

But his dad was right. Like it or not, that baby changed everything. Being closer to home might help, especially since he'd have access to a newborn support group and mentoring for new dads. Besides, Marquette might be open to giving him a decent academic scholarship. Maybe they could even work with him on housing and childcare. But what really sold him was the accelerated civil engineering program that would let him get his master's degree at the same time.

It's worth a try, he thought. He scanned the application again, making small tweaks as he worked. He finally reached the end of the document and hit 'send' with a sigh of relief.

Worst-case scenario was that he stayed at Northwestern and had to file an appeal to try to get his scholarships reinstated. Being forced into fatherhood should definitely fall under the 'extenuating circumstances' category!

Chapter Sixteen

"Alright, y'all," Theo growled. "Settle down. We've got a lot to talk about tonight."

Sam eased down into the closest chair, wincing as his strained stomach muscles protested. It had been four long days since the labor simulation and his body had still not forgiven him.

He looked around. Mike had sat down exactly opposite him in the small circle. He glared in Sam's direction, refusing to make direct eye contact. *Yeah, blame me*, Sam thought. *I'm not the one who pushed Deuces. I'm just the one that got caught.*

Jacob slid into the chair next to him. "Hey, man," he grunted. "How you doing?"

Sam shrugged. "Recovering," he told him as he shifted his weight to try and get comfortable. "How 'bout you?"

"Can't believe they lied to us," Jacob said as he rubbed at the sides of his lower abdomen. The movement strangely reminded Sam of Rylee, and he vaguely wondered if that helped her with the pain. "I think I tore something during that science experiment. Generally safe, my ass!"

Sam chuckled, then winced at the sudden stab of pain. "Me, too," he admitted.

Theo took the last spot in their circle and looked around. "You may have noticed that Tyler is missing tonight." Sam scanned the faces in the circle. A small thrill of fear raced up his spine, and he looked over at Mike. Mike frowned and shook his head. He didn't know what happened, either.

"Tyler was arrested yesterday afternoon," Theo told them. It might have been Sam's imagination, but Theo looked even more pissed than he had at Sam's hearing. "The Court subpoenaed Tyler's text messages with Devi. There was enough there for a referral to criminal court."

"What the hell?" Mike exclaimed. "Is it against the law to talk about adoption now?" he demanded.

Theo turned his glare at him. "Careful, Mike," he growled. "The only part of this that concerns any of you is a reminder that the Court takes threats to both your partners and your unborn child very seriously."

"He threatened Devi?" Matthew leaned forward, shaking his head as he spoke. "That doesn't sound like him, Theo."

Theo glanced down at the floor for a moment. He looked frustrated as he weighed his next words carefully. "The information that I'm going to provide you with is in the criminal complaint and is available to the public. But I have to tell you that this is the first time that I've had a client arrested for rape."

"Rape?"

"No way!"

"She's claiming he raped her? A bit late for that, isn't it?"

Without looking up, Theo held up his hand for silence. Gradually, the group settled down and Theo looked up. After a long pause, he said, "Two phrases stick out from the rest: *Sorry you were drunk and I didn't stop,* and *do you want me to run down to Illinois to get you some Plan B?*"

Sorry I didn't stop? Sam thought. *What the hell does that mean?*

"According to the DA, the text confirms witness testimony that Devi was a victim of rape," Theo told them. "She was too intoxicated to give consent. Tyler has been charged with first-degree sexual assault due to non-consensual sexual contact that resulted in pregnancy." He paused for a moment; lips pursed. "If convicted, he's facing up to sixty years in prison."

"Sonofa—" Sam muttered. Tyler could get sixty years in prison for having sex while Devi was drunk? He blinked. Maybe that's why Judge Olson had been so angry when they talked about consent at the hearing. If Rylee had said . . . he could have been arrested, too!

"Now is a good time for each of you to take a hard look at what you are saying and doing with your partner," Theo told them. "How many of you have been muttering about how unfair it is to be saddled with your baby momma and offspring? How many of you have tried to convince her that adoption will set you both free? How many of you have tried to be the tough guy behind closed doors and done the bare minimum to get ready for the next phase of your lives?" He snorted at the group. "Most of you? All of you?"

Sam couldn't make eye contact with Theo, and he knew that he was not alone. Maybe Rylee was right, and he was being an ass. But he still had rights. Didn't he?

Sam barely listened as Theo talked about what to expect during postpartum. Most of it, he already knew. Encourage rest and self-care. Check. Encourage bonding time with the baby. Check. Take over household chores like cooking, cleaning, and running errands. Heh. He wouldn't be surprised if there was a team of hired help just waiting for the baby to be born so they could step in, but whatever. Check!

"You've had it drilled into you that postpartum was a critical time for both the woman and the baby, but there's very little out there about the impact to you," Theo told them.

Sam shifted position. Impact to him? His back and stomach might not agree, but it wasn't like *he* was going to give birth!

Theo chuckled. "Yeah, I know," he told them. "I'm not having a baby, so why would I be tired?" He looked around the small circle. "You might already know this, but that baby is going to change everything. Your stress level is going to go up because that baby wakes up every couple of hours to demand food, a dry diaper, and some quality time with their parents."

Matthew chuckled in agreement, ruefully shaking his head. "Ain't that the truth!" he said.

"As if Julia is going to let me get anywhere near that baby," Max replied, crossing his arms as he slouched lower in his seat. "Her *abuela* has already told me that my only job will be to bring in more money to support her *nieta* and that's it."

"That's part of it, Max," Theo allowed. "But adjusting to fatherhood means spending real time with your newborn, finding a balance between your job and your new responsibilities, and understanding that you may experience a wide range of emotions, like anxiety, depression, or feeling inadequate, just like your partners. So that's what our focus will be in March."

A low groan swept through the group. "Before we call it a night, I just need to let everyone know that I have some time off coming up," Theo announced. "I'm moving our March 9th meeting to the day before. Make sure you update your calendars so that you attend." He looked around. "Alright, get outta here!"

Sam folded up his chair and walked it over to the rack as the rest of the class wandered out. Theo followed suit, then turned to look at him.

"How're you feeling, Sam?" he gently asked. "I didn't want to call you or Jacob out in front of the group, but it looks like you're still feeling it, huh?"

Sam nodded. He went and grabbed another chair.

Theo followed. "Something you need to get off your chest?" he finally asked. Sam looked down.

"Talk to me, Sam," Theo urged.

"I don't even know where to begin," Sam told him. He refused to look up.

"There's not a lot that I can do unless I know what the problem is," Theo reminded him.

Sam stirred. "Fine," he finally said. "Rylee wants to hire a nanny."

Theo pursed his lips. "Really?" he drawled. "I didn't think the two of you could afford that."

"We can't," Sam said. "Or at least I don't think we can. Rylee got access to her trust fund and thinks that she can pay for it on her own."

Theo smiled, biting his lip. "She does, does she?"

Sam nodded. He didn't trust his voice right now.

"Well, she can think that all that she wants but, I gotta tell you, the law is pretty firm on sharing expenses equally," he told Sam. "Very few exceptions are allowed."

"I know," Sam said. "I've tried to get through to Rylee, but she won't listen to me." He closed his eyes and threw his head back. "Rylee always gets her way, Theo. If anyone can find a way to get the Court to allow her to have a nanny, it's her."

"Maybe you're looking at this the wrong way," Theo told him.

Sam dropped his head, staring at the worn carpet. "How so?" he asked.

"Stop thinking about what you don't want and start thinking about what you do," Theo said.

Sam looked at Theo. "What I want?" he asked.

"Yes," Theo firmly told him. "If you could have everything you want, knowing that you'd still have Rylee and that baby in your life, what would that look like?"

Sam threw Theo a puzzled look. No one had asked him that this entire time. "What would life look like?" he murmured.

"Yeah," Theo told him. "Rylee and you have a child together. Do you live apart? Together? What does your normal day look like?"

Sam folded up another chair and looked off into space. "Well," he said, uneasily. "I guess I'd rather have my own place, you know? Maybe a small two-bedroom condo, and close to downtown."

Theo nodded. "Good start," he said. "Big city? Small city?"

"I'm not sure," Sam admitted. "I don't really want to live in a huge city like New York, Houston, or Chicago. Too many people." He paused. "Maybe something a bit smaller, like Atlanta, Memphis, or . . . " he trailed off.

"Milwaukee?" Theo prompted, a small smile lighting up his face.

Sam chuckled, slowly shaking his head. "Maybe . . . " he said, then thought about it for a minute. "Yeah, probably. I applied to Marquette's accelerated civil engineering program, but I don't think I'll get accepted. Too much competition and my grades aren't that great this year."

"Don't sell yourself short, Sam. Marquette is a great school, so let's keep going," Theo suggested. "Milwaukee, a smaller metropolitan area. You want a condo close to downtown. That means it's closer to the Marquette campus, to events, the theater, and to restaurants, right? Everything you need is within walking distance or a short bus hop. What else?"

"Um," Sam thought about it. "Definitely need a decent daycare nearby so that I can drop Allison off when I'm in class, but they need to have decent hours because I still need to work a part-time job so I can afford things."

"What about Rylee?" Theo asked. "Is she local?"

Sam shook his head. "No," he admitted. "Rylee wants to move to the East Coast and eventually live in New York City."

"So, no Rylee," Theo said. "But you still see having Allison as a part of your daily life."

Sam blinked. "Yeah, at least for some of the year," he replied. "I think it's important that she gets to know her grandparents and cousins."

Theo clapped him on the shoulder, a rare smile lighting up the old biker's face. "It really sounds like you know what you want."

"I—guess I do," Sam admitted. "But Rylee has a completely different plan for our future. I'm never going to get what I want."

"That, my friend, is something that I can help you with," Theo told him, grabbing the last chair and placing it on the rack. "If you have some time, we can grab a cup of coffee and get this documented for the guardian ad litem."

"Why would he want to see that?" Sam asked as he picked his jacket up from the floor.

"Part of his job is to work with the arbitrator on child placement," Theo told him. "And you need to be a part of Allison's life just as much as Rylee does."

Chapter Seventeen

The next couple of weeks were rough. Once Rylee got past her thirty-fourth week of pregnancy, she seemed to start arguments for the strangest things, like waking him up in the dead of night to complain that his mom had refused to give them the rocking chair that had been in Sam's family for generations. Other nights, they fought because he was out late making deliveries.

The screaming fits were endless. He found himself spending as much time as possible at the library, opening himself up wide for deliveries, and seeking out Lucas on the weekends. She couldn't yell at him if he wasn't there.

The last straw was when she stormed after him, as he was leaving for his weekly mentor meeting. He could hear her slowly stomping her way down the stairs, screaming in high rage, as she tried to chase after him. He tried to ignore the abject wailing as he walked out to the garage.

"Sam!" she yelled after him. "This isn't over!"

He stopped, took a deep breath, and turned around. "Rylee, give it a rest!" he yelled back. "These meetings arc fucking mandatory and I'm not spending any more time in jail because you made me miss one!"

"Bullshit!" she shrieked. "Your meetings are on Friday nights, not Thursdays! You're going down to that bar again, aren't you?!"

Why, oh, why had he finally given in and told her about what happened at Deuces? It was bad enough that most of his mentoring group hated him because Mike had been forced to accept a six-month sentence plea deal for their little exercise. But Rylee had turned the entire incident—and the labor simulation—into a weapon meant to hurt him.

He glared at her, the icy cold seeping into his jacket. "Rylee, I already told you that Theo had to move this week's meeting because he has to go out of town for the weekend! What the hell else do you want?" he demanded. "A note signed by the Court?"

Rylee moved closer, fists clenched as she tightly hugged the sweater she'd thrown on when she ran after him. "The truth, Sam! Allison and I just need the truth!"

He looked down at her. He could almost feel the rage coming off of her in waves. "Rylee—"

A police siren went off in the alley, followed by the flashing blue and red lights that bathed the twilight around them. Sam shot her a dirty look. "See what you've done?" he muttered. "One of the neighbors finally called the police because of you."

"Me?" she shrieked. "You're the one who started this!"

"How?" he demanded, turning to watch as two police officers moved into the backyard, carefully avoiding the iced over puddles. "I was just leaving. You're the one who started screaming."

Anything that Rylee wanted to say was lost as the officers approached. "Good evening," the older officer said, his hand casually propped on his gun for a moment. "What seems to be the problem this evening?"

Sam took a deep breath. "We're just having an argument, Officer," he said. "I'm late for a mentor meeting and my partner doesn't seem to believe that the date was changed."

"That right, miss?"

Rylee hesitated. "Why don't we have a talk over there, ma'am," the younger officer said, gently guiding Rylee to the picnic table to have a seat. The first officer beckoned, and Sam followed him to the back of the garage, just far enough away that he couldn't hear Rylee's conversation.

"So, let's start with your name," the officer said.

"Sam Maxwell, officer," Sam responded quietly. He held out his hands to either side, fingers spread so that the cop would know he didn't have a weapon. He just knew that Rylee was going to claim he'd done something stupid. It would be his word against hers and they'd haul him back to jail. Only, this time, he'd land up in criminal court and no one would be able to help him.

"I'm Sergeant Moore," the officer responded. "And, how do you know—" he said, pointing in Rylee's direction.

"Rylee. We live together," Sam admitted. "We're in the Wisconsin Individual Family Education program. I don't have a choice."

Sergeant Moore's graying eyebrows arched, and he grunted.

"Look, she's almost nine months pregnant, officer," Sam told him. "She's always had a short temper, but her pregnancy has made it worse. A lot worse. I have to attend a weekly meeting, and, for some reason, she seems to think that I'm lying so that I can go down to the bars."

"Which would be against the law."

"Which would be against the law," Sam repeated earnestly. "Look, can you just call my mentor to confirm my side of the story? The meetings are mandatory, and I don't want to get into any more trouble than I already am."

"Any history of physical or verbal abuse that I need to know about?" the officer asked, looking back at the table where Rylee was having an animated conversation with the other officer.

Sam found himself looking down at the ground, shoulders slumped against the inevitable. "No, sir," he told him as he looked up. "I wouldn't call this verbal abuse. It's just how she is."

The sergeant pursed his lips. Sam knew that's not what the cop meant, but he let it pass. With the new law in place, he was sure that there were a lot more domestic disputes being called in.

"Okay," the sergeant finally said. "Can I see some ID, please?" Sam pulled his wallet out of his back pocket and handed over his driver's license.

"Thank you," the sergeant said. "Wait here, please." He walked toward Rylee, head to his shoulder radio. "I need to run priors on Samuel Maxwell, address 31 . . . "

Sam backed up against the side of the garage and found himself huddling against the siding. They were going to find out that he'd been arrested for going down to Deuces earlier this year. Which meant that they were going to believe whatever Rylee told them. He was going to jail. He shivered as the icy cold pummeled him.

He pulled out his phone out of his jacket pocket and texted Theo: *Rylee pitched a fit and the cops are here. I think I'm going to miss tonight's meeting.*

Sam slid his phone back into his pocket, looking over at Rylee. She was crying, almost yelling at the poor cop as she tried to make her point.

He sighed, his heart pounding. He was so screwed. The meeting started in just under a half-hour. Theo probably wouldn't see his message for a couple of hours because of his 'check your phone at the door' rule.

He pushed himself away from the garage, shivering in his light jacket. If they were going to arrest him, he'd rather face them like a man instead of cowering against the wall.

His phone rang. Sam froze. Who the hell would be calling him?

Fuck it. He struggled to pull his phone out of his pocket, then answered the call before it even registered that it was Theo. "Hello?"

"Sam, missing our weekly meeting is not an option," Theo said.

"Wh—wh—what do you want me to do?" Sam stuttered. "Just leave?"

"No, *vlákas*," Theo told him. "Who is the officer in charge?"

"I'm not sure. Sergeant Moore, maybe?"

"And you're still at the apartment, right?" Theo growled. Sam nodded. "Yes."

"Hold tight, Sam." The call dropped.

Sam looked at his phone for a moment, then shoved it back into his pocket. He stared into the alley and tried to think. Maybe he should call Olivia. That's what people do when they're arrested, right? Call their lawyer?

After about five minutes, Sergeant Moore walked over to Rylee. He looked pissed as he beckoned the other officer off to one side. He gave Sam a hard look, then Rylee, as the two officers talked.

Finally, he waved Sam over as they returned to the picnic table. "We've confirmed that you are both enrolled in the family education program," the sergeant told them, making significant eye contact with each of them in turn. "Since there is no corroborating evidence of domestic violence and no outstanding warrants for either of you, we're going to issue you both a citation for disorderly conduct."

Rylee started to protest, tears streaming down her face, but Sergeant Moore held up a hand. "If we get called again, one or both of you could be arrested and face criminal charges." He stared at Rylee. "Do you understand?"

Sam looked at Rylee. She looked crestfallen as she searched the officer's faces for any sign of reassurance. "A citation?" she whispered.

Sergeant Moore nodded. He turned to Sam. "I believe you have a meeting to attend. Better get going."

Sam mentally shook himself as he reached into his jacket pocket for his keys. "Thanks, Sergeant Moore," he said. He ignored Rylee for the moment.

"You're welcome," the sergeant replied, handing Sam the ticket and his driver's license back. He walked with Sam back to the garage. "A word of advice?" Sam nodded as he opened the door to the garage. "You might want to bunk somewhere else for a few days until this cools down."

Sam looked at the sergeant, seeing the compassion in his eyes. "Yeah. I think I'm going to hit up a friend. I'm not sure how much more of this I can take."

Sam couch-surfed for over a week, starting with Lucas. Lucas had been hesitant, but reluctantly agreed to let Sam stay for a few days. His off-campus apartment wasn't very roomy, with five people sharing two bedrooms and a bathroom. It was also a rather painful reminder of what he was missing out on, so he hit up Ethan, one of the few members of the mentoring circle that was somewhat sympathetic about his issues with Rylee.

Ethan and Lauren had a sweet three-bedroom condo in Brewer's Hill. Ethan had converted the first-floor bedroom into an office so that he could work at night and not disturb Lauren. The foldout couch in the office was not quite as comfortable as his bed at home, but he'd rather avoid both of the women in his life while he had the chance.

Sam tried to stay out of their way as much as possible. They seemed to be the happiest couple in their small group, and he didn't want to overstay his welcome.

Today, he found himself wandering aimlessly around at the Mequon Library, looking for a table so that he could crack his laptop open for a few hours. He had a paper due for his sustainability class and he hadn't even started yet.

He really missed the main library at Northwestern. He could always find a quiet corner in the south tower's student lounge, pop his earbuds in, and get to work. A few hours at most and then on to the next project.

Sam found a table off in a corner and sat down. He stared at his laptop for a moment but couldn't seem to make himself open it. With a sigh, he pushed the laptop out of his way, crossed his arms on the table, and buried his face.

He was just barely passing his current classes, and that was a huge hit to his GPA. He still hadn't taken the last online class about what to expect during Rylee's postpartum and he found himself really not caring. *Maybe I should just drop out until this is over*, he thought.

Two other guys in the program had dropped out of college to make it easier on them. Max had told him that it was just a strategic decision: better to give himself the space he needed now, so that he could focus on his education later.

Hunter had a different take on it. *Maybe he wasn't meant to get a college degree,* he'd told Sam. Maybe there was a better way to make a living. All Sam knew was that Hunter seemed happier in his apprenticeship program than he had before he dropped out of school.

Sam sat up and opened the laptop so that he could log into the library's Wi-Fi. He pulled up Northwestern's website but couldn't make himself look up how to withdraw from the school. Yeah, he could call the Registrar's office, but he couldn't find the energy to pull out his phone and make the call. And who knew what this would do to his application to Marquette?

He closed his eyes, listening to the quiet hum of conversation in the distance. Drop out? Was that his only choice? Was this who he was now?

Sam opened his eyes and glared at the screen. *No,* he thought. *This is not who I am.* He'd worked too damn hard to give up now. He hadn't heard anything from Marquette University's Admission Office, but it was still early days. There was still a chance that they'd approved his transfer into their Civil Engineering program for this fall. Maybe not the accelerated program, but even the regular program would be a good move.

Marquette had rolling admission, he reminded himself. So, if he didn't get in this fall, he could try again for the spring semester. If he could just find a way to pass this quarter.

He pulled up his notes from class and tried to focus. Time to lean in and get this damn sustainability paper written. And then, it was time to go back to the apartment. His days of running away were over.

A week later, Sam was in the zone. It was almost 5:30 pm, the golden hour of meal deliveries. He was on his second delivery of the evening. If he was lucky, he could grab four or five more dinners back-to-back and call it an early night.

He strode into El Hogar's, dodging through the small crowd waiting to be seated, until he got to the front counter. His phone vibrated as he sorted through the pick-up bags on the cantina's counter. Sam fished his phone out of his pocket to check. Rylee, again.

Sam pushed the call to voicemail and grabbed the bags for his current delivery. He didn't have time to talk to her right now. He needed to make as much money as he could over the weekend. It was a great time to pick up extra deliveries, so he'd opened his delivery schedule as wide as possible.

He hurried back to his car, pausing only long enough to drop the dinners into the insulated bag that had become the essential tool of his trade. Anything to get better tips. Then, he found the client's address and put his car in gear. Time to go.

Sam's phone buzzed again. He ignored it as he pulled into traffic. Yesterday had been a pretty good day. Rylee's due date was coming up, so he really had to push himself to get as many deliveries as he could. As it was, he'd already decided to not take any courses over the summer. If Allison was anything like her mother, there wouldn't be much time for sleep, let alone homework.

He found the house, but parking was non-existent. Didn't matter. He pulled as close as he could to the parked car next to him, threw it into park, hit the flashers, and bolted up the short hill to pop the bags on the front porch. Took the obligatory 'See, I delivered it!' picture. Then, back to his car in record time and ready to make himself available for the next delivery.

As he pulled into traffic, his phone buzzed yet again. He took the next right into a not quite empty parking lot. Rylee again. This time, it was a text. *Allison is coming, please come back to the apartment. We need you.*

Sam read it again. *No way*, he thought. Rylee was only thirty-seven weeks pregnant. Too soon. He punched her number on his phone.

Rylee answered with a breathless, "Hello?" followed by a grunt.

"It's me," he replied. "How far apart are your contractions?"

"I don't know," she told him, her voice edged with panic. "Maybe twenty minutes apart? But it hurts, Sam, and I'm afraid my water's going to break any minute now!" She paused, waiting for him to respond. When he didn't, she started crying. "Please, please come home!"

Sam licked his lips nervously. "Okay," he replied. "On my way." It sounded like the contractions were too far apart, but what did he know? She could be in preterm labor.

It took more than a half-hour to get back to the apartment. It was still technically winter, but people were making the most of the spring-like temperatures. He raced up the stairs to the apartment and found Rylee on her hands and knees in the living room, rocking back and forth, crying.

He dropped his stuff on the kitchen table and helped get her back on the futon couch. Then, he propped a few pillows behind her lower back so that she could try to relax.

"When did they start," he asked, mentally going through the delivery checklist from class. From what he could tell, her water hadn't broken yet, but that didn't necessarily mean anything.

"A few hours ago," Rylee told him, panting. "The cleaning service didn't show up today, so I decided to do a bit of vacuuming. At first, I thought that maybe I'd overdone it. My muscles felt tight right around Allison, and when I put my hands over her, it felt like my skin was getting hard to the touch. So, I sat down and waited to see if it would happen again."

"Which it did, right?" Sam could hear the doubt in his own voice.

"Yes, but they seem to be completely random and, when I have a contraction, it seems to last forever," she told him, pushing one hand against the baby. "I just don't know what to do!" She looked up at him intently. "Oh, I think it's happening again!"

She reached for him, and Sam found himself holding her hands as the contraction hit. Rylee held her breath, and he found himself falling back on what Abby had done with him during his labor simulation training. "Breathe, Rylee," he told her. "Come on, just breathe with me. In and out. Nice and slow. It's going to be okay."

When it was over, Sam took out his phone and placed it on the coffee table. He started the timer so he could start keeping track of the contractions. Then, he grabbed his iPad to take notes.

After a while, he turned on the TV and found something mindless to stream. He kept an eye on Rylee, periodically asking how she was feeling.

Thirty minutes went by. He was just starting to get annoyed when Rylee gasped and reached for his hand. He hit the button to restart the timer and grabbed his iPad to note the time.

She pushed his hand onto her belly. "See," she gasped. "See how hard it feels?" Sam gingerly rubbed at her taut stomach. He felt Allison kick against his hand in protest. That was reassuring, even if this was the first time he'd felt her do it.

Rylee started hyperventilating. "Oh, my God, Sam!" she moaned. "It hurts. It really hurts!"

"Breathe, Rylee." Sam said, trying to cut through her panic. "Come on, breathe with me."

Rylee focused on Sam's face and slowly started to match his breathing. The contraction cut out and Sam updated his tracker with when it started and how long it lasted. Then, he restarted the timer and settled back on the couch to wait for the next one. And the next one. And the one after that.

It was almost 7:30 when he realized that neither of them had eaten dinner. He got up and made some sandwiches for them before settling back on the couch to monitor her.

"I can't take this much longer, Sam."

"Rylee, you've only had six contractions," Sam told her, trying to push his annoyance down to a more manageable level. "I'm pretty sure it's going to be a while before you are in active labor." Besides, he added to himself, his own 'contractions' had been far more intense. Had to be Braxton-Hicks.

"At least try calling the doctor," she begged him.

Sam could hear the panic in her voice. He looked around. "Where's your phone?"

"Kitchen," she told him. Sam grabbed her phone off the counter and brought it back into the living room. Rylee found Dr. Zastrow's office number, then handed it to him. He put it on speakerphone as he touch-toned through the after-hours menu.

"After hours triage, this is Katie," a friendly voice announced. "How can I help you?"

Rylee grabbed the phone from Sam. "This is Rylee Williams and I'm having contractions. They seem kind of erratic," Rylee told the nurse. "Anywhere from ten minutes to thirty minutes apart."

"And how long do they last?" the nurse asked. Sam could hear her typing.

"Almost a minute," she replied. Sam shook his head. The longest contraction had been about forty seconds.

"Rylee, I know it can be a bit scary," the nurse told them. "But you're not in active labor yet. You need to call us when your contractions are coming regularly at four minutes apart. Each contraction should last at least one minute and, this is the most important part, they have been following this pattern for at least one hour."

"But they are so sharp," Rylee complained. "It feels like what they told us real labor would feel like!"

"I understand, Rylee," the nurse said, sounding sympathetic. "But until they are about four minutes apart and the contractions last at least a full minute, you're not ready to deliver. But, just to be safe, we'll schedule you a follow-up with Dr. Zastrow tomorrow morning. Can you hold while I access tomorrow's schedule?"

"Sure," Sam replied. It was going to be a very long night.

The next morning wasn't any better. The receptionist told them that Dr. Zastrow was running late because several patients had gone into labor. "Not entirely unexpected," she told them cheerfully. "Thanks to the governor, we're having a bit of a baby boom."

Sam snorted. He'd heard that a lot in the past few months. But, as much as Wendy liked to blame the governor for the sharp increase in Wisconsin's birth rate—and the tax increase that went with it—there wasn't a whole lot that anyone could do about it. It's like a former Wisconsin senator had said: if you didn't like how our state handled things, you could always move.

Yeah, right, he thought. He'd moved out of state and still landed up in the system.

As they sat, he kept an eye on Rylee. Her intermittent contractions had stalled overnight, but they seemed to be back this morning. Worst part? They were entirely random. Sometimes they were sharp enough to bring Rylee to tears. Other times, she barely seemed to notice.

After almost an hour's wait, the nurse took them back. "Sorry for the wait," she told them. "We're a bit backed up right now."

"We know." Sam sighed. "How much longer will it be before we can see the doctor?"

"Not much longer," they were told. "Dr. Zastrow just arrived and will be with you shortly. Why don't you get undressed from the waist down and we'll take a peek at how you're doing?"

Sam tried to duck out of the room, but Rylee refused to let him leave. Between the two of them, they were able to get her undressed.

Sam tried not to really look at the changes to her body. Her distended belly button was surrounded by dark fissures, her skin overly stretched to accommodate the baby, and her feet were so swollen that he could barely see her ankles. They had removed the GPS tracker a few weeks ago due to the swelling.

Rylee grimaced as Sam helped her get settled on the exam bed. He handed her a small sheet to cover her lap. She struggled to lie back on the bed, and Sam moved to help. He grasped her left hand in his and carefully eased her into a reclined position.

There was a tap on the door, and the nurse came into the room.

"I'm really worried about the contractions," she told the nurse. "Please tell me that Allison's okay."

"We'll take a closer look, Rylee," the nurse replied. "But I'm sure she's fine."

The nurse carefully pushed the sheet further down on Rylee's lap, spread the obligatory goop onto her belly, and ran the flat wand all the way around the baby bulge. Sam tapped his foot impatiently. The baby was right there. Why did she need to hunt all over the place for it?

"Ohh," the nurse cooed. "There she is!" She pulled the screen a bit closer with one hand so that they could take a closer look. The baby was upside down, her eyes clenched tight, and her thumb firmly planted in her mouth.

"Allison is head down, Rylee," the nurse said as she moved the wand higher up on Rylee's belly.

"Oh, that's good, right?" Rylee replied. "She keeps kicking me right under the ribs, especially when I have a contraction."

"Perfectly normal," the nurse responded. "Lungs are fully developed and she's just about ready to take her first breath any day now."

"Let's not get ahead of ourselves too soon," Dr. Zastrow said as he entered the room. "You're in your thirty-seventh week, right?"

"Yes," Rylee responded, her entire focus on the screen. "Is my baby okay?"

Doctor Zastrow changed places with the nurse and began to methodically move the wand over Rylee's belly. "So far, I don't see any concerns," he told her. "You might be feeling less movement now. She doesn't have much room to move around in."

Rylee sighed. "That's a relief," she whispered.

Sam found himself drawn to the screen. The black-and-white image had become somewhat blurry, with an oblong shape that twitched rapidly in the center of the screen. "What's that?" he asked the doctor. Whatever it was, it didn't look right.

Dr. Zastrow looked over at him. "That's your baby's heart," he told Sam in a gentle voice. "Based on what we're seeing, she's doing fine."

"Oh." Sam didn't know what to say.

The doctor continued to move the wand, periodically stopping to take measurements. He kept up a running dialogue on what they were seeing with one final view of the baby's face. Sam watched, fascinated, as she took her thumb out of her mouth and yawned. He couldn't quite say what he was feeling. It was starting to feel very real, somehow.

Then, the doctor moved the wand away and handed Rylee a cloth to clean the gel off of her skin. He cleaned the wand and had a seat.

"Before you leave, I'll check to see how dilated you are, Rylee," he said. "Based on what we see on the ultrasound, I'm not overly concerned. We still have a few weeks to go."

"What about the contractions?" Sam asked.

"Most women experience contractions as they approach their delivery date," the doctor told them. "First-time mothers can find them to be . . . "

"Frightening?" Sam offered.

"Unsettling." The doctor looked at Rylee. "This is the time to try and rest up, Rylee. I know that some of the contractions may feel intense. Think of these contractions as a way of warming up your muscles, getting you ready to give birth."

Rylee started to protest, but the doctor held up his hand. "Let's get your feet up in the stirrups and take a quick look at your cervix." He unfolded the stirrups and helped guide Rylee's feet. Sam stayed on the other side of the bed, trying to ignore things as the doctor slid some sort of metal device between Rylee's legs and peered inside of her before popping back up.

"As of right now, your cervix is dilated less than one centimeter," he told them. "We have some time."

"But it hurts!" Rylee protested.

"I understand, Rylee," the doctor reassured her. "However, until they get more intense and, more importantly, the contractions begin at the top and feel like they're pushing down on the baby, you're not in active labor." He smiled at Rylee's disappointed pout. "You'll get there, I promise. In fact, if we don't see any progress in the next few weeks, we can always induce labor. But it's always better to let things happen naturally," he'd told them and sent them on their way.

Sam wandered into the kitchen to grab a soda so he could wake up a bit before hitting the books. Last night had been rough. *Braxton-Hicks, my ass!* Rylee's contractions might not be active labor, but some looked almost as painful as what he'd gone through in the labor simulation. He was just glad that Rylee was still sleeping when he checked in on her. He needed some time alone.

He grabbed a box of granola from the cupboard, a bowl, and some milk. He was starving, he realized, as he started wolfing down heaping spoonfuls of the stuff. As he ate, Sam went through the unopened mail on the table. Bills, obviously, but one of them caught his eye: Marquette University's Admissions Office.

Sam dropped his spoon, barely noticing that it clanged against the bowl, and splashed some milk on the table. It was a thick envelope, much thicker than if it was a simple rejection or even a waitlist notification. He ripped it open, holding his breath in anticipation.

He only got through the first sentence before he sat back with a huge sigh of relief. "Congratulations! We are pleased to offer you admission into the Civil Engineering Accelerated Degree Program . . ." There were things that needed to be done, he knew, but for now, all he wanted to do was savor this moment.

He'd done it. Even with all of the competition to get into the Civil Engineering program, Sam had managed to score one of the few coveted spots for transfer students. Not only that, but the program would allow him to take classes that met the requirements for both his undergrad and master's degree.

He pushed his bowl aside and quickly sorted through the packet. Important steps that all incoming students had to take, transfer student orientation dates, how to apply for on-campus housing, access to the student portal, scholarship information.

Whoa. He'd snagged a small academic scholarship. Probably only enough to pay for books, but it was a start, right? Applying for a tennis scholarship was out of the question for now. It all depended on the child placement negotiations, and those wouldn't even begin until Allison was a few months old. Plus, if it was his turn for custody, he had no idea how to travel with an infant, let alone who would watch Allison during a match.

He picked up the paperwork and moved into the living room, his breakfast completely forgotten. He needed to verify the scholarship information and find out when he had to get his enrollment deposit in. He grabbed his iPad so he could log into the student portal.

Two months. He had two months to get his deposit in to hold his place. Sam pulled out the acceptance letter. It was almost a week old.

Damn it. He should have been the one picking up the mail, not Rylee. She piled things up on every single flat surface because there wasn't enough room in the apartment to put things away. There was no question that he wanted to go. Needed to go.

The only thing that stood in his way was his mom. She couldn't stop him from using money from his college fund, but there was only about $40,000 in that account. Before, he'd been able to balance things out with his scholarships, but now he wasn't sure he could make things work without taking on a huge amount of student debt.

Sam carefully placed the iPad down on the table. His mom might think he was a failure and that he'd ruined his life by getting Rylee pregnant. She may have cut him completely off financially. Maybe even cut him out of her will, for all he knew. But there had to be a way to make this work.

Think, Sam. Think. He stared at the acceptance letter for a moment.

Okay. His first step was to get an appointment with the financial aid office. After that, time to dig into his current workload so that he actually passed his current classes with flying colors. That 3.5 GPA was his ticket to changing schools, and every class counted!

Chapter Eighteen

S am had just finished loading the dishwasher when Rylee abruptly sat down at the bistro table, groaning. She arched her back, both hands clamped to the edge of the table.

"Another contraction?" Sam asked. He took a quick note of the time, then picked up his phone from the counter and hit the timer to track how long it lasted.

Rylee slowly nodded. She bit her lower lip, trying to breathe. "It feels like Allison is pushing down right up against my pelvis. She really wants to come out," she told him.

Sam nodded. Over the last two weeks, Rylee had moved from Braxton-Hicks contractions to the on-again, off-again early stages of labor.

He reached for the air fryer bin and began to scrub it out. This afternoon, the contractions started coming more frequently but lasted less than a minute. Rylee was just under forty weeks now. Allison could come at any time.

Rylee relaxed, breathing deeply. "It's over."

Sam leaned over to check the timer. "That was over a minute, Rylee." He stopped and looked at her. "Did you want to log that?"

She gave him a tired smile, then pulled his iPad over. He told her the time it started and the exact length. "I hope this is over soon, Sam." She pushed herself into standing. "It really feels like Allison is ready to come home."

Sam nodded. In theory, the baby's room was set up, and the apartment was ready for whatever the next few months were going to throw their way. But it didn't feel like they were ready. None of the information they'd been drowning in over the last six months seemed to have made a difference.

You don't know what you don't know, Sam thought.

Rylee stood, then slowly waddled into the living room, her hands gently rubbing her belly in a circular motion. She picked up her 'go bag' from the coffee table, then sat down and started going through the contents again. Suddenly, she gasped, "Sam!"

"Another contraction?" he asked.

"Yes," she groaned through clenched teeth. "It feels like I'm being stabbed here."

Sam dropped the dishrag into the sink and grabbed his phone. He hit the timer as he followed her into the living room. "Are you breathing?" he asked.

Rylee gave him a dirty look, blowing out her breath, then slowly inhaled. Her hands crept to her back, fingers digging into the muscles.

Sam sat down next to her. He mirrored her breathing. Breathe in through the nose. Pause. Out through the mouth. Pause. And again.

As they breathed together, Sam found himself studying the curve of Rylee's lips as she blew out her breath. How her messy braid was carelessly flopped over one shoulder. That determined look on her face. They might not be deeply in love anymore, but he knew that there was something there. He just didn't have a word for it yet.

Rylee carefully got up and started pacing in the small space between the kitchen and the living room. "Dammit," she moaned. "That hurts!"

"Walking doesn't help?" he asked. He hadn't been given the opportunity during the labor simulation, but had been told repeatedly that it might help during one of the birthing modules.

"No, it's not." She paused and looked down at him. "How long was that one?"

Sam checked his phone. "Almost a minute and a half."

"Help me find my shoes," she told him, her tone deceptively quiet. "I don't care what the doctor said. We're going to the hospital. I need my doula. I need my phone. And my mom."

Sam looked at her for a moment. Rylee seemed just a bit too calm for someone who was in active labor.

"Now!" she barked, rubbing at her back. *And there she is,* he thought as he got up. Probably should grab his laptop and the extra charger. Her contractions were averaging just over five minutes apart. If they didn't send them straight home, they were in for a very long night.

It seemed to take longer to get Rylee into the car and settled in the front seat than it actually took to drive to the hospital. He had it memorized: Commerce to Pleasant Street. Right on North Palmer, then left on Vine. Quick turn down Second Street to the hospital's emergency entrance.

Traffic was lighter than expected, but it was still a nerve-racking drive. All of the lights were against him. He tapped the steering wheel with impatient fingers.

What if Rylee was right? He'd had it hammered into him repeatedly that she knew her body best, and that, above all, he needed to trust her instincts when the time came. But her contractions were only five minutes apart, and the doctor had clearly said four minutes meant she was in active labor.

The worst-case scenario was they were sent home. Of course, Sam could see Rylee arguing with the hospital staff until they just gave in and admitted her.

Rylee moaned in frustration as she juggled her phone, looking for her mom's phone number. "Come on," she moaned.

"Maybe that can wait until we get there," Sam told her, glaring at the red light on Palmer. "It's not too far now."

Rylee ignored him as she put the phone to her ear. "Hi, Mom," she breathed. "We're on the way to the hospital. It's time."

Rylee pulled the phone away from her ear. They both winced as Rylee's mom yelled in excitement. "Mom," Rylee said, trying to interrupt. "Mom, I've got another contraction coming on. I gotta go." She ended the call, then dropped the phone onto the car's floor. She braced herself against the glove box, moaning as another wave hit her.

Sam sped up as he made the turn on Vine. He didn't want to risk pulling out his phone, but that one was definitely less than five minutes from the last one.

"Sam, I'm feeling something squishy," she managed to get out.

"Squishy?" he asked as he glared at the car in front of him. *Get out of the way!*

"Mm-hmm," she replied. "Not gushy wet like my water broke, but something very, very strange."

Sam spared her a quick side glance. She was pale, her lips peeled back as if she was silently snarling.

He made the turn on Second, and they were there. He pulled in front of the emergency entrance, threw the car in park, then ran in to grab a wheelchair from the vestibule. He waved his hand to trigger the inner automatic door. "Need a bit of help here," he yelled. "My partner's in active labor!" He didn't wait for the nurse at the check-in desk to respond before he turned back to the car.

Rylee was already struggling to stand up, bracing herself against the car. Her 'go bag' had opened, spilling everything that she'd so neatly packed all over the ground, including her purse. The ground was littered with her phone charger, the bag with the two delivery gowns that she'd bought with her, the box of breast pads for her nursing bra, assorted socks, several changes of clothes, her make-up bag, and her brand-new breast pump.

Sam raced back, stopping just short of the car. He put his arm around her and helped her sit down in the wheelchair. He looked up as the attendant closed the distance between them.

"I hear you're in labor?" she asked, leaning down to talk to Rylee.

"Yes," she hissed. "Four minutes apart. I need my doula!"

"Great!" she told Rylee. "Let's get you checked out in triage." The attendant didn't wait for Sam as she quickly wheeled her inside. Sam quickly scooped everything up and followed, attempting to stuff the remaining items into the cloth bag as he tried to follow them.

"My phone!" Rylee cried over one shoulder. Sam doubled back to grab the phone from the car. He turned toward the emergency entrance, but double-backed to grab his backpack. He stopped only long enough to hand his keys off to the valet before heading deeper into the hospital in search of Rylee.

The front desk pointed him down the hall. Sam picked up his pace. There, up on the right. Triage #3.

He could hear Rylee's voice coming through the partially open door. He gently knocked and then slid into the empty seat next to the nurse.

No, Rylee hadn't called her doctor or doula before making the decision to come to the hospital. Yes, her contractions were just over four minutes apart, lasted over a minute, and had been consistent for more than an hour. No, walking or changing her position didn't help. Yes, the baby was moving a bit less than she had previously, but she was still giving Rylee an occasional kick right up under her ribs. And, yes, her back ached almost continuously.

Sam silently shook his head, but decided it was better to not contradict Rylee in front of the nurse. Her contractions were closer to five minutes apart.

"Why can't you just admit me?" Rylee complained. "The pain is getting worse!"

"Let's get your vitals and take a look, shall we?" the nurse said, a slightly condescending look on her face. "You may not be far enough along for us to admit you tonight."

Sam was booted to the hallway while the nurse checked Rylee's dilation. *This is really happening*, he thought as he frantically went down the list of people he might call. Rylee had a group text ready to go once she was settled in a room, but that only included her friends and family members. Sam was on his own.

He walked further down the hall until he could no longer hear Rylee arguing with the nurse. Then, he pulled out his phone and called the only person that he could think of: Theo.

Theo answered almost immediately. "S'up, Sam?" he asked. He sounded tired.

"Hey, Theo," Sam said, nervously. "Looks like I will probably miss this week's mentoring meeting. We're at the hospital. Rylee's still being evaluated, but she might be admitted."

"That's great, man!" Theo said. "You're at the Birthing Center, right?"

"Yup."

"I'll let the group know. Let me know if you need anything, okay?"

"Thanks, Theo."

Sam leaned up against the wall and studied his phone for a moment. He was on the verge of calling his dad when the nurse beckoned him back to the room. "We're moving her up to the eighth floor. If you'll come with us?"

Sam grabbed their gear and fell in behind the triage nurse as she pushed Rylee's wheelchair to the elevator. On the way, they passed the family waiting area. Several people were clustered around the large fake gas fireplace on the far wall. A few of the couches were taken, and at least one person had fallen asleep in a chair by the windows. Looked like a nice upgrade from the usual waiting room he'd expected.

Two nurses staffed the Birthing Center's front desk. One of them moved around the desk to greet them as they stepped off the elevator. "Ms. Williams, welcome," she said. "Sounds like you're in active labor. Why don't we get you settled?" She didn't wait for Rylee to respond as she moved behind the wheelchair to take over from the triage nurse. "This way, please."

If he remembered correctly from the website, the original Birthing Center had started with just twelve delivery rooms. Given the sharp increase in the birth rate over the last few years, it had more than doubled its capacity. Sam had expected to hear echoes of women screaming in pain, with staff running around in surgical gear, medical carts in tow. Instead, the floor was strangely quiet.

The nurse slowly pushed Rylee's wheelchair down the hall. Sam followed a few steps behind, overloaded with both of their bags and her purse.

"Here we are," she said as they entered the room. "You're currently dilated to four centimeters, so we'll need you to get you changed into your delivery gown." She pointed to the bathroom. "If you'd like to grab a shower first, towels are already laid out for you."

She helped Rylee stand, then turned the wheelchair around to leave. Rylee stopped her. "What about the whirlpool tub? I would kill for a chance to just relax for a while."

The nurse shook her head. "I'm sorry, we have just the one and it's currently in use." She held up her hand. "I can put your name up on the board, but I'm not sure when it will become available. One thing to keep in mind, though. You can't use the whirlpool if you have an epidural."

Rylee looked crestfallen. "But I was hoping that I could get that done quickly."

"The anesthesiologist should be by to visit in the next hour, Rylee. If the whirlpool becomes available before then, I'll let you know."

Rylee winced, hands moving to her lower back. "Thanks."

"In the meantime, why don't you make yourself comfortable," the nurse said with a smile that was meant to be reassuring. "The Wi-Fi password and TV remote are on the counter. I'll be back soon."

Rylee took her 'go bag' from Sam and placed it on the bed. She rooted through it until she found the bag with her delivery gowns and a pair of soft, fuzzy socks. "I just want a nice, hot shower," she told him.

Sam nodded, and she retreated into the bathroom.

He looked around. It was a large room, with lots of space around the birthing bed. A compact fake leather couch and a small recliner were on the far side of the room, near the windows. Assorted medical devices and an IV stand stood ready in one corner of the room. A long counter spanned the length of the room across from the bed, with a TV and an ancient Blu-ray player on the wall.

There was a small basket on the counter. In it, he found assorted brochures, including the menus and locations of the places to eat within the hospital campus, a map of the Birthing Center, and the Wi-Fi password. Score!

Sam grabbed the card, picked up his backpack, and headed over to the couch. He pulled his laptop, snacks, a water bottle, and chargers out of his backpack and placed them in one corner of the couch. He heard the shower start in the nearby bathroom.

He sat down, opened his laptop, and stared at the screen for a long moment before setting it aside. *This is it*, Sam thought nervously. They were finally here. At the hospital.

He tried to figure out what he was supposed to do next but drew a blank. Rylee had called her parents already. He'd let Theo know. The hospital had notified Rylee's doula and Dr. Zastrow.

He pulled his cell phone out of his back pocket and stared at it for a moment. Should he text Josh to let him know? What about Lucas?

Sam snorted. Lucas was more likely to start a betting pool about the paternity test than to really care about the fact that Rylee was in labor. Of course, knowing Lucas, that betting pool was already up, and Sam didn't want to feed into it.

Who else? He scrolled through his contacts and found his dad's number. He studied it for a moment and hit the button to place the call.

His dad picked it up on the first ring. "Hey, Sam," his dad said. "Is it time?"

Sam looked across the room at the birthing bed. "I think so, Dad," he told him. "We're at the Birthing Center. Rylee's been admitted. Contractions are about four minutes apart, and I have no idea what to do."

"Would you like me to come down?" his dad gently asked.

Sam hesitated. Rylee's parents were so overprotective that they might be camped out in the family waiting area already. Asking his dad to wait down there with them, after everything that had happened with Wendy, seemed wrong, somehow. But . . . "Yeah, Dad. I could really use the support."

"Say no more, son," his dad told him. "I'm on my way."

Chapter Nineteen

Rylee stepped out of the bathroom. The room's dry air sucked in the humidity from her shower, leaving behind a slightly floral scent. She had dressed in the pink delivery gown, holding her white fluffy socks in one hand as she walked barefoot across the room.

"I couldn't get these on," she said as she eased herself onto the oversized bed. "Can you help me?"

"Sure." Sam put down his phone and made his way over to the bed. He took the socks from her and got down on one knee to gently place them on her swollen feet.

Unexpectedly, Rylee giggled. He looked up.

"Isn't this where you're supposed to pull a ring out of your pocket and ask me to marry you?" she asked, a sly smile lighting up her face.

Sam shook his head in amusement. "Probably," he agreed. But he knew that as close as they'd gotten over the past few weeks, it wouldn't last. They just wanted different things out of life.

Besides, all hell would break loose if he suddenly demanded that the Center's chaplain marry them right before the baby was born. Wendy would eat him alive, and Rylee's parents would probably point out that, without an actual license, the marriage had no legal standing.

The smile turned into a hiss. "Oh, boy. This one's pretty bad. Where the hell is that nurse?" she demanded.

Sam stood up. "I'll go check," he said.

Rylee grabbed his hand. "No," she whimpered. "Please stay. Diana should be here soon."

"Okay." He helped her lie back on the bed, then pulled away long enough for him to grab the recliner and move it closer to the bed. He sat with her, nervously waiting for the next contraction.

There was a knock on the half-open door. A woman with long, brown hair streaked with blond highlights stood in the doorway. "Hi, I'm Dr. Drexler. Rylee, isn't it?" She waited until Rylee nodded. "I'm one of the anesthesiologists on staff." She beckoned to the two younger women hovering in the doorway to join her. "May we come in?"

Rylee nodded and grabbed Sam's hand for comfort. Sam squeezed back, then slowly released her hand.

"I'd like to talk about your birth plan," the doctor told them. "But, before I begin, can I confirm your full name and date of birth?" Rylee gave her the information, trying to breathe as another contraction took hold.

"Thanks," she said. Then, she turned to Sam. "And you are?"

"Sam Maxwell," Sam told her. "I'm the dad." He blinked. Even saying it out loud seemed strange. *Dad. I'm going to be a dad.* Somehow, just saying that made it feel real.

"Nice to meet you, Sam," Dr. Drexler said. She gestured to the women with her. "This is Janet and Bethany. They are working on their clinical rotation with me. So, Rylee. I need to confirm this: your plan calls for an epidural, but you would like to defer it for now because you'd like to try the whirlpool. Did I get that right?"

"Yes, please," Rylee told her. "My sister gave birth here last spring, and she was able to spend some of her early labor in the whirlpool. Chloe said that it helped so much that she almost didn't need the epidural. I really want to give that a try."

The anesthesiologist nodded. "We can wait," she told Rylee. "But just be aware that an epidural may take as long as thirty minutes to take effect once it's administered."

"Oh, that long?" Rylee asked.

"Yes, and we won't be able to administer it once you're fully dilated and ready to deliver," she continued. "So, I'm going to recommend that you don't wait too long to request one."

Rylee nodded.

Dr. Drexler smiled. "Then, why don't we get that IV started. If you'd like, I can give you something to take the edge off until you're ready for the epidural."

"That would be awesome," Rylee responded. "Thank you so much."

"Let's get that IV set up, shall we?" Dr. Drexler beckoned to the students. Janet rolled a small metal table over while Bethany brought over the IV stand and hung a bag of saline from one of the hooks. "After this, one of the doctors will need to check to see how far dilated you are," she added.

Sam stood up and walked to the window. Maybe it was time to open that laptop and see if he could crank out some homework.

He sat down and pulled his laptop over, trying to ignore the fuss Rylee was making about how much she hated needles. There was a sudden yelp of pain. Sam looked over, but Rylee seemed to be over the worst of it. Janet quickly taped the flexible tubing down along Rylee's arm as Bethany hung a smaller bag on the stand and connected it to a port on the IV tubing.

"There you are," the doctor told her as they finished up. "It should take effect in a few minutes."

"Thank you, Doctor," Rylee said, wiping her face with her free hand.

He'd only gotten logged into the Wi-Fi when Rylee started squealing. "Diana!" Sam looked up and saw an older blond woman, maybe in her mid-fifties, briefly paused in the doorway before she launched herself across the room and into Rylee's arms.

"I'm sorry I'm late, dear one," Diana said, moving to sit on the edge of Rylee's bed. "Lactation visits can be just a bit time consuming, especially when it's twins!"

"Oh!" Rylee breathed. "Are the babies alright?"

"Perfect little angels," Diana assured her. "Just a bit challenging to breastfeed in tandem." She paused and studied Rylee's face for a moment. "I was told that you were about four centimeters dilated at the time of admission. How's the pain?"

Rylee frowned. "Real intense," she complained. "I can't have the epidural until after I try the hot tub and I can't try the hot tub because it's in use right now!"

Diana patted her shoulder. "Did they give you something for the pain?" she asked.

Rylee nodded her head. "Just now," she told her.

"Well, I'm sure it will take effect soon," Diana reassured her.

A team of nurses stood in the doorway. "Well, why don't I get out of the way, Rylee," she said. "We'll know more once they've verified how dilated you currently are." She looked at Sam. "Let's step out into the hallway."

Sam followed her out, perplexed by the request. "Don't you usually stay in the room for this kind of thing?" Sam asked. He gestured at the closed door behind him.

Diana smiled. "Doulas aren't medical professionals, Sam," she told him. "We can't perform vaginal exams. Can I monitor them? Absolutely. But, in reality, my job is more of an emotional and physical support."

Sam nodded. That's exactly what Abby had told him. "Got it."

"I've heard a lot about you over the last few months, Sam, but we haven't been properly introduced," Diana told him. "As I understand it, you're Rylee's partner."

Sam frowned. "For now," he allowed.

"I also understand that you're an 'involuntary dad,'" Diana drawled.

"Meaning?" Sam demanded. He'd been with Rylee almost every step of the way, damn it!

Diana gave him a half-smile. "Meaning that neither of you plan to remain together as a couple once Allison is born."

Sam nodded and looked down the hallway. He wasn't sure where this was going.

Diana sighed, glancing down for a moment as she crossed her arms. "That complicates this just a bit, Sam," she admitted. She looked up. "Normally, I encourage partners to actively participate in their child's birth. I can give you some direction on how to support Rylee, how to reassure and comfort her during this time." She looked up, searching his face for a moment. "Frankly, based on what I've been told, I was surprised to see you actively involved back there."

Sam stared at her for a moment, surprised at her candor and just a bit pissed at what she'd heard.

"What do you want me to say?" he finally asked. "That I'm excited to become a father? That all I want in this world is to give Rylee her happily ever after?" He could hear the resentment in his voice and struggled to rein it in. "It's a bit more complicated than that."

It was Diana's turn to nod. "Yes, it is, Sam." She cocked her head to one side, leaning up against the wall. "So, I need to know how I can support you during this time. Specifically, what do you need to make it through the next few hours?"

"I-I-I don't know," Sam stammered. "I thought this was all about Rylee." Wasn't that what Abby told him during his simulation? He struggled to remember.

Diana smiled. "A doula—a good one—sees her role as part-emotional support, part-pain management, part-sanity check. That includes both the woman giving birth and their partner." She pushed herself away from the wall. "Give it some thought and let me know."

"Okay," Sam replied, uncertain what to make of the conversation. He silently followed her back into the room. He couldn't remember the last time anyone asked him if he needed anything. He'd spent so much time just trying to survive each day as it came that he had no idea what he really needed.

Rylee pushed herself upright as they entered the room. "Whatever they gave me is starting to work," she told them. "I need to walk."

"Sounds good," Diana said. "We'll need to stay on the delivery floor, though."

Rylee pouted. "My mom expects me to check in, Diana."

Diana slowly shook her head with a small smile. "You can call or text them, but they aren't allowed to visit," she told her. "The

Birthing Center has a firm rule. You're only allowed to have your partner up here. If they're not available, only one other family member can join you. And you're not allowed to leave delivery."

Rylee looked at her phone laying on the bed but made no move to grab it. "So, it's just us for now?" she asked.

Diana nodded. "Once you're moved to the post-delivery floor, close family members will be able to visit. Just not all at once!"

Sam was almost relieved that Rylee's mom wasn't allowed up on the delivery floor. Since that disastrous lunch, the only time they'd even made eye contact had been at church and even then, it had been unpleasant.

"Oooh . . . " Rylee groaned. "My back is killing me. I need to walk." Diana moved to the bed and carefully helped her stand.

"Sam," Diana said, turning to him. "Can you walk with Rylee? I'm going to check to see when they expect that whirlpool tub to become available."

"That would be awesome," Rylee said, trying to breathe during the contraction. "Thank you so much, Diana!"

Sam took Diana's place and helped her move across the room to the door. Once they were out in the hallway, Rylee dropped his hand and started slowly walking down the hall, pushing the IV pole with the other hand. He wasn't sure what to do, so he walked right next to her, one hand hovering behind her back as they passed the other women in the hallway.

"I hope that Diana is able to get me time in that whirlpool," she told him. "Once I have the epidural, I know that I won't be able to move around anymore."

Sam nodded. Probably best to just let her talk it out.

"Normally, I'd text my mom, but I really don't want to," Rylee confessed. "As much as I love her, I kinda feel like this just needs to be us, you know?"

"Why just us?" Sam gently asked. Regardless of how he personally felt, Rylee had always been close to her mom.

Rylee bit her lip. "I know that she's still struggling to accept what happened," she confided. "But like it or not, my parents are going to have to accept that their baby girl is growing up. And that means accepting that you're always going to be a part of my life. Of *our* lives."

"It's a nice thought," he told her. "But they're never going to accept me, Rylee. You know what happened at church."

"Yeah, Mom's BFF got it in her head that I was too innocent to actually enjoy sex," she said with a wry smile. "Either way, there's going to be a baptism in our future."

Rylee's smile turned into a hiss. She stopped and put her hands up against the wall, leaning forward. Sam tentatively rubbed her lower back, slowly moving his hands in tight circles. Her skin beneath the delivery gown was as hard as stone beneath his fingers.

Diana joined them. "Rylee, I have great news," she said. "They're almost done cleaning the tub out. By the time we get there, it should be ready for you."

Rylee took a deep breath and slowly straightened. "That's the best news I've had all day!" she told them.

They slowly made their way down the hall, Sam trailing behind them. At the end of the hall, Diana directed Rylee into the large bathroom. An oversized whirlpool tub sat in the corner, surrounded by shaded windows.

"Why don't you have a seat, Rylee," Diana said as she helped her to the side. "I'll get that tub filled." Rylee sat down in a nearby chair with a sigh.

Before long, the tub was full, and Diana had used an automated bath lift to settle Rylee into the warm water. Rylee moaned in relief. "Chloe was right," she told them. "This feels so good against my skin."

Sam's phone vibrated. He slid it out of his pocket to read the text from his dad. *I'm in the family waiting area, Sam.*

Finally. "My dad's here," he told Rylee and Diana. "I should go out to see him."

Rylee nodded, more focused laying back in the whirlpool than on what he was saying. He made eye contact with Diana and exchanged nods. Then, he made his way to the main floor.

The family waiting room was crowded. With over thirty birthing rooms, it was inevitable that friends and family members would overwhelm the small space. He looked around, then spotted his dad standing by the fireplace.

"Hey, Dad," Sam said, waving one hand as he threaded his way through the crowd. His dad looked up from his phone and met him halfway.

Sam was not expecting the hearty hug, though. He felt himself relax into it for a moment, then stepped back. It had been years since his dad had hugged him like that and he needed it.

His dad clapped him on the shoulder and stepped back. "So, how's she doing?" he asked matter-of-factly. "It's going to be a long night, right?"

Sam nodded. "She was at five centimeters last time they checked," he told him. "She's in the Center's whirlpool tub and is hoping to delay a need for the epidural."

It was Sam's dad's turn to nod. "Let me guess. Her birth plan did not include one, but she changed her mind once she went into labor." He smiled. "Your mom was the same way when she had Josh. She was going to have a natural childbirth. Drugs? She didn't need drugs. She was much stronger than that!"

They both laughed. "Actually, Rylee wanted an epidural as soon as they admitted her," Sam told him. "But she also wanted to sit in the hot tub for a while to see if that would make a difference."

"I saw Rylee's parents earlier," his dad told him. "Her mom seemed quite unhappy. Apparently, they didn't realize that the Birthing Center would enforce the 'partner' mandate."

Sam's heart sank. "Yeah, well . . . " Sam said, looking around. "Rylee called her mom, but we didn't know that they were already here."

"You probably need to find them so that they get a first-hand update," his dad told him. "I've already called my office to let them know that I won't be in tomorrow. I'm going to grab some coffee and I'll be back, okay?"

Sam nodded. As much as he didn't want to talk to them, they were Rylee's parents and he should probably give them the update, even if he didn't have anything to tell them. He took a deep breath. "Before you go, I just wanted to let you know that I've been accepted to Marquette for the fall semester."

His dad grinned. "I'm happy to hear that, Sam," he said. "I know Northwestern was your top choice, but to be honest, I'm relieved to hear that you're moving closer to home."

Sam looked down. "Yeah." He didn't really have the words to explain why he wanted to come home yet. He just knew that it felt right.

"Hey, it's going to be okay. I promise," his dad said, putting his hand on Sam's shoulder. "We can figure this out. Have you met with the financial aid office yet?"

"I have an appointment coming up next week," Sam admitted. "I was notified that I got a small academic scholarship, so that's something."

"That's great news, Sam," his dad said. "I can come with you to the financial aid office to get this sorted out if you want. Just let me know."

Sam nodded, then took a deep breath. "Thanks, Dad."

His dad gave him one more clap on the shoulder and went in search of coffee. Sam turned to scan the crowd, but didn't see anyone who looked familiar. He pulled out his phone. Maybe he could just text Rylee's dad and be done with it.

Before he could even find the number, he heard a loud, "There he is! Finally!" yell from across the room. He looked up, just in time to see Rylee's mom push through the crowd toward him, her husband trailing after her.

"Well?" she demanded, her gray eyes almost flaring with outrage. "We've been waiting out here for over a half-hour. It's about time you came out."

"I'm sorry, Mrs. Williams," Sam told her, trying not to cringe. "Rylee didn't tell me that you were here already. But, really, there's nothing to report. Rylee's at about five centimeters and they don't expect any change for a few hours."

"Hmmph." She pushed a short strand of blond hair behind her ear as she turned to her husband. "Do you think we should talk to the nurse?" she asked.

Rylee's dad studied him. "No," he finally said. "Unless they decide to give her something to speed up delivery, I'm fairly certain it will be a while." He held up a hand with a knowing look as Rylee's mom started to protest. "Remember how long Chloe was in labor?"

She nodded. "Well, obviously, we can't wait here," she said. She gestured to the crowded room.

"Why don't we see if one of the restaurants is still open?" Mr. Williams asked, tucking her hand into his elbow to guide her away. "You have my cell phone number, right, Sam?" He gave Sam a meaningful look.

Sam nodded, then pulled the restaurant brochure from his back pocket. "Would this help, sir? It's got all of the hospital restaurants in it, including hours of operation."

"Yes, it would." Rylee's dad took the brochure with a small smile. "Thank you." And with that, they melted back into the crowd. Sam turned to go back to the elevator but stopped as a sudden celebration broke out to one side. An older man stood waving his phone to show off pictures of a newborn.

"Woohoo!" he exclaimed. "She did it! Seven pounds, four ounces! My first grandbaby!"

Sam paused for a moment, watching them celebrate with a rueful grin on his face. He couldn't imagine his mom hugging Rylee's mom or anyone in either family urgently passing the phone from one to another as they tried to get just a glimpse of their granddaughter.

He walked down the hall to the elevator. The best he could hope for is that the two women set aside their disagreement for now. And he doubted that would happen.

Sam wandered around the floor, trying to find the Aquatics Room again. A passing nurse was able to point out the back hallway he'd missed that led to the room, but it was empty. *Strange*, Sam thought, *I wasn't gone that long.*

When he finally got back to the room, Rylee was propped up in the birthing bed, surrounded by medical staff. He knew that the Birthing Center was attached to a teaching hospital, but this seemed to be a bit much. Wasn't the birth of a child supposed to be a private thing?

"What happened?" he asked, quickly moving around the bed so that Rylee could see him. Diana had moved the recliner out of the way and was standing next to Rylee, holding her hand.

"The whirlpool didn't really help," Diana said as she stood up. "Rylee has asked for the epidural. Switch places with me."

Sam moved to stand near the bed, uncertain as to what to do. One of the nurses brought over a pair of wide elastic straps and some electrical pads that disturbingly reminded Sam of TENS pads.

"What are those?" he demanded. Part of him knew that the hospital probably didn't have one on the delivery floor, but he was very unsettled by the similarity.

The nurse looked down at her hands. "This? We're just hooking up the fetal heart monitor, that's all."

Heart monitor. That made sense, Sam thought. He rubbed his suddenly damp hands against his jeans.

The nurse covered Rylee's thighs with the blanket, then flipped her gown up to expose her belly. She handed the straps to Diana. "I'll help pull Rylee up if you can get this underneath her," she said. Between the two of them, they were able to get the straps under Rylee's back with each end hanging down the sides of the bed.

"This is called a transducer. We use it to listen to the baby's heartbeat," she told them. "That way, we can detect any fetal distress." She squirted a clear gel on Rylee's abdomen, then she placed a large, light blue disc on her belly with a cord that was attached to a small monitor. The nurse moved it around for a while and then pointed to the screen.

"Ah, one-twenty," she said. She quickly moved to attach the upper strap to the transducer to keep it in place.

"That's a good number," Diana reassured them as she stared at the monitor. "Normal range is one-ten to one-forty."

The nurse held up a dark gray disc. "We use this one to measure your contractions, Rylee. It will give us a much better picture of how productive your labor is." She quickly attached the gray disc to the lower strap.

Rylee wiggled around a bit.

"Are the straps too tight?" the nurse asked. "I can adjust them."

"No," Rylee told her. "I think we're good."

"Alright," the nurse responded, "then, I'll leave you to it."

She started to turn away. "Wait," Rylee said. "Where's the anesthesiologist? I asked for an epidural."

The nurse gave a quick shrug of one shoulder. "We put in a request, Rylee. They should be along shortly," she told them and quickly left the room.

Diana frowned, then shook her head. Obviously, it was going to be awhile. She turned to Sam. "Could you turn on the TV, Sam? We have some time before Allison is ready to arrive."

Sam grabbed the remote off of the countertop and handed it to Rylee. Then, he wandered over to the couch. He sat down and popped open his laptop again. After a moment, he closed it down. There was no way that he was going to get any homework done tonight.

Rylee didn't see anything she wanted to watch, so Diana dug a few movies out of her purse. "I thought you might enjoy something light, like a rom com," she told Rylee. She spread a handful of discs on the bed. "You choose."

Rylee giggled. "Some of these are older than I am!"

"*Groundhog Day*, it is!"

Sam stood up. He felt restless. There was no way that he was going to be able to sit through a movie while they waited for Rylee's labor to progress. "I'm hungry," he told them. "I'm going to take a walk."

Diana smiled at him. "That's fine, Sam," she told him. "I'll text you if something changes."

Sam slowly walked down the hall back to the elevator. He thought about trying to find his dad, but maybe he just needed some time alone. Things had gotten so out of control that he really hadn't had a lot of time to think through what his options were.

He got into the elevator and punched the button for the first floor. Life had made a whole lot more sense before Rylee had gotten pregnant. Maybe a soda would help clear his head.

He scrubbed at the top of his head with both hands. Rylee. It always came back to Rylee.

The door opened, and he instinctively turned right instead of left. He wasn't sure if Rylee's parents had gone back to the family waiting room, but he didn't have the patience right now. He was tired of being blamed for everything that had gone wrong in the last nine months.

He found himself walking a bit faster as he passed different departments, all of them dark and empty. He smiled, shaking his head in amusement. For a hospital that prided itself on being open and available twenty-four hours a day, it looked like most of it was shut down overnight!

Near the end of the hall, he saw light coming out of a half-open door. Sam paused and pushed the door open a bit more. A few scattered tables, a fridge, a coffee maker and microwave on the counter, and a small vending machine. A breakroom. Score!

Sam pushed his way in and walked over to the vending machine to check out his options. A few sandwiches, the random candy bar, a scant row of microwavable popcorn. Not a lot of variety. No soda machine.

He found himself yawning and realized that he was more tired than hungry. He pulled his phone out of his back pocket to check the time. Strange. It was just after 10 pm. He shouldn't be this tired.

He looked at the coffee maker. The pot was more than half-full and there were a few clean coffee mugs drying on a faded kitchen towel. He rarely drank coffee this late, but he knew it was going to be a long night, so he poured himself a cup and had a seat.

He buried his face in his hands. What was he going to do? There were so many moving parts in his life right now. Adding a newborn to the mix might just break him.

"Are you okay?" a voice asked.

Sam looked up. An older woman stood in the doorway, a pink surgical mask dangling from one hand as she looked over. Her white jacket was stitched with blue lettering. Dr. Laurel Mason.

"Yeah," he said, picking up his coffee mug. "I know I'm not supposed to be in here, but . . ."

Dr. Mason smiled and walked over to the coffee maker. "I understand," she said. "It's late and sometimes all of this," she gestured with her hands, "can be overwhelming."

Sam nodded and took another sip of coffee.

She poured herself a cup of coffee and sat down across from him. "First time?" she gently asked, cradling her mug in both hands.

"Yeah."

"First babies are hard," she told him. "People around you can have very strong opinions. Cloth diapers or disposables. Breastfeeding or formula. Unpaid parental leave or daycare. It's tough."

Sam grimaced. "What about 'nanny or no nanny?'"

Dr. Mason laughed. "There's that, too," she said and took a sip, her elbows resting on the table. "Which side are you on?"

Sam picked up his mug and stared into it for a moment. "I may not be ready to be a dad, but I don't think that someone else should raise my kid," he admitted. "It just feels wrong."

"I take it that your wife—"

"Partner," he corrected her.

"Your partner has a different opinion?" Dr. Mason carefully placed her mug on the table, then brushed a strand of gray hair behind one ear.

Sam nodded and took another sip of coffee. It didn't seem to matter what he wanted. Rylee believed that she was moving to Massachusetts in August. For all he knew, she had a team of lawyers working on it right now. His only choice was to either move out east and give up everything he'd worked for to ensure that Rylee didn't hire a nanny or to hold firm and accept that a nanny was inevitable.

The doctor leaned forward. "Want a bit of advice?" she asked.

"Sure," Sam mumbled. *Not that it would do any good*, he thought.

"Parenthood can be a delicate balance between what each parent believes their child needs to be successful," she told him. "Each of you needs to look at what you believe is essential and what you can compromise on."

"And if there's no way to compromise on this?" Sam asked.

The doctor smiled, picked up her mug, and sipped at it. "There's always room for compromise," she told him. "It all depends on what you're willing to give up to get what you really want."

Sam frowned. As long as he'd known Rylee, she'd never been willing to compromise. "And if I don't know what I want?" he asked.

"Having a baby can complicate any relationship," she told him. "What separates great parents from the rest of us is that they put their child's needs ahead of their own every time."

She stood, then drank the last of her coffee. "Time for me to get back to work," she told him, then took her mug over to the sink to wash it out.

After she left, Sam sat for a long time and thought about what the doctor had said. *Put my child's needs ahead of my own*, he mused. He'd worked with Theo to submit his own proposal to the Court about custody arrangements, and he felt that it was a good starting point for the arbitrator. One of them needed to be close to their extended family. It was the right thing to do.

He stretched for a moment, then collected his mug to clean it. Regardless of how things turned out, he was absolutely certain of one thing: Allison did not need a nanny.

Diana was standing right outside of Rylee's room when Sam made it back to the delivery floor.

"Sorry I was gone so long," he told her.

Diana smiled. "No worries," she told him. "Rylee's dilated to six centimeters. They are administering that epidural." She handed him a blue hairnet to match her own.

"I was gone for almost an hour," he said, frowning with concern. "What took so long?"

"Sounds like there was a shift change and Rylee's request stayed on the board much longer than usual," Diana said, with a small frown. "But they're here now and she's okay, Sam."

He frowned and put the hairnet on. "Did they kick you out?"

"It's a medical procedure," she told him. "They kick everyone out for this. Don't take it personally."

Sam snorted, then pushed the door open just a bit so that he could see what they were doing. There was a small gap between the wall and the privacy curtain. He could see Rylee laying on her side, facing away from the door. Her delivery gown had been pulled up to expose her back. The anesthesiologist moved directly behind Rylee, blocking his view.

"Rylee, I'm going to numb the area and then we'll get started," he heard Dr. Drexler tell her.

Sam couldn't hear Rylee's response, but she sounded scared. "Good," the doctor said. "Now, you may feel a pinch for a few seconds, and then a feeling of pressure when we start the medication." She paused. "How are you doing?"

Another almost inaudible response. "I know," Dr. Drexler said in a soothing voice. "Here we go."

"Oww . . . !" Rylee shrieked. "That hurt!"

The doctor nodded, making some adjustment that Sam couldn't see. "How's it feel now?"

"Better."

"We're ready to start the epidural, Rylee," the doctor told her. "You should feel a bit of pressure . . . now."

"Oh," Rylee exclaimed. "That feels so strange!"

"Let's go ahead and get you on your back, Rylee," Dr. Drexler said. The nurses helped Rylee roll over into a more comfortable position and replaced the baby band monitors. "You should feel some relief in about twenty minutes, although it may take a bit longer to feel the full effect." She raised her voice and said, "You can come back in now."

Diana grabbed Sam's arm and gently pulled him around the gaggle of nurses and student doctors huddled around the bed.

Rylee smiled when she saw them. "It's weird," Rylee said. "My legs are starting to feel all warm and watery, like they're falling asleep." She gave a small laugh. "No, more like they're still in the whirlpool!"

"The epidural isn't supposed to completely numb you," Diana told her. "It just pushes the pain aside so that you can work with Allison when she's ready to come out." She looked around the room as the crowd moved out into the hallway. "Now, what movie do you want to watch?"

Rylee laid her head back against the pillow. "I don't care, Diana. Dealer's choice."

Diana rummaged around the movies that lay on the counter. "*Ghost*, it is, then!"

Chapter Twenty

"Sam!" Rylee's hand squeezed his arm, jolting him from a light doze. "Wake up!"

Sam groaned, trying to reorientate himself in the dim room. He must have fallen asleep in the recliner. "She's coming, Sam!"

He blinked, and Rylee's face swam into focus. Her eyes were wide with anxiety, and he could hear the real fear in her voice. Her hand was shaking. For the first time in a very long time, she looked so . . . vulnerable.

He looked over her shoulder. Diana was standing on the other side of the bed, gently massaging Rylee's neck.

"Sorry," he said, struggling to sit up. "Didn't mean to fall asleep."

Diana smiled. "You're fine, Sam," she told him. "Rylee's in transition. She's fully dilated, and her contractions are less than one minute apart."

Sam felt a surge of adrenaline as his body reacted. "Transition," he muttered. He tried to think. "That's the hardest part of labor. When the pain is the worst, right?" He forced himself upright in the chair, gripping the arms as his stomach muscles tightened. The air around him seemed to evaporate, and he could almost feel his stomach muscles burn in sympathy.

"It's okay, Sam," Diana told him. "Her epidural is stopping most of the pain."

He barely heard her as he closed his eyes tightly. *No*, he thought. *I am not doing this. Not now. This is not the labor simulation*, he told himself. *What did Abby tell him to do? Breathe, right?*

Sam took a deep breath. In through the nose. Breathe into the belly. Out through the mouth. He felt his back and stomach muscles relax a bit. He took another and slowly opened his eyes. Diana studied him for a moment, concerned.

He nodded at her. She turned back to Rylee.

"Oh, I think I'm having another one," Rylee whispered. She pulled up her delivery gown and put one of his hands on her belly. Her entire stomach flexed, hardening as if it had become a solid piece of muscle. He glanced over at her heart monitor. It was as if Rylee was running a marathon, but she was just sitting there. It was amazing and terrifying at the same time.

"You're doing very well, Rylee," Diana told her. "So is Allison." She pointed at the fetal heart monitor. Sam watched the baby's rapid heartbeat with concern.

"Is Allison in distress?" he asked, slowly removing his hand as he started to get up. "Where's the doctor?"

"Allison's heart rate is absolutely normal, Sam," Diana reassured him. "And the doctor is making his rounds. He should be back to check on us very soon."

Rylee moved her feet. "Oh, I think I feel another one!"

Sam sat down, then reached for her hand. "It's going to be okay, Rylee," he told her. "You've got this. Just one contraction at a time."

Rylee groaned. "Is it time to push yet?"

Diana moved behind her, gently massaging Rylee's legs with long strokes of her hands. "Not yet, dear one," she told Rylee. "It's not quite time for you to push."

"But it feels like it's time," Rylee protested. "Really, it does!"

"I know, sweetie," she crooned. "But we're almost there." Diana arranged the pillow under Rylee's head, then pulled the light blanket up over her enormous belly.

"It won't be long," Diana told her. "Breathe with us."

She sucked in her breath in two short bursts, then panted it out in two short but hard exhales. "You can do it, Rylee!" Diana told her. Then, she nodded at Sam, and he followed her lead.

Rylee gripped Sam's right hand and used her other hand to slowly rub at her belly in a slow circular motion. She sucked in her breath, a renewed look of determination on her face. Then, she blew it out again, two short bursts of breath.

Dr. Zastrow pushed past the privacy curtain, masked up and wearing an all-too-familiar surgical gown. Several nurses closely followed behind him. Sam blew out one last time and stood. He tried to pull away, but Rylee held fast to his hand.

"Hi, Rylee," the doctor warmly said. "It sounds like we're just about ready for you to deliver."

Rylee pushed a stray strand of hair behind her ear. She nodded and stopped the breathing exercise mid blow. "Are we done yet?" she asked plaintively.

"Let's take a closer look," he told her, and waved a few of the nurses forward. Rylee reluctantly let go of Sam's hand as he pulled the recliner out of the way. He watched the nurse move around the bed almost as if the team had done this so often that their movements were carefully synchronized.

One of the nurses pulled out the boot-like stirrups from beneath the bed and moved them into position as another pair helped Rylee scoot further down on the bed. Her feet were guided into the padded boots as the bed was moved into a reclined seated position. The pillow was removed from behind her head.

Diana nudged Sam back to his place next to Rylee as the doctor rolled into position between her legs and pushed the blanket up past Rylee's knees. Rylee grabbed for his hand. Her skin felt hot and sweaty in his.

After a long couple of minutes, Dr. Zastrow looked up and nodded. "Rylee, you're doing great. I can see the baby's head. It's time to push."

Rylee blinked furiously at the doctor. "What?" she asked. She turned to Diana. "I wanted to push before, and you told me not to!"

"Rylee, honey, it's okay," Diana crooned. "It's time now."

Rylee flopped back on the bed. "I'm so tired, Diana," Rylee said. "I can't anymore. If he can see the baby, can't they just pull her out?"

"No, sweetie." Diana told her. "You need to push now. Allison is exactly where she needs to be. And, you'll hold her in your arms very soon."

Diana held Rylee's other hand. "Now, with your next contraction, we're going to breathe like we practiced, right, Sam?"

She looked at Sam. He nodded. "You've got this, Rylee," he told her.

"Here's another one," Diana announced, her eyes on the contraction monitor. "Breathe in, Rylee. Now, push, Rylee! Push!"

Rylee grunted, bearing down as she struggled to push. "I can't, Diana!" she said, panting as she tried to catch her breath.

Sam squeezed her hand. "Yes, you can, Rylee," he told her. "Push!"

Rylee shook her head. "It's too hard," she complained.

"Come on, Rylee!" he encouraged. "It's time for the big push, remember? Breathe in and tighten those abdominal muscles, just like we practiced in class! You can do this."

"The big push," she repeated, her head sagged against the mattress, eyes closed. She moaned, almost snarling as she pushed.

"Good job, Rylee," Diana interjected. "The contraction is subsiding. I need you to breathe with us, Rylee. Breathe . . ."

Together, they worked to slow Rylee's breath down.

"I need you to open your jaw for me, just a bit," Diana told her. "Let's see if we can get you to relax into this next one."

"Relax," Rylee laughed just a bit. "It feels like I've got a beach ball down there, and it's stuck!"

Diana nodded. "I know," she reassured her. "Okay, we have another one starting. Deep breath. Now, push for me! Push for Allison!"

Rylee leaned forward as much as she could while she pushed, a deep guttural sound cutting through the otherwise quiet room. This time she didn't lay back until it was over.

"Now, with the next one, I need you to remember to focus on relaxing your pelvic floor while you push," Diana told her. "We're going to take deep relaxing breaths."

Rylee moaned in frustration, shaking her head from side to side in exhaustion.

Diana looked at the monitor. "Another one is starting. Take a deep breath. Let it out. Now take a breath and push into the pressure. That's right!"

Rylee hung onto their hands as she tried to pull herself up. Sam put one hand beneath her shoulders to support her, his other firmly squeezing her left hand. She had that 'Get out of my way!' look on her face that had been known to send retail clerks and teachers scrambling.

"Almost there, Rylee. The baby is crowning," the doctor reported. "I'm going to need you to relax and stop pushing for a moment."

"What? Why?!" Rylee demanded. A bead of sweat rolled down the side of her face.

"We're going to let your perineum stretch a bit," she was told. "Otherwise, I'll need to do a quick episiotomy to reduce the chance of a tear."

Rylee flopped back on the bed. "First, you tell me to not push. Then, I have to push. Now, you tell me to stop!" she complained. "I need to push! I need this to be over with!" she yelled.

Diana leaned forward until her forehead was touching the side of Rylee's head. "I know, dear one," she said. "Let's breathe through this. Nice and slow." She raised her head, looking over at Sam as if she expected him to take the lead with Rylee.

Rylee whimpered, and he looked down. Her determination seemed to have vanished, leaving behind a scared and needy girl. "That's right, Rylee," he said. He took a light breath, then blew it out. He looked at her and gestured for her to do the same. "Come on, Rylee. Breathe with me."

Soon, Sam, Diana, and Rylee were breathing in unison. Sam studied her as they breathed. He remembered those feelings of helpless exhaustion. Loss of control. The need to just make it stop so that he could rest. He squeezed her hand in sympathy.

Of everyone in the room, he was the only man who truly had an idea of what she was going through.

"Rylee," the doctor said. "Get ready to push again on the next contraction. We're just about there."

Sam slid his right hand under Rylee's shoulder. He could feel her body trembling. "It's going to be okay, Rylee," he told her. "Just a few more minutes."

Rylee squeezed his left hand, leaning her cheek against the back of his hand for just a moment.

"Alright, Rylee," Diana said. "Take a deep breath. Now, let it out. Take another and push!"

Rylee pulled herself up on their hands, grunting as she gave it everything she had left. There was a flurry of activity as a nurse moved in to help the doctor guide Allison the rest of the way. Another nurse began to quickly wipe the baby off and her umbilical cord was cut.

A shriek of newborn outrage filled the air. "Oh, my God," Rylee breathed as she lay back. "It's over, right?"

Diana squeezed Rylee's hand. "For the most part, yes," she gently told her. "Just a few more pushes to deliver the placenta."

Allison was whisked off to the electronic all-in-one baby heater and bassinet in the corner by one of the nurses. "Initial Apgar looks good, Doctor," the nurse reported. Sam could see them weighing a fussy Allison, trying to get her height while wiping her down, and finally loosely wrapping her in a blanket.

The machine pinged, and in Sam's exhausted state, he had to chuckle. "Sounds like she's done, Rylee."

Rylee smiled, then made one last push to deliver the placenta. "So am I," she said, laying back.

"Apgar is a solid ten," the nurse reported. She brought Allison over. "Time for some skin-on-skin cuddling, Rylee," she said.

Diana pulled down the delivery gown and the nurse carefully placed Allison on Rylee's swollen breasts. "Oh," she breathed.

Diana grabbed a soft blanket and covered both of them up. Allison snuggled closer to Rylee's breast, one clenched fist near her mouth.

Sam stepped back. He couldn't quite describe how he felt in this moment.

"Sam?" Rylee gestured. "My mom's going to want some pictures. Can you . . . please?"

Sam nodded. *Pictures. Of course.* He grabbed his phone off of the couch and snapped a few close-up pictures.

"I can send these to our parents," he told her. "Are you okay if I duck out to give them the good news?"

Rylee nodded. "Have fun," she said with a sleepy smile.

Sam shed the hairnet and quickly made his way down to the family waiting area. The crowd had thinned, so he was able to spot Rylee's parents almost immediately. His dad was nowhere to be found.

"There he is!" Rylee's mom exclaimed. She dragged her husband across the room and began peppering him with questions. Why had he stopped responding to their texts? Was Rylee okay? What about the baby? Why hadn't he come down sooner? What time did Rylee give birth? Pictures, where were the pictures?!

Speechless, Sam took out his phone, pulled up the pictures he'd taken, and surrendered his phone to her parents. He felt a hand on his shoulder and looked up. His parents stood behind him, along with Josh and Theo.

"Theo. Mom. Josh!" Sam exclaimed. "I didn't expect you all to come down here!" His mom grabbed him for a long hug. He looked over his shoulder at his dad, who just smiled at him, then at Josh. His brother gave him a goofy grin and a double thumbs up.

"Of course, I came," Wendy scolded him, pulling away to look at him. "I made your dad come get me just as soon as I heard you were at the hospital. We've been here all night." She looked over his shoulder at Rylee's parents, frowned for a second, then turned back to him and gave him a strained smile.

"I don't un-understand—" Sam stammered. "I would have, I mean, I could have called—" He looked around and tried again: "Josh, when did you get in?"

Josh smiled. "I was in Minneapolis for a business trip," he told him. "I knew that Rylee's due date was coming up, so I decided that I'd take a few weeks of vacation and surprise you by coming home. I didn't think my niece would be born a week early!" he said with a grin.

Sam laughed and grabbed him for a hug. "It's so good to see you, man!" Then, he turned to Theo. "Theo—"

"What kind of mentor would I be if I didn't check in on you?" Theo said with a gruff smile. "How's Rylee doing?"

"She's doing great," Sam told everyone. Rylee's mom came to stand next to Wendy and passed Sam's phone to her. "They should be moving Rylee and Allison to another floor, and I think you'll be allowed to visit."

Wendy scrolled through the pictures rapidly, then paused to take a closer look at one. Josh leaned over and dragged his fingers across the screen to make it bigger. Wendy covered her mouth with one hand, blinking back tears. "Adorable," she whispered.

"They won't move her off the delivery floor for at least a few more hours," Theo told them. "So, it's probably a good idea for everyone to go grab a few hours of rest. Sam can call you when they're settled into the new room."

Rylee's mom looked like she was going to protest, but Theo gave her a look that said it was probably better to not mess with the old biker dude.

Sam's dad held up a conciliatory hand. "Agreed," he said. "We can all come back this afternoon."

His mom handed Sam's phone back to him. "Yes, we can," she replied, eyeing Rylee's mom warily. "It's been a very long and exhausting night." She reached out to hug Sam again, and he awkwardly returned it.

Then, his mom looked over at Rylee's parents. "We'll see you later," she said before she grabbed her husband's hand and slowly walked away. Josh shrugged and followed them out.

Rylee's mom looked after them. "I guess we should get going too," she said. Then, she turned back to Sam. "Please send us those pictures as soon as you're able to," she told him, not quite asking. "I'd like to get an announcement out in the next few days."

Sam nodded. "Will do," he said.

Rylee's dad reached out to shake his hand. "Welcome to the family," he said. And, with that, he turned to tuck his wife's hand into his elbow and guided her out of the room.

Sam stared after them for a moment. *Welcome to the family? When did that happen?*

He turned to Theo. "Were you here all night?" he asked.

Theo pursed his lips, then nodded.

"Are you going to tell me what happened last night?" Sam slowly asked. He could not imagine what Theo could have done to stop Maternal Armageddon.

Theo smiled. "Come on, Sam," he chided him, nudging him to walk with him to the exit. "You know that I can't break client confidentiality." He paused and looked over at Sam. "They will tell you in their own good time. Until then, it's really none of your business." He clapped Sam on the shoulder. "Now, get back to your own family, okay?"

Family? Sam wasn't sure that he would go that far, but it was probably the closest word he had to what they were building. "Thanks, Theo. I don't know if I could have made it this far without you."

"That's what a mentor's for, kid!" Theo told him and walked down the hallway to the entrance.

In a daze, Sam found his way back to Rylee's room. Allison was fussing in the heated baby caddy as a nurse struggled to put her into a newborn onesie and cap.

When she was done, the nurse handed Allison to Sam, swaddled in a generic white blanket with a pink stripe along one edge. He looked over to Rylee, who gave him an exhausted smile, then closed her eyes.

He awkwardly cuddled the baby's warmth against his shoulder, her knit cap pressed against his chin. Rylee had wanted the name Allison because that was Rylee's favorite grandmother's name. Isabelle was Sam's. He thought about it for a minute.

"Allison," he breathed. "Allison Isabelle Williams Maxwell." Yeah, that was a perfect name for a perfect baby girl.

He shifted her position a bit as he walked to the window, looking out over the parking lot. The sun lit up the trees in the distance. It was going to be a beautiful day.

Looking down at his newborn daughter, Sam felt something that he couldn't really explain. Part of it was sheer amazement that they had brought this new life into the world. Some of it was relief that this part of the journey was over. But something else nudged at him and wouldn't stop. In that moment, he knew that the DNA test didn't matter.

Allison twitched in her sleep, her tiny fists snuggled against her cheeks where they poked out of the blanket. Her little frown faded as her tongue poked out, making tiny sucking motions.

He bent forward and planted a light kiss on her cap. *I'm a dad,* he realized. *Holy shit, I'm a dad!*

Sam took a deep breath. He realized that it didn't matter what he had to do, he was going to do everything in his power to make sure that she was happy.

"Welcome to the world, little one," he whispered, looking back over at Rylee as she slept. "I promise you that I'm going to do everything in my power to give you a safe place that you can always call home."

Sam carefully sat on the couch, cuddling a fussy two-week-old Allison against his chest with a careful hand. He leaned back against the futon and held up the bottle to check that the nipple was screwed on correctly. He didn't want to risk another spill.

He brushed the nipple against Allison's lips to get her attention. She was so engrossed with her fussing that she barely noticed. "Come on, baby girl," he told her quietly. "I know you're hungry."

Finally, the nipple got her attention and Allison latched on, guzzling that warm milk for all it was worth. Sam sighed and settled against the cushions. It had been a quiet night.

He heard Rylee moving around upstairs. It was hard to believe that they'd found a schedule that worked. Sam went to bed immediately after they put Allison down for the night, the door closed so that he could get some decent shuteye. It felt like such a luxury to sleep in a bed after so many months of crashing on the couch, if only for a few hours. Sometime after midnight, Rylee would wake him up and he'd spend the rest of the night on the couch looking after Allison.

The rest of his day was spent in a blur of homework, housework, and deliveries. In all honesty, if it wasn't for the fact that Rylee's mom was paying her housekeeper to come over for a weekly clean, Sam had no idea how they'd keep it together.

Rylee quietly came down the stairs. "There she is," she breathed. "Coffee?"

Sam nodded. "I started some as her bottle was warming up," he told her.

Rylee padded into the kitchen. A short time later, she returned with two mugs. She carefully sat them down on the coffee table and settled down on the rocking chair next to the TV.

"How'd she sleep?" Rylee asked before taking a careful sip from her mug.

Sam yawned. "Pretty good," he told her. "She woke up a few times but quickly settled down, so I was able to get a few naps in."

Rylee gave him a tired smile. "Still think that having a nanny is a bad idea?" she asked.

Sam looked down at Allison. Her tiny fists tried to clutch the baby bottle almost as if she was claiming it as her own. *My bottle!*

He sighed. "Look, I know that this is hard, Rylee, really I do," he said. "But handing our daughter off to some stranger—"

"A carefully vetted stranger," Rylee interjected.

"Fine," he responded. "A 'carefully vetted stranger' brings a whole set of worries that I'm just not comfortable with."

Rylee took another sip of coffee. "Tell me," she commanded. "All of this would be so much easier if we could get some help around here."

Sam paused to reposition Allison. "We can't afford a nanny," he told her. "Yes, I know that you have access to money from your trust fund and this wouldn't make a dent in what your parents gave you." He could hear the bitterness in his voice.

"It doesn't matter how much money you have. We have to split our finances evenly. And, every single receipt, every deposit, everything that we spend every month has to be reported to the guardian ad litem until Allison is six months old. They know how many hours I work and how much I'm able to provide. We're barely making ends meet now, Rylee, because I can't pull more hours, help with Allison, and get my homework done. Can you imagine what could happen if the Court found out that you were paying for a nanny?"

Allison started fussing, pushing away the bottle. Her dark eyes glared up at him as if it was his fault that the bottle was empty. Rylee put her mug on the coffee table and stood. "Here, let me take her," she said. "She might be a bit gassy now."

Sam carefully handed Allison over and watched as Rylee settled the baby against her shoulder. She began to gently circle her hand against Allison's back as she carefully walked across the small room.

"My mom and dad have offered to pay for the nanny," she told him.

Sam carefully placed the baby bottle on the coffee table before grabbing his coffee mug. "What?" he exclaimed. "That can't be legal, Rylee!"

Rylee turned around and walked back across the room, swaying a bit. "There's nothing in the current law that forbids them from doing that," she told him. "The money wouldn't go to us. It would directly go to the nanny as their employee."

"What about the whole 'grandparents can't raise their grandkids' thing?" he asked.

"Well—" Allison interrupted with a well-timed burp. Rylee laughed. "Good girl," she crooned. "Technically, it would still be us raising our daughter. Just with some well-timed assistance. Think about it, Sam. Most daycares accept six-week-old newborns. What is the difference between dropping her off at a center or having someone come here to take care of her during the day?"

Sam snorted. "We can't afford that, either."

Rylee sat down in the rocker and positioned Allison on her lap, facing Sam. She held up Allison's hands, her tiny fists clenched around Rylee's fingers, and gently bounced them up and down as she sat. "At our current income, the state provides a subsidy allowance for daycare, Sam. We could afford a few hours per week and have a nanny take care of her the rest of the time."

Enough. Sam stood, glaring down at Rylee. "No nanny. Period."

"Why not?" Rylee demanded. "This is a very simple solution. Allison gets a bit of social interaction, and we can get on with our lives!"

Sam nodded, scooping up the baby bottle and his mug as he stalked away. "It always comes back to that, doesn't it, Rylee?"

he growled. "Allison is not just a speed bump on your way to Wellesley. She's our daughter!"

"What is that supposed to mean?" Rylee exclaimed. The sudden spike in volume startled Allison into crying. "See what you've done?!" She turned Allison around so her head was on Rylee's shoulder and started rocking her. "It's going to be okay, baby. Momma's got you . . . "

Sam spilled out the last of his coffee and loaded the cup into the dishwasher. Then, he carefully took apart the bottle to wash it and placed it in the drainer. He thought hard about what he needed to say next.

He turned around to face her. "I'm transferring to Marquette in the fall," he told her. "You're still planning to go to Wellesley. I can't imagine that your parents will pay for a nanny when you're not here."

"What are you saying?" she demanded. "The nanny will stay with Allison, no matter where we live." She turned Allison back to her shoulder and rubbed at her back. Allison found her fist and settled down.

Sam walked back into the living room. Rylee seemed to be under the impression that she'd be taking Allison with her. Time to play hardball. "Do you really want to have Allison move every month so that she can have equal time with both of us when you move out East?" he asked quietly.

"No—"

Sam cut her off. "If you push for the nanny, I'll insist that Allison come home every other month so that I keep joint placement."

"You wouldn't!" Rylee snarled. She stalked into the kitchen and put Allison in the baby bouncer on the floor near the table, pausing only long enough to strap her in before turning to glare at him.

Sam moved to the table and sat down. He watched Allison for a moment, then looked up. "There has to be a way for both of us to get what we want, Rylee," he told her. "And it starts with not having a nanny in our future."

Rylee poured herself a fresh cup of coffee. She carefully stirred in some cream, then sat down at the table. "Fine," she said, then took a sip. She grimaced at the hot liquid. "Let's talk."

Epilogue

S am gazed out the conference room window, relaxing for the first time in a long time. Halloween might not be for a few weeks, but Allison had already celebrated the trick-or-treat holiday this weekend, in style. He'd found a cute little baby lobster outfit that fit snugly over his forward-facing baby carrier, complete with lobster claws and a hat with enormous eyes and antennas. She'd had a blast giggling as people told her what an adorable baby she was as they'd walked down the hallway of his new apartment near campus. He'd even had to turn down a few party invitations because *someone* had a firm 7 pm bedtime.

Today was the day. The final settlement. After they were done here, Sam was a free man. No more stringent Court oversight. No more submitting a copy of each and every receipt and paycheck for review. No more worrying that he'd missed something. Nope, today was going to be a great day!

Both of their attorneys, the ever-present guardian ad litem, the arbitrator, Rylee's mentor, and Theo, sat around the conference room table. Rylee had joined via video conference and observed the room from the monitor at the far end of the room.

Sam was still amazed that the judge had allowed her to move to Massachusetts two months before their probationary period was over, but the arbitrator had agreed to the accommodation. *Extenuating circumstances,* she'd said. *Great lawyers,* Sam thought.

He looked down at Allison as she napped in the carrier on the floor. Six months old today. She had Rylee's black hair and pout. His hazel eyes and a joyful smile. And an easy disposition that was all her own.

The door opened. Judge Olson entered, smiling as she carried a rather thin folder and her tablet. Everyone at the table stirred when the stenographer placed her device in the corner and sat down. Rylee smoothed her braid over one shoulder and set aside her phone so that it was no longer visible. The judge sat down at the head of the table and took a long moment to scan the group, and verify that Rylee was logged in to the teleconference, before she opened the folder in front of her.

"Mr. Mueller," she said in a quiet voice. "The settlement that we have before us is quite unusual. Are you certain that you are in agreement with it?"

"Yes, Your Honor," he replied. "I believe that this is in my client's best interests."

Judge Olsen looked at the arbitrator. "Ms. Rodriquez, as the arbitrator assigned to the case, can you walk us through the agreement at a high level?"

"Of course, Your Honor," she replied with a smile. "This case was unusual in that, while both parties are enrolled in universities, one of them had been accepted out-of-state. This complicated the usual placement rotation."

The judge waved her hand, silently urging the arbitrator to get to the point.

Rodriquez cleared her throat. "Both parties have agreed that Ms. Williams Maxwell, aka Allison, will live with Mr. Maxwell until Ms. Williams has completed her undergraduate program at Wellesley University. During this time, Ms. Williams will pay 100 percent of their child's financial expenses. This includes half of Mr. Maxwell's housing expenses, reasonable child care expenses, and all of Allison's food, clothing, medical, and educational allowance."

The judge held up a hand. "Educational allowance?" she asked.

"Educational books and toys, Your Honor," the arbitrator clarified. "Both parents have expressed an interest in Ms. Williams Maxwell learning a foreign language."

"Ah. Continue."

"During this time, Ms. Williams will have to return home during school breaks to assume custody. Once Ms. Williams has completed her undergraduate program, Allison will move to her mother's residence until she's ready to attend elementary school. This will allow Mr. Maxwell to travel, if he chooses, or pursue employment outside of the country. He will, however, be responsible for fifty percent of their child's reasonable expenses during this time."

"Interesting." Judge Olson tapped her pen against the folder. "Why is Mr. Maxwell responsible for only fifty percent?"

"Because Mr. Maxwell has agreed to remain in the state so that Ms. Williams Maxwell is able to regularly visit with her grandparents and extended family," Rodriquez told her.

"Anything else?"

Rodriquez nodded. "Both parties have agreed to a weekly video call so that Ms. Williams Maxwell is comfortable with both parents, and annual reviews with the guardian ad litem, in person, to ensure that they remain in good standing with the program."

Judge Olson turned to Theo. "Mr. Petropoulous, any concerns?"

Theo smiled, a sly but relaxed grin as he looked up at the monitor where Rylee watched the proceedings. "Is there a no-nanny clause, Ms. Rodriquez?"

Rylee made a choking sound, flushing at the question.

The judge looked from Rylee to Theo. "Is there something I should know, Mr. Petropoulous?"

Theo shook his head as he looked at Sam. Sam tried to hide a smile behind a casually placed hand, but failed. "No, ma'am," he finally said. "Sorry. Just a private joke, Your Honor."

Judge Olson laughed. "Someday, someone's going to let me in on the joke, right?"

"Absolutely, Your Honor," Theo said. Sam nodded.

The judge turned to Rylee's mentor. "Any concerns, Mrs. Meyer?"

Rylee's mentor shook her head. "None, Your Honor."

She turned to Sam. "Mr. Maxwell, do you have any thoughts that you'd like to share with this Court before I make a final judgment?"

Sam pursed his lips for a moment. "Your Honor, this has been a wild ride. In all honesty, I never expected to become a dad this early in my life and I never expected that I would fall so completely in love." He looked down at Allison as she stirred in her sleep.

"Children will do that to you," the judge replied with a smile. She glanced at the monitor "Okay, Ms. Williams, do you have anything that you'd like to add?"

Rylee sat up a bit straighter, pulling her long French braid to hang over one shoulder as she leaned forward. "I'm just glad that we were able to come to a reasonable accommodation,

Your Honor," she said. "I agree that Allison's placement and the financial support are exactly what our little family needs to have in place to ensure her future."

Not to mention that, once again, Rylee got exactly what she wanted, Sam thought, shaking his head. Of course, in many ways, so had he.

"Does anyone have any other information that needs to be taken into account before I issue my final ruling?" Judge Olson asked as she took one last look around the room.

At that moment, Allison woke and started fussing. Sam looked at the judge, smiling. He quickly pulled the baby out of her carrier and settled her on his lap.

"Ah, you're awake, Ms. Williams Maxwell," the judge said. "Do you have anything to add?"

Allison spit out her pacifier and yawned.

"Alright, then," the judge said with a laugh. "Based on the feedback I've received, this settlement goes into effect today, October 8, 2029. Both parties are expected to meet with Ms. Williams Maxwell's guardian ad litem, annually, to make any necessary changes to placement and financial support until she has reached twenty-one years of age. So, ordered. Case closed."

There was a collective sigh as people started to gather their things to leave. "Thank you, Your Honor," Rylee said. The video ended.

Judge Olson leaned forward and took Allison's hand. "Congratulations, little one. I'm so happy for you."

Allison smiled, then started babbling, a bit of drool falling down her chin. Sam pulled a soft cloth out of his pocket and carefully wiped at her chin. "Thanks, Your Honor," Sam said. "From both of us."

He gently held Allison close as he stood. She blew raspberries at him, fussing as he tried to grab her carrier from the floor. Theo came around to his side of the table, placing the carrier on the table in front of them.

"You did good. I'm proud of you, Sam," Theo said, as Sam placed Allison back in the carrier with a practiced hand.

Sam looked up. He didn't quite know what to say.

Theo clasped Sam's shoulder, then dropped his hand. He looked down at Allison. "Don't be a stranger, you two," he said, then walked away.

Sam checked the straps to make sure Allison was secure. "Well, baby girl, I guess we may have to invite your Uncle Theo to your first birthday party," he told her. "What do you think?"

Allison stuck her tongue out, fussing. Sam popped her pacifier back into her mouth and rocked the carrier for a few seconds until she settled down.

"Come on, you," he said, lifting the carrier up. "Time to get you some lunch!" He carefully made his way to the door.

He looked back at the room. A year ago, he felt trapped and abandoned by a system that treated him as both a criminal that needed governmental oversight and as a lost child in desperate need of an education. Turned out, he needed a bit of both and a solid kick in the ass from Theo!

Allison interrupted his thoughts, kicking her legs against the carrier. Sam laughed. "Okay, I get it. I'm going, already!"

Stay updated! Join my mailing list at www.mewright.com to receive notifications about new releases, exclusive giveaways, and exciting updates. By being part of our community, you'll be the

first to know about upcoming projects. And, if you found my book engaging, please take a moment to leave a review. You play a crucial role in reaching a wider audience and encouraging fellow readers to explore my work.

There are two sides to every story...

Curious about what Rylee went through during her pregnancy? Here's the first chapter of **The Motherhood Mandate**.

Rylee carefully pulled into the parking lot and scanned for Sam's car. A few vehicles were scattered around the large lot. She spotted Sam's distinctively dark blue hybrid at the far end, near the trail that led through the tree-lined path to Tietjen Beach.

She pulled in next to his car, sighing as she checked her watch. Just after 8 a.m. So much for being early.

Of course, he'd picked the beach. Grabbing a nearby picnic table and talking things out would have been so much easier.

No. Sam was not going to make this easy for her. Nothing said 'we're done' like a forced march along the worn asphalt trail to remind her of happier times. After all, Tietjen Beach had been their special place.

Rylee blinked back tears as she exited the car, automatically locking it and tucking her keys into a pocket as she walked over to the northern trail entrance. She knew where to find him. He would be waiting for her on the farthest access point to the beach, far away from anyone taking an early morning walk.

A slight chill seeped past her loose linen sundress and the damp wind caressed her bare arms. The forecast had called for a chance of rain later in the day, but it had been so warm at home that she hadn't thought to bring a wrap.

Rylee glanced through the window into the backseat. She didn't see her spare sweater. *Dammit,* she thought. By the time she got to the beach, she'd be freezing.

No help for it. Time to get going. With any luck, Sam would agree to continue their conversation over breakfast at a nearby restaurant.

She could feel the random pebbles and irregular pavement through the thin soles of her leather flats as she walked. The trees overhead flickered in the damp breeze, birds happily chirping as they greeted the morning sun.

As she followed the trail deeper into the forest, all Rylee could think of was how crappy it was that Sam had chosen this place to meet. It felt like the ultimate punishment. So many memories, good and bad.

She could feel the tears starting again. She wiped at her face with the back of her hand and kept walking.

The summer beach parties with the robotics team. That time someone had lit up the entire lakefront with a bunch of possibly illegal fireworks.The community barbecue the summer before her senior year, when she first thought he might be interested in her.

Their first kiss had happened right along this trail, during last year's Winter Wonderland Hike. These trees had even witnessed their last fight.

Rylee stopped walking, stretching her neck to look up at the tree canopy. *No!* she thought. She was not going to give him the satisfaction of seeing her break down. Not now.

Maybe she should just go. He didn't love her. Maybe he never did. Maybe all she had been to him was someone who gave him sex on demand, like some anonymous plastic sex doll.

She wiped her face with both hands. *That wasn't true*, she told herself. Somehow, she knew Sam had genuinely cared for her, even if he could never bring himself to say the word 'love'. Cared? Yes. Needed? Absolutely. But never loved.

Rylee crossed her arms, blinking back tears as she rocked back and forth for a long moment. There was only one way to find out if he could help, and that was to keep going. Besides, she could see glimmers of the beach peeking through the trees up ahead. No sense turning back now.

As she approached the beach, she noticed the small details. His vague silhouette stood against the backdrop of the calm lake waters, his faded blue t-shirt and old jeans making him blend in. His dark red hair was a vivid smudge against the shades of blue around him.

Sam stood with his back to the trail, the small waves lapping up against the monochrome shoreline at his feet. He was staring off into the horizon, to that place where the sky kissed the shimmering lake water.

He might have been lost in thought. Or, more likely, he was avoiding even looking at her.

She stepped off the trail and onto the beach, if you could call it that. Sandy pebbles littered the shoreline, with larger stones and pieces of driftwood scattered around as if Mom Nature had had another temper tantrum with the last storm.

"Dammit!" she cried out, bruising her toes as she tripped over a small tree branch. "Why the hell did you want to meet on the beach when there are perfectly good picnic tables closer to the parking lot?" she complained as she got her balance and looked down at her shoe. A shallow scrape marred the dark leather.

She looked up, annoyed. Sam hadn't even noticed her distress. Of course, he hadn't.

Rylee made herself continue walking until she reached his side. "Sam, I'm cold," she told him. "Can't we go someplace else?"

When he didn't respond, she reached for his hand as she tried to make a connection.

He pulled away, shoving his hands into his front pockets as he took a step away from her. "Just tell me what you want, Rylee," he told her, his voice dark with anger. He continued to scan the horizon, eyeing the dark clouds that were gathering out over the lake. "We broke up. It's over. There's nothing more to say."

"It's really chilly out here," she whimpered, rubbing her cold hands against her arms to ward off the chill. "I can't talk when I'm freezing to death!"

Sam knew how sensitive she was to the cold. Once upon a time, he'd cared enough to put his arms around her against a sudden chill. Not now, though. She felt the tears threaten to start again and held up one hand under her nose to try to hold back the sniffle.

Sam turned to her, his hazel eyes blazing with unspoken rage. "Let's go," he snapped. Before she could do more than blink, he grabbed her by the arm and dragged her across the beach to the trail that led through the woods behind them.

She stumbled after him, tripping over another small piece of driftwood. His fingers flexed, painfully gripping her bicep, as he kept her from falling. She struggled to pull away from him and he abruptly let her go as they slowly made their way through the overgrown trail to the stairs that led to the bluff overlooking the beach.

The limestone steps were nearly overrun by wild grapevines, goldenrods, and various weeds. They made it nearly impossible for her to reach the ancient wooden handrails as they headed for the bluff.

As soon as they reached the top, Sam moved to one of the benches that used to overlook the beach below. Over the years, the forest had taken over the bluff, obscuring the once picturesque view.

He sat, leaning back against the bench as if the very sight of her disgusted him. "Tell me what's going on," he growled.

Rylee slumped onto the closest bench. There were so many things that she needed to say, but the words just wouldn't come out. "We can't break up, Sam," she finally told him, brushing her tangled, black hair out of her face. "I–I need you." *I need your help.*

Sam's expression hardened and he turned away, staring at the random foliage around them. After a long moment, he told her the words she didn't want to hear. "Rylee, it's over." He leaned forward, staring at the sandy ground between them. "You broke up with *me*," he spat. "We're done."

His words hit her like a backhanded slap. She sprang from her seat, fists clenched at her side. "No!" she cried out. "You don't understand. We made a mistake!" She choked back a sob; the words 'I think I'm pregnant' stuck in her throat.

Sam leaned back and eyed her, scorn etched into his pursed lips. "How many times do we need to break up before you finally accept that it's over, Rylee?" he asked mockingly. "Two more times? Five?" He glared at her. "Breaking up was your idea." He paused for emphasis, then barked, "Both times!"

Rylee swallowed a sob, screwing her eyes shut as she turned her face upward. "I was wrong," she whispered. She opened her eyes, wiping the tears from her face with both hands as if she could wipe away her fear. "Things have changed, Sam."

He rolled his eyes. "What things?" he demanded. "I'm really tired of this, Rylee! Tell me what's going on!"

She collapsed against the bench as she covered her eyes with one hand. She didn't have the words to stand against his rage. This wasn't him. Couldn't be him. Not the Sam she loved.

Rylee took a deep breath and then looked up at him. It was obvious she couldn't expect any help from him. "It doesn't matter, Sam," she finally told him. "I'm probably worried about nothing."

Sam glared at her for a moment, then sighed as he stood. "Fine," he growled. And, with that, he sauntered away.

Rylee collapsed into tears, wrapping her arms around herself as she cried. Her last hope was gone. He really didn't care.

After a long while, she wiped away her tears and tried to pull herself together. Time to find some answers.

She fumbled for a moment as she pulled her phone out of her pocket, then hit the button for the AI assistant. "Who can help figure out why I have been feeling nauseous?" she asked in a low voice.

"Hello, Rylee," her phone answered. "According to your MediTrack app, your last menstrual period was July 16th. It is highly recommended that you seek out a gynecologist to rule out pregnancy before pursuing an alternative medical diagnosis."

She thought about it for a moment. Her regular doctor was out. Dr. Marrow might contact her mother and she couldn't have that. Not yet. Not until she figured this out. She tapped the app button again. "Where can I find a gynecologist that will see me today?"

There was a pause. "There are five gynecologists within a thirty-mile radius. One of them offers same-day appointments and confidential consultations."

Rylee took a close look at her screen. The Faith and Prayers Pregnancy Crisis Center. According to her phone, it was just a few minutes away in Fox Point.

She stabbed at her phone to make the call. *It was early*, she thought. *Maybe they could get her in now.*

Don't miss out on the next chapter of The Unborn Child Protection Act series. Get your copy of *The Motherhood Mandate* today!

Author's Notes

April 23, 2023

The novel *The Fatherhood Mandate* is set in a dystopian future. A place where pregnant women who are either unmarried or, in the midst of a divorce, are detained if a fetal heartbeat is detected. Where the State of Wisconsin takes the idea of personal responsibility to such an extreme that the men that got them pregnant are held physically and financially responsible for their offspring. A place where society is ill-prepared for the consequences imposed by the state legislature and the United States Supreme Court.

So, how did we get here? Our story begins the moment that women in the United States lost their right to self-determination.

On June 24, 2022, the United States Supreme Court overturned Roe v. Wade, the landmark ruling that made access to abortion a federal right in the United States. This decision dismantled over fifty years of legal protection, paving the way for individual states to restrict or outright ban a woman's right to bodily autonomy.

Justice Alito delivered the High Court's opinion[1]. "We hold that Roe and Casey must be overruled. The Constitution makes no reference to abortion, and no such right is implicitly protected by any constitutional provision, including the one on which the defenders of Roe and Casey now chiefly rely—the Due Process Clause of the Fourteenth Amendment. That provision has been held to guarantee some rights that are not mentioned in the Constitution, but any such right must be 'deeply rooted in this Nation's history and tradition' and 'implicit in the concept of ordered liberty.'"

Prior to 1973, abortion had been illegal in 30 states and was only legal under specific circumstances in the remainder. Justice Alito pointed out that common law had long recognized abortion as a criminal offense, in at least some stage of pregnancy. Common law as early as the sixteenth century declared that abortion was a crime, at least after 'quickening'—i.e., the first movement of the fetus felt in the womb.

Other federal rights that relied on the Fourteenth Amendment were also put in jeopardy by the ruling, including interracial and same-sex marriages, as well as religious and gender-related discrimination.

---

1. The Associated Press. June 22, 2022.
   https://apnews.com/article/abortion-us-supreme-court-health-racial-injustice-gun-politics-e38479715c763a4972a85cc4003d73f9.

Following the Supreme Court ruling, Wisconsin abortion clinics halted elective abortions[2]. Many of them relocated over the border in neighboring states, as women who needed abortions traveled across state lines to receive them. Planned Parenthood launched a mobile abortion clinic initiative to cut down travel time, and the costs associated with seeking abortion care.

Governor Evers called a special session of the Wisconsin State Legislature on October 4, 2022. He requested that the legislature create a pathway to repeal Wisconsin's 1849-era criminal abortion ban. In response, Wisconsin's Senate convened for 15 seconds, long enough to gavel in and adjourn without taking action.

Milwaukee County circuit judge Janet Protasiewicz's election to the Wisconsin Supreme Court in Spring 2023 tipped the Court to a 4-3 liberal majority. However, the election of conservative Dan Knodl[3] handed Republicans a supermajority in the state senate. This injected a high degree of uncertainty into state politics, as this would allow Wisconsin's senate to impeach state officials, including a state supreme court justice.

---

2. McCabe, Samantha. Here's what to know about abortion access in post-Roe Wisconsin, Wisconsin Public Radio, September 9, 2022.
https://www.wpr.org/heres-what-know-about-abortion-access-post-roe-wisconsin.

3. Levine, Sam. Wisconsin senate supermajority win gives Republicans impeachment power, The Guardian, April 5, 2023.
https://www.theguardian.com/us-news/2023/apr/05/wisconsin-senate-supermajority-impeachment-power.

These events are the foundations that *The Fatherhood Mandate* is built on. From here, we move into the dystopian future that may come to pass. History may diverge as the story unfolds.

In this universe, the state legislature declined to repeal or amend the 1849 Wisconsin Criminal Abortion Statute, which had been in place shortly after Wisconsin had been admitted to the Union as a state. The statute[4] reads in part:

Any person, other than the mother, who does either of the following is guilty of a Class E felony:

(a) Intentionally destroys the life of an unborn quick child; or

(b) Causes the death of the mother by an act done with intent to destroy the life of an unborn child. It is unnecessary to prove that the fetus was alive when the act causing the mother's death was committed.

A series of lawsuits were made against the state and individual legislators, claiming that the statute clearly stated abortion was legal before sixteen to twenty-four weeks of gestation when movement could be felt. Others pointed out that the statute allowed medicinal abortions, as the mother could voluntarily ingest medications that would end her pregnancy. The medications prescribed for this, mifepristone and misoprostol, are generally considered to be safe to use up to the eleventh week of pregnancy.

Due to legislative inaction, the legal question of abortion remained in place until the 2024 election. In response to retaining a veto-proof supermajority in both Assembly and the Senate, Republicans replaced the 1849 abortion bill with one that declared life began at conception and outlawed abortion

---

4. Wisconsin State Legislature Statute 904.04: https://docs
   .legis.wisconsin.gov/statutes/statutes/940/i/04

if the pregnancy was viable. This included pregnancies due to rape or incest. Once a fetal heartbeat was detected, there were very few options available to protect the life of the mother.

In December 2024, a video captured a prominent pro-life state legislator's daughter as she was transported by ambulance to Illinois to undergo a life-saving abortion following an unexpected complication late in her pregnancy. The video went viral and prodded the legislature to take action. The law was amended to include that ectopic pregnancies and specific instances where the embryo or fetus is determined to not be able to survive to be medically necessary.

It's important to note that according to this legislation, the health and safety of the mother were secondary considerations. Women were routinely denied cancer treatment until after they had successfully delivered their babies and women died because care was delayed until their life was confirmed to be in danger. In addition, it did not include severe birth defects that would result in the newborn dying after birth.

Section 1 of the state constitution was amended to reinforce the state law that life began at conception: *All people are born equally free and independent, and have certain inherent rights; among these are life, liberty, and the pursuit of happiness; to secure these rights, governments are instituted, deriving their just powers from the consent of the governed. The term 'person' or 'persons' shall include every human being from the moment of fertilization, cloning, or the functional equivalent thereof.*

By early 2025, the legal age of 'adult' was standardized to occur at age twenty-one. Legally, anyone under the age of twenty-one was no longer allowed to vote in local or state elections, or allowed alcoholic beverages, to purchase tobacco or CBD products, or even marry without parental consent.

A measure to raise the age of consent for statutory rape from age sixteen to eighteen was introduced. It was a difficult law to pass, but the need to protect children was heavily used in advertising and media talking points.

Wisconsin's birth rate began to increase, straining the already shaky healthcare system. This especially impacted the poorest residents, who were unable to afford to travel outside of the state for abortions. More fathers found themselves taken to court for child support, but the standard guidelines remained paltry: only 17% of income for one child, 25% for two children, and 29% for three children. As child support did not cover all of the costs of raising a child, the number of fatherless families applying for FoodShare Wisconsin and other state support programs dramatically increased around the state.

Various tax measures were considered—and rejected—in response to the increased pressure on the state budget. Instead, the legislature quickly passed a series of measures in early 2027 which were designed to reaffirm the core principle of 'personal responsibility'. These included:

- The Unborn Child Protection Act, which had been originally designed to allow pregnant individuals to be detained if they were suspected of substance abuse, was amended to allow unmarried, pregnant women to be taken into custody to determine if they posed a risk to their embryo, provided that a fetal heartbeat was detected.

- Unborn citizens gestated by an unmarried woman, or one who was suing for divorce, automatically became a ward of the state. This was designed to prevent women from traveling outside of the state for an abortion.

- Child support guidelines were replaced with one that called for each parent to contribute half of all offspring's reasonable expenses until age twenty-one. The exception was if either parent was convicted of rape, domestic violence, or was deemed to be a risk to the life and safety of the child. In this case, the convicted parent was responsible for 100% of their offspring's reasonable expenses.

- The Wisconsin Individual Family Education program, which had been a voluntary program designed to facilitate an unmarried couple's transition to parenthood, was made mandatory under most circumstances. This included couples that were in the process of divorcing and those that were pursuing adoption after their child was born.

- The 'No Means No' initiative changed all rape charges to state felonies. No misdemeanor charges remained in state statutes. Rape kits were required to be processed within seventy-two hours, or three calendar days, of the reported event and the state's attorney general was required to provide a quarterly report on the progress the state made in securing rape convictions.

Conservatives felt that these measures were a good start, but didn't go far enough. A new bill was introduced to codify the idea that every child was entitled to have a father and a mother. Backers knew that they couldn't force unwed couples to marry, but felt that cohabitation during the child's first months of life might improve marriage rates.

Under the new law, unmarried couples were required to live together from the third trimester of pregnancy until the child was six months old. Courts could wave this for several reasons, including but not limited to a history of physical or emotional abuse, where rape is suspected but not reported, and in very limited child support and custody cases. In all things, the child's needs were placed above the needs of the parents.

The state was immediately sued, and the case was fast-tracked to the Supreme Court. In anticipation of the conservative majority prevailing, staffing for family courts around the state greatly increased and the number of guardian ad litem positions tripled.

In May 2028, SCOTUS declined to hear the case and Wisconsin began immediately enforcing the new laws. And this is where *The Fatherhood Mandate* begins.

Acknowledgments

No author lives in a vacuum. There are so many people in our lives that provide the encouragement we need to create that next manuscript. I am deeply grateful for the people who have supported me along the way.

First and foremost, I want to thank my loving husband and daughter for their unwavering support. Your belief in me has been the fuel that kept me going during the long hours of drafting and editing. I am grateful for your patience, understanding, and unconditional love.

Heartfelt thanks to my sisters, who cheered me on and provided me with much needed feedback on college scholarships. I also want to thank my dad, who instilled in me the belief that I could do anything, as long as I had faith in myself.

A big shoutout to my Cafe Crew at Immersed's VR coworking space, who graciously let me bounce ideas and dialogue off of them as I worked to bring this story to life. Your feedback and camaraderie were invaluable in helping me to shape and refine this narrative. And, to my editor and my online tribe who gave me feedback on that all-important first draft: you rock!

About Author

M.E. Wright is a Midwest native with a passion for delving into the realms of fiction and nonfiction. As a social scientist and writer, she starts each project with a simple question: 'What if...'

She loves diving into dystopian and speculative science fiction, where she doesn't shy away from the brutal realities of a world shaped by shifting ideologies. With a knack for social commentary and a talent for creating characters you can't help but root for (or against), she's all about crafting stories that make you think, laugh, and maybe even cringe a little.

On a personal note, Wright prefers soda to pop, measures the distance between places in time rather than driving distance, and has been known to cheer the Bears, even though she currently lives in Packer country. Her website is www.mewright.com.

www.ingramcontent.com/pod-product-compliance
Lightning Source LLC
Chambersburg PA
CBHW070657010826
48975CB00014B/1941